Sam Dawson is a journalist, ex-campaigner and volunteer medic. A spare time cave guide and first aider, his interests include history, films, books, martial arts, and investigating places that are odd, old or underground.

THE RUNNING

By Sam Dawson

(Front cover by Mark Hetherington, based on photographs by Sam Dawson, internal pictures by Sam Dawson)

Other Side Books

This edition published in 2025 by
Other Side Books
Glasgow G51 3SJ

www.othersidebooks.co.uk

Copyright © Sam Dawson 2025

Cover illustration © Mark Hetherington 2025

ISBN: 9798286931316

All rights reserved.
No part of this publication may be reproduced, stored or transmitted in any form without the express written permission of the publisher.

The moral right of Sam Dawson to be identified as the author of this work has been asserted by him in accordance with the Copyright, Designs and Patents Act 1988.

The moral right of Mark Hetherington (front cover) and Sam Dawson (inside illustrations) to be identified as the artists of this work has been asserted by them in accordance with the Copyright, Designs and Patents Act 1988.

For my father

Contents

Chapter One 13
Chapter Two 14
Chapter Three 17
Chapter Four 20
Chapter Five 25
Chapter Six 28
Chapter Seven 34
Chapter Eight 37
Chapter Nine 44
Chapter Ten 48
Chapter Eleven 52
Chapter Twelve 57
Chapter Thirteen 62
Chapter Fourteen 64
Chapter Fifteen 70
Chapter Sixteen 75
Chapter Seventeen 80
Chapter Eighteen 87
Chapter Nineteen 91
Chapter Twenty 96
Chapter Twenty-One 98
Chapter Twenty-Two 104
Chapter Twenty-Three 109
Chapter Twenty-Four 114
Chapter Twenty-Five 120
Chapter Twenty-Six 127
Chapter Twenty-Seven 133
Chapter Twenty-Eight 139
Chapter Twenty-Nine 146
Chapter Thirty 150
Chapter Thirty-One 152
Chapter Thirty-Two 158
Chapter Thirty-Three 163
Chapter Thirty-Four 168
Chapter Thirty-Five 172
Chapter Thirty-Six 173
Chapter Thirty-Seven 174
Chapter Thirty-Eight 178
Chapter Thirty-Nine 182

Chapter Forty 184
Appendix 187
Hidden Depths 187
George Nathan 199
The Second City...210
Further Reading...210

Illustrations
1. Alice's, Portobello Road, page 23
2. British Museum Underground Station, 1900, page 52
3. Tomb, Kensal Green Cemetery, page 57
4. Ruined church, Belchite, page 104
5. Street in the village, page 118
6. House in the village, page 122
7. The cemetery, page 124
8. Wood and flint harrow used as door, page 152
9. River Fleet, mid 19th Century, page 189
10. River Fleet outfall, Blackfriars Bridge, page 191
11. River Walbrook outfall, page 193
12. Clay pipe dating guide, page 194
13. Jacob's Island, mid 19th Century, page 197
14. George Nathan, page 199
15. Four Nathans, page 201
16. WW2 toilets, Chislehurst Caves, page 213
17. Chislehurst Caves, page 215
18. Hell Fire Caves, page 216
19. Wall carvings, Hell Fire Caves, page 217
20. Farthing Lane Underground Station, page 230
21. Endpiece, page 235

Chapter One
Castilla La Mancha, Spain, autumn 1995

You get an eye for it. Something that interests you teaches you to see things differently from other people. Take a collector of toy soldiers, or china or 1970s plastic tat – anything really – to Portobello Road antique market. Tell five non-collectors that they must find, say, a Dinky car. They'll scour the stalls and miss specimen after specimen. Ten minutes later the collector will stroll past, stop and take two steps backward, having somehow X-rayed the desired lost toy hidden under the detritus of doorknobs, old *Picture Posts* and James Last albums.

I'm interested in hidden underground sites: deserted tube stations, forgotten and sealed air raid shelters, bunkers, dungeons, tunnels. Any place dark and lost that promises adventure. Which means that I've become sensitised to the clues on the surface that show there's something down below.

It's a harmless talent with a whiff of the anorak about it.

So how come it's left me crouching in the darkened kitchen of a little house in a Spanish village, wondering if I can run to a shotgun that I'm not even sure how to use, without being dragged out through the window and killed in the street?

One candle lights the room. The church clock is striking eleven; an hour till tomorrow, my 34th birthday. Which I might get to see if I can move fast enough.

If I can put that candle out.

If no one shoots through the glass.

If the gun is loaded.

The clock strikes again.

Time to make a wish.

Chapter Two
London, the previous year

"I wish I was somewhere else. Thomas, you're going to have to do something about this." I began the working week with the familiar Monday morning personal rebuke that came with entering the office of Montressor Publications, publishers of *World Transport Industry News* magazine.

In not much more than seven months I was due to leave off being 33 and hit 34. Which wouldn't matter if I didn't think that at that age I should be doing a job a bit more challenging than this one.

Tom Drummond. (Current) occupation: trade journalist.

I swiped in, late, up in the lift, over to my desk. My coworker, Roger, a genuinely funny guy with a gift for impersonation, greeted me with the smallest lift of an eyebrow. All that was needed to express our mutual feelings about beginning another day.

"Guv," (Roger to me: Good morning)
"Guv," (Morning)
"Guv, can I have a word?"
"What is it, George?"
"Coffee, you slag?"

Without conscious decision it seemed that what was going to get us through the day was Sweeney talk. Another time it might be to speak in quotes from favourite films ("Today, Mathew, I am going to be Bob Hoskins in Mona Lisa"). We were roughly the same age. Politics divided us but seventies television united us.

Then the voice of Cecil, one of the advertisement account directors, travelled over the low partition that separated us from the magazine's ad sales team. He was beginning the first call of the day. By the second one he had committed Roger to a joint early morning visit to a possible advertiser's Dudley head office.

Roger mimed despair, throwing me a pleading look, then putting his head in his hands and slumping over the desk.

It was no good him looking to me for sympathy. I was The Sweeney, and I hadn't had any dinner. "Get your trousers on," I told him. "You're nicked."

We began to work. Roger picked up a file thick with unsubedited company descriptions. "Um, all this week at Sunshine Desserts we have the annual third-party logistics suppliers' report to do. Which do you want to take," he asked, "A to M or N to Z?"

"Like Vienna to Ultravox, it means nothing to me."

He brightened immediately. "He was on the telly the other night, talking about losing out to Joe Dolce." Roger was an ex-New Romantic, so after working with him for several years I knew that "he" was Midge Ure, remembering how his song Vienna was beaten to number one in 1981 by Dolce's Shaddap You Face.

"Serves him right for not knowing what the capital of Austria was."

We could go on like this for a surprisingly long time. We once put together a whole issue of the magazine in which every headline was a song title. Nobody noticed. Other times it was sack-worthy double entendres and messages hidden in the dropped capitals at the beginning of paragraphs. Same reaction.

In ways such as these we held off the boredom of being employed by a once-respected company that was now tumbling downhill fast, following its takeover by the former sales director, who thought that nothing should stand in the way of increasing the advertising revenue. Editors were an overeducated, bolshy distraction, whose product should be eliminated wherever possible in favour of more money-earning adverts and advertorials. Despite the sublimation of everything to this pursuit the firm was noticeably in decline, with a steady drip of previously profitable titles being closed down.

Our answer was to take refuge in rambling conversations and verbal games, always looking for an opportunity to drop a line from a film or a song into the conversation – or the magazine. Like Roy Orbison singing Pretty Woman, we asked daily for mercy, even if we couldn't make the endearingly silly growling sound.

Although today was a Sweeney day, historical necessity meant the introduction of Michael Caine quotes was inevitable. In time one of us would manage to steer a conversation round to the point where it was begging for the classic "You're a big man, but you're out of shape. With me it's a living. Now behave". By the time this happened we should have got through a reasonable amount of writing. When this point was reached it was usually time to stand up, stride to different parts of the office looking important and carrying papers, and then sneak out to the nearest arcade to play video games. If there weren't too many rather younger truants hogging them.

And so, the day passed until 5.30 came and real life took over.

Chapter Three

What was good about the job was that you clocked on, you clocked off. At the end of the day it was vroom, out the door without a thought. That part of my life dropped away. About the rest I had no complaints. I was comfortably single, following a fairly amicable recent parting that put me in the year-off part of the relationship pattern of choice – go out with someone for a year or two, stay unattached for a year or two.

The job just about paid the rent on a very, very small (not my fault), very, very crowded (my fault) bedsit flat in one of west London's less trendy parts. Ten minutes jog from Wormwood Scrubs if I fancied a run, and a few miles walk from Portobello Road and Ladbroke Grove for almost everything else. In a good week I buried myself in books, practised martial arts once and swam twice. Occasionally, despite feeling like a nineteenth century toff, I went to a fencing club.

As often as I could get myself organised, I would travel out to the countryside. Usually carrying a small rucksack holding lunch, camera, a few cigarettes, first aid kit and a folding spade. The last because I'd never lost the eye for spotting the traces of human habitation I developed in my teens when digging for Victorian bottle dumps. It was surprising how often I would still stumble over lost remains, from the gone-wild rose brambles that revealed the site of a long-gone cottage's garden, to refuse pits, an overgrown icehouse or a nettle-buried air raid shelter. Oh, and in my pocket a keyring torch, because I have never been able to resist exploring any ruined building, whether it's above the ground or below it.

It was the end of the week, so I planned a good long swim after work. Sunday night was booked for going out for drinks, leaving that Friday after the pool free up to one AM, when Vampire Circus was on the TV. I vaguely thought about getting out of London, maybe taking just a sleeping bag and flysheet and making my own space in some woods for a day or two, but knew that I wouldn't be up in time to make it worthwhile. I put a ready meal in the oven, found the half bottle of wine from last weekend and decided to treat myself to one of the favourite films that lived among teetering boxes of records, books and collectibles in the "spare" room.

The Night of the Hunter was in the four-year danger area (never kill a great film by watching it too many times). I'd re-read *The Maltese Falcon* recently, which meant the film was barred, since the superb dialogue was still rolling around in my head. Not long before we'd parted, I'd lent my last girlfriend Missing, which meant it now was. What else did I have? Our Man in Havana? Something with Cagney in it? Or Sim? No, something darker. Perhaps The Black Cat, the only true Art Deco horror film. Unless I could find The Bride of Frankenstein. That would be an excellent Friday night flick. If I could find it. If. *If.*...

If.... There it was. Lindsay Anderson's explosive parable of violent rebellion at a despotic English public school. I first saw it on BBC2 late one night when I was thirteen, and it was a revelation. Electrifying. No film I knew retained as much of the visceral impact it had on first viewing the way that one did. It was probably four years since I'd last seen it and I picked up my food and wine and sat and let it overwhelm me: the extraordinary, almost animalistic, physicality of Malcolm MacDowell. The power and beauty of the cinematography: a BSA 650cc Lightning chasing the sun across the Gloucestershire countryside, "the girl" standing on its saddle, her arms outstretched like an angel's wings. The claustrophobia of the school's regime and the hatefulness of its prefects.

By the time the end music played I was fairly drunk, having followed the wine by having a good go at the decanter of whisky I kept for special occasions.

Once there would have been no question of having such a thing. Before the flat I'd lived in a shared house where there were a couple of Spaniards who hosted a stream of visiting cousins and friends. When they asked if the rest of us minded queuing for the bathroom and giving up space to guests for a couple of weeks, we set the price of listening to a fortnight's Andalusian moaning about pubs closing early and why we have double taps instead of mixer ones at a bottle of Spanish brandy and a carton of Fortunas. All the drink and too many of the cigarettes would be consumed in a chokingly smoke-bound, international conversation in the kitchen the first evening they arrived. The idea of a bottle of spirits surviving beyond one night still smacked of novelty.

The combination of alcohol and film made it inevitable that I'd think about the fairly desolate place that being thirteen years old had seemed and what kind of a life I'd imagined back then that I'd have now. Turning it over in my mind I decided that I wasn't doing too badly. Yes, I needed to change my job, if only to prevent a creeping loss of self-confidence and respect, but there were many things I wasn't ashamed of. I'd saved two lives and risked my own several times. I'd put myself in situations and done things many would consider impossibly reckless, but which, to me, had been for good enough causes to justify the danger. It wasn't something you advertised back in England, but I'd stared down the barrels of guns pointed at me and still carried on because I'd believed there were principles worth defending. By the age of 30 I'd done most of the things that I dreamed of as a teenager, and then some more (although, obviously, I never actually did go out with any of Pan's People).

If I'd been told that I had an incurable disease I would have known I'd had a good run and faced up to what was coming, not gone under shaking my fist at God. I didn't like the fact that the things that made me feel OK about what I'd done with my life were all in the past, but there was still time to do something about that. I had some great memories, and I was still in reasonable shape. If I looked in the mirror, I'd see a pretty healthy six-foot and a bit bloke. Not the haunted-looking whip-thin youth who stared self-consciously out of old photos, comforting cigarette always in hand, but not too out of condition either.

I knew that when I wanted one, I could probably find a girlfriend, and I knew that one day I was going to die happily single. No one had ever persuaded me into marriage or a lifetime relationship. And no one ever would.

Chapter Four

The next day I met Elena.
I was up by one in the afternoon and decided to treat myself to a bacon sandwich to deal with the slight hangover. White bread, four rashers light to medium done, marge, ketchup. A couple of bites then made sure no one had crept into the flat and was watching and gave way to my terrible, since-childhood secret vice by dunking it in my tea, while bent over a novel. Delicious. Showered. With no reason to dress up and no desire to iron, I threw on boots, trousers, jacket and a t-shirt, and set off for Portobello Road.

It was immediately obvious she was Spanish. The clothes and the stance gave it away as much as the face. Petite, mid-20s, long brown hair, very brown eyes, regular features, well-groomed, and dressed in too-warm clothes. She was distractedly studying a piece of paper, then a street finder, then looking all around for the missing someone who, odds on, was her boyfriend.

Which might make it alright to break the Londoner's rule of never helping anyone unless asked. Even though you only have to get lost in a foreign town to appreciate how much a little assistance from a local means. Although it was daylight this wasn't the best area to be female, foreign and alone in. I put on my best non-murderer's face.

"Excuse me. Are you lost?"

"Oh! Is that I am to meet my friend, at Ladbroke Grove estation y...." She tailed off helplessly.

She pronounced it *ess-station*. The inability to say an s without putting an e in front of it confirmed it. I asked, "¿Española?"

Relieved, she answered in a breathless rush that as best as I could I put together as something like: "Sí, sí. Es que intentaba reunirme con mi amiga pero cogí un autobús y pedí al conductor que me avisará cuando llegáramos y el me dijo que sí, pero no lo hizo...y luego él se enfado..."

I commiserated over why bus drivers who say they'll tell you when you get to your stop rarely do, and then get arsey when you ask if you've come too far. Then, in my adequate but not brilliant Spanish, told her that she could risk a bus back or if she didn't mind walking a few kilometres – she was lucky she had got off when she did – I could give her directions. I took a breath. Or she could come with me.

No Londoner, she opted for the latter.

It was a cold but piercingly clear and sunny day in autumn, London's best season, and a chance for a chat, fresh company and to practise my Spanish without any need to try and make a good impression was just about the best way to pass the walk I could think of.

We swopped names. Hers was Elena, pronounced the Spanish way: El-lane-ah. She kicked off the conversation.

"Your Spanish is very good."

"Me defiendo". I defend myself. A correct answer which made me smile the first time I heard a Spaniard say it and had the same effect on her.

"Where did you learn it?" My Spanish actually wasn't particularly good, but this was an inevitable part of this kind of conversation, as much a set question as me asking how long she was here for and where she came from in Spain. I explained that I'd served as a volunteer shantytown medic in South America, a major event in my life. For the sake of brevity I didn't go into how I had also travelled there to support those fighting a military dictatorship.

My grasp of her language was a bit better than hers of mine, so we stuck to Spanish.

"And you, are you on holiday here?"

"No, I am learning English. I am here three months more. I live with a friend in Dorking. In Surrey."

Friend, amiga, female. "Yes, I know it. Is it her you are meeting?"

"No, another. An amiga from Spain who has family in London. Ay, how late I will be!"

"What part of Spain are you from?"

"I live in Valencia with my boyfriend, but we are from Castilla La Mancha originally. Do you know it?"

"I spent a few days in Valencia one time when I was on my way to Barcelona…"

"Pff. You English, you all love Barcelona! I do not. Uy, Catalunya! Some of my family lived there. The Catalans treated them very badly for being Spanish."

Oops. "Oh, yes? I don't really know any towns in La Mancha. Are you from one of the big ones?"

"No, Soy de pueblo," I am of the village, a phrase loaded with meanings in Spain. Her voice lifted, "We still visit. It is very, very, umm. It is difficult to describe to an English person. Old fashioned. No, not just that. A different world. Really a different world. You cannot imagine".

We passed the walk in a pleasant amble. She was simpática. Nice. Safe to talk to. Despite my slowing down my normal impatient stride to her more relaxed and short-legged pace we arrived at Ladbroke Grove tube quicker than expected. Ready to say goodbye I pointed the public phones out to her but stayed trapped by good manners that said I couldn't go till she was taken care of.

She made her call and rang off. "She forgot we were to meet," she said. I would learn that this was typically Spanish, "Not important".

So, we stood for long seconds while each waited for the other to issue a goodbye or an invitation. If we hadn't established the lack of any attempt at a pickup I couldn't have done it, but we had, so I did: "Look, I'm just here to take a coffee and stroll around. Do you want to accompany me?"

"¿Sí, cómo no?" Yes, how would it be no?

So, we wandered at leisure among the stalls, stopping for Portuguese coffee and cakes, since you cannot make Spanish people walk for long without refreshment, and ambling along while I occasionally rambled on about the area. Pointing out where Michael Caine's character's flat was in the Italian Job (at the back of Alice's antique shop at number 86, but she'd never heard of the film); George Orwell's house at number 22; and where you could get the best curried chips in west London, though we settled on German sausages for lunch.

Portobello is about a mile long and runs roughly parallel to Ladbroke Grove for as long as the mood takes it. From south to north, it has a mild gradient which acts like an economic mirror. A gradual creeping shabbiness the further you go from the Bayswater Road's tourist and embassy-fed prosperity, and the nearer you get to the end of the road, which is nicely metaphorically overstated by the wonderful Victorian excesses of the nearby Kensal Green Cemetery.

Sunday to Thursday it can be surprisingly quiet. But on Friday and Saturday, especially Saturday, it undergoes its weekly self-rediscovery. The atmosphere becomes charged by the activity of the antique and fruit and veg markets and people blur into two sides, vendors and visitors. The first – market traders, buskers, Trot paper sellers, shop workers and drug dealers – chat and work at a pitch dictated by how much they want to offload their stock before going home time. Meanwhile, on the visitors' side, everyone, local or tourist, forms part of the increasingly slow, milling crowd that's come to talk and walk and look. And only maybe to buy.

And though sometimes I have to get pissed off with the area – its gentrification; one particular nationality's tourists' innate talent for spotting a vital access point then blocking it; the unwashed trustafarians at a table next to you always crapping loudly on about their latest video or art installation or photo exhibition; the fact I can't afford to live there, and they can – you can't beat it as a source of life and variety and vitality. And my pleasure must have been evident, and Elena's was too, as she saw a bit of England that was new to her. So, we were both happy, and the weather was fine, and we ended up in the chill sunshine of the garden of the Earl of Lonsdale pub, before I walked her to Notting Hill Gate to begin her journey home. We swopped numbers and I told her that if she was up in London again sometime, she could give me a ring on the Friday and if I was free, we could meet up again. And it had been a good day, and from these combinations things develop.

Chapter Five

She phoned the next day. Unusually, I wasn't too worried by this. She thanked me for the walk then rang again at work on Monday, saying she had the next Sunday free, and did I too?
"Yes, I think so. Did you want to see more of London?"
She did. I tried to put together a quick mental itinerary that would cover a few different places without being too rushed or too expensive. Had she been to Buckingham Palace, had her photo taken with a friendly PC at Parliament, all the usual stuff? Yes, luckily, she and a girlfriend had done the London bus tour that took in the major landmarks she needed to see, leaving me to show her the places she otherwise wouldn't. Where would be easy to meet and to go on from, a tourist must-do that she might not have visited yet? Covent Garden? Had she been there? No? How about outside the tube then, Sunday, say 12:30?
She was an hour late, but there are worse places to be kept waiting than while watching the world pass at Covent Garden. We strolled a bit, looked at the performers, bought postcards at the London Transport Museum shop, then moved on to the Royal Academy. Not to actually go in, but to have her jump on and off a Routemaster bus while they're still there. And then see something nearby that's in no guidebook, the first red telephone kiosk, the 1924 full-size model Sir Giles Scott built for the competition to find a design that would one day grace every town and village in Britain and provide a trademark of nationhood. All that before he went on to design Battersea and Bankside Power Stations and Waterloo Bridge.
"The first? Could you take a photo with me in it?"
"The first ever, ever. Look, see where it says Telephone? The words were cut out by hand, so that air could circulate when the door was shut. Later they used glass. Has your camera got a flash? It's quite dark under here. Oh, bloody hell." The inside was covered with prostitutes' ads. We had to pull out and hide handfuls of them so they wouldn't spoil the picture.
We took more photos in nineteenth century shopping centre and one-time crinolined streetwalkers' boulevard Burlington Arcade, with its ultra-quaint top hatted beadles,

who are meant to enforce the rules against running, whistling or otherwise behaving in an urchinly manner. Then, having done enough of the tourist bit, we journeyed into a patch of personal London.

I fell in love with the South Bank when I moved back to West London in my early 20s. Walking the Thames or seeing a band at Jubilee Gardens, broke but childishly overcome by the view from the middle of Hungerford Footbridge. The Thames taking the place of a grand continental avenue, flanked by St Paul's, Cleopatra's Needle, Parliament and County Hall, all with an untypically wide expanse of sky above. A great vista that made me feel I was in the centre of a world-class city.

I liked it best in the summer when, no matter how chokingly hot the rest of the capital might be, a whisper of air skims the top of the water, bringing a breath of coolness all the way from the sea to the middle of the metropolis.

It was too cold to sit at the tables outside the National Film Theatre, a good spot in the sun, but just a little too gloomy and shaded by Waterloo Bridge running over it when skies are grey, so we had coffee and sandwiches inside.

How was my work going? Yeah, fine, fine. And hers?

"Yes, alright. Hard work, but I love the old people." When not studying she worked as a care assistant in a private nursing home in Epsom. "Some of them are so sweet. It is lovely to see them smile when I come on duty. Only, I don't know if I should say this about your country…"

"Of course, go ahead."

"It's just it is very different from at home. We don't really send old people away. Grandmothers live with the family. Maybe it isn't better, some of them are working till the day they die, cleaning and cooking for the grandchildren, even when they have grown up and are just sitting around smoking dope," (Spanish style, she called it "chocolate"), "But, where I work, the fees are very high, yet there is only just enough food. The owners make all this money but sometimes at night I find one of the grannies in the kitchen trying to find something to eat because they are too hungry to sleep. We are meant to report them when we find them doing it. Can you believe it?" She hastened to temper the criticism: "I am not saying it is bad here. There are many freedoms you have because you have a different idea of family."

I asked her about her own family. "I have seven brothers and sisters. The youngest eighteen, the oldest forty-five. They do different things. A builder, a carpenter, a waitress, a mechanic, a teacher, a torero."

I didn't know the term and for once decided not to pretend I did, then carry on and hope to guess from what followed. "Torero?"

"In la corrida. The running."

"What's that?"

"You know. La corrida de toros. The running of bulls."

"What, a bullfighter? Really?"

"Yes, that. I know how you feel about it in this country. It was his way to get away from my father and spending his life in the factory or the fields. In Spain it was the route to escape from poverty, for those who could. Many tried. Alicio worked hard and succeeded. He is an intelligent man; he might have been many things, but my father took him from school when he was eight and sent him to work on the land."

"At *eight*?"

"Yes, he wanted to stay, he was a good pupil, and he tried to argue with my father, but..." She made a fist of her hand and, with a resigned look, mimed a punch.

"Bloody hell. At eight. Could he do that?"

"It was the days of Franco. The head of the family could do anything. It was the same for the wives and daughters, you learned not to speak back. If you did..." Again, the fist. "I was lucky, I was born ten years after Alicio. I was allowed to stay at school till I was fifteen. But enough. Today it is your turn to tell me things. Tell me about your family. No. Better. Start with your childhood."

Chapter Six

What kind of a childhood did I have?

"I was born in the 1960s and it was a good time to be a growing up, for me, anyway. Happy. It's difficult to try and describe Britain at that time to someone who wasn't there."

(Not much traffic, being allowed to go anywhere; pillboxes and washed-up mines on holiday beaches; Doctor Who, Thunderbirds, Captain Scarlet, the great brassy intro of the Avengers theme calling the family to pack round a big black and white television with doors; wearing shorts whatever the weather and not minding; your pee smelling of penicillin; the Beatles; Airfix kits; Sean Connery; George Best, Gordon Banks, Alf Ramsey; The fact that our fathers had fought Nazism to a standstill; the British film industry; Aston Martins, Jaguars, Mini Coopers; the Triumph Saint (Stops Anything In No Time) police motorcycle; VC10s, the English Electric Lightning, Concorde; the Post Office Tower; the feeling that we were citizens of a Britain that was a powerhouse of cultural and technological development.)

I paused while one of the counter staff came to clear our tray away. Elena said no to another coffee, still new to the idea that you have to keep buying to stay in most English cafes.

"There was so much going on. Every week a new icon – a film, a car, a song, an actor or band. To a boy it seemed natural. And we had so much space to play in. It's a silly story, really, but I remember when I was about five and my brother eight we went to buy cigars for my father. It was nighttime, pitch black. I'm not sure why he didn't go, maybe we volunteered to be helpful and not to have to go to bed, or he was exhausted from work. Anyway, it was nearly a mile and off we went in our shorts and wellies and zip-up grey woollen pullovers, and it seemed the most natural thing in the world for two little children to be out at night innocently buying tobacco from an off licence. My brother carried my Dad's torch, one of those big black rubber Ever Ready ones – did you have them in Spain? I think they gave them to men at maternity hospitals: 'New father? You'll be needing one of these, then' – and he pointed the beam up at the stars and said that it would be a million years before it reached one of them. I imagined a little pool of light falling on the darkened surface of a planet far, far in the future, and that night and street and space and life and family seemed like they would go on forever: endlessly wide and timeless and full of wonder and potential."

As the memories appeared they tumbled out into speech: "Oh and we had floods and power cuts. And fogs. Fogs like in American films about London. They don't exist now, they were because most houses used to be heated by coal, and factories used it too. There was a law, the *Clean Air Act*, before that people were dying in what they called smog. But it took, oh, ten or fifteen years for the atmosphere to clear, and where we lived, near the Thames, there were still these fabulous impenetrable pea soupers. We would go out to play and you could stretch out your arm and you couldn't see your hand. At night a torch beam would disappear in inches. I can remember how when you breathed it in the mist in your nose tasted of excitement and the end of the year coming. And other smells from that time. In summer, sky blue PVC, these folding paddling pools with little wooden corner seats and metal legs people used to have. And in autumn, dry leaves, that peppery, dusty scent they have when they first fall and you walk through the piles, kicking them up in the air. We'd go down the road with my father and a wheelbarrow to gather them up to stuff a Guy with, it's an effigy that you burn on a bonfire. And the bonfire you'd stuff with leaves too. And with fireworks when the adults weren't looking. Oh, and then there's the smell of fireworks..."

I didn't mention music, perhaps because I still don't understand the emotional mechanisms. Many songs from that time I can take or leave. But those on the records my parents used to play – A Whiter Shade of Pale, Downtown, Moulin Rouge – evoke a painful nostalgia for lost times and innocence. I'm considered a pretty hard and self-contained man, but Feed the Birds from Mary Poppins can make me cry almost helplessly. I don't know why. Presumably it's an echo of the completely forgotten effect it had when I first saw it, aged three, when our beings are built around loving and being loved.

There's a great piece of music called High Wire that I would very occasionally hear, and it would be like a punch of concentrated sadness in the stomach. I didn't know where the tune or the effect came from. It was only a few years ago that I learnt that it was from Danger Man, one of those programmes that the country would come to a stop to watch on a Saturday afternoon. Not too long out of nappies I'd be toddling around, my brother would be playing with his Dinky toys or Lone Star pistols, my father would be cutting the lawn, or reading in a deck chair, and my mother would call out that it was on, and we'd all rush in to sit together and watch it, not knowing that Dad only had a few more years to live.

"Then there were the 1970s, maybe not so good. There was a loss of cohesion, I suppose you could say. An opening of fault lines in society that would be widened for ideological reasons and political gain in the next decade. The things we had felt proud of seemed to be falling apart or turning into an international joke." (The opportunity to educate yourself in film, courtesy of BBC2 and their Cagney, Rathbone and Bruce, and sexually-charged foreign film seasons, set against the Morris Ital, football hooligans, Love Thy Neighbour, the Franco-admiring Major next door stockpiling rifles in his attic, the National Front, tank tops, centre partings, strikes, the three-day week, shortages, crap disco, the Silver Jubilee, we love the Rollers, Brut aftershave and Brutus jeans.

A short equation would be:

1960s = The Avengers. The Rolling Stones. The Prisoner. Films starring Finch, Finney, Caine, Connery, Hemmings, Baker, O'Toole, Courtenay, MacDowell.

1970s = The New Avengers. The Boomtown Rats. The Professionals. Films starring Robin Askwith.)

"Then in the 1980s I hit my twenties. That was the time of Margaret Thatcher, and I was always broke, working too hard for political campaigns, scraping by on the dole or doing labouring and decorating work in between. Getting deeper and deeper in debt, drinking too much, smoking too much, going out too much. Doing other things too much, eating too little. It was great."

It was as much talking as I'd done to anyone for quite a while, a stream of consciousness that was censored only by the difficulty of explaining many of the references and because I hate to sound or feel self-pitying when I have so little to be self-pitying about.

I finished. "Maybe someday you could meet my mother. She and my brother are very similar to each other. Physically and emotionally. I've been told that I take after my father more."

"Maybe one day you will meet my family too if you come to Spain. Maybe even to the village. You would be fascinated, I think. You will never have seen a place like it."

She paused. "Mind you I prefer to visit, not to live there. It was very, very difficult to leave the village. Girls were not expected to look for their own futures and I had no confidence. All my brothers and sisters are marked one way or other by my father's personality and that was mine. It was Paco, my boyfriend, who helped me become my own person. Before that I was too shy. He is older than me and that helped; he knew more of what I was going through. He's a good man. He had left the village years before and was living in Valencia. It was only because we moved in together that I was allowed to leave home. Mind you I had to tell my father that we had married. Not my mother, I wouldn't lie to her. We all had our different ways to escape my father, you see. With Alicio it was the bulls. With me a pretend marriage."

She smiled wryly. "It's different now; Spain has changed. The young ones in the family. Ouf! They do what they want. You wouldn't believe."

It was her turn to talk, and I steered her towards speaking about her own hopes for the future and reminiscences of the past, her work and the difficulties of learning English – all the time watching the emotions play across her face, especially when it was her family she was discussing.

Afterwards we wandered up to Bankside Power Station, Sir Giles Scott's deserted "cathedral to energy", squeezing through a gap in the fence and racking open the doors as far as their padlock and chains would allow so that Elena could see the vast, sleeping, Molochian turbines within.

Later she leaned, tip-toed, over the Embankment wall and watched the water passing for a long minute, before deciding. "Yes, I like this place, I didn't know there was somewhere in the middle of London with so much space. Explain to me the river. What is its history? And why is it so muddy?"

They were easy questions. I used to work for a London listings magazine where, until it went bust, in my spare time I would write and photograph articles on things that interested me, like London's social and political history, the ghost stations on the tube, and its river history*.

"The Thames *is* London." I told her, "There wouldn't be a city here without it. It only looks filthy because of the clay and silt being moved by the tide. Once it was three times as wide as this. You have to imagine London as a valley with a broad, shallow river spilling over onto miles of marshes, with hills floating above it to the north and south. This part, Southwark, was still islands in a bog when the Romans came. Even in the nineteenth century it was waterlogged and pestilential, a mix of taverns, breweries and stinking tanneries with cesspits and ditches running between them. The air was foul and the water black with chemicals or red with blood and guts from the slaughterhouses. Look, the tide's out, come and we'll see if we can find some old London."

We took the steps down then picked our way along the muddy shore. Within ten minutes I had found animal bones, a shard of Roman hypocaust tile, a clay tobacco pipe and the broken stems of several others.

"The bones will be from the tanneries and slaughterhouses. The pipe looks seventeenth century. They're called plague pipes because people, even children, smoked to keep the disease away and there're usually hundreds of them in with the bodies in plague pits. Scary, eh? The river is like a constant archaeological dig, scouring out its sides and showing its history to anyone who's there at the right moment before it's washed out to sea or sinks in the silt again. Incredible finds still turn up. Ancient armour sacrificed to some sinister bogside god, live German bombs. From where we're standing, we would once have been able to see brothels, slums, prisons, a bear-baiting arena and a leper hospital. Oh, and a bullring; that went on here right up till the nineteenth century. Just down the river was an island so hellish that when Charles Dickens wrote about it most London readers thought it was fictional. Do they get you to read him in your course? *Oliver Twist*? No? There's a film, a musical of it, the scenic design is fantastic, it gives you a real idea what it was like. Hovels with weeping walls teetering above filth and mud. The river was contained in that century, and they began to clean it up before it became the death of the city. But you can only channel a river, you can't stop it moving, and this one still has to be controlled so it doesn't burst its banks." I pointed out the bronze lions heads on the Embankment that are meant to signal the flooding of London if the water rises high enough for them to drink from it, "and you can't stop it scratching away at London and revealing its two thousand years of secrets."

Sometimes I talk too much. But sometimes I get away with it.

She wrapped the clay pipe in a tissue, and we walked to Waterloo. Mindful of our status, I put her, glowing, on a train home; even though it would have been more convenient, but maybe just a little dangerous too, to have her stay over at my place.

*See appendix

Chapter Seven

Just as I was thinking it would be nice if one of us phoned to fix up another meeting, she did, interrupting an attempt by Roger and I to spend the whole day speaking only in West Country accents.

I'd had girlfriends I saw less than this, but I didn't mind. It made sense to enjoy each other's company while we had it.

"One of my cousins and her boyfriend have found a budget break to London. One week, last minute. You know, a special offer. It's their first time abroad. If someone could show them around a little it would make it much better for them. Would you mind very much if I asked you?"

I went to say something, but she rushed on, "They say the hotel is very small and dirty and cold, they don't really want to stay in too much. I wouldn't ask you if they weren't family. I like your country, and I would like them to like it too. And to tell people back home that everything is fine here for me."

It was actually quite inconvenient, and I didn't fancy chaperoning a couple of strangers around all day by myself. "Will you be coming with them?"

"Sí, cómo no?"

"In that case I'll see what I can do."

We met at Ladbroke Grove. Elena was late, Sol and Raúl were later. They showed no curiosity about our relationship, accepting me for what I was. Just someone Elena had met, who fortuitously happened to live in the capital.

We paired off by gender, with the girls in front talking away at a speed that I would have been unable to match. Raúl was reserved. Young, Spanish, male and proud, typically fast to complain and at pains not to seem surprised by anything London could throw up. Maybe a little nervous too, and by tradition not allowed to show it. He was a builder, he said. And me, what did I do?

"Journalist," I noticed Sol look around approvingly, "But not a real one".

Portobello could have been made for Spanish tourists. The crowds make walking at anything above an amble difficult, and painfully long periods can be happily passed looking at clothes or goods that they're not going to buy. They loved it.

Raúl's determination not to be impressed broke down when a resident drove by in his army surplus armoured car. Visitors swivelled their cameras or nudged their friends, but few locals gave it a second glance. "Sometimes I love this city," Elena said, "You can wear what you want and do what you want, and no one looks twice. What freedom you have."

Slowed down by too-frequent snack and coffee stops we had to hurry to fit in quick looks at Buckingham Palace, Trafalgar Square and Westminster. Each time I stepped up to buy tickets or ask the price of something Elena would rush past me and do it in the best and clearest English she could manage. I glanced at her, then at the others, who were obviously to take news of this back to Spain, and then at Elena again. When they weren't looking, I raised an eyebrow. She answered with an expression of complete innocence. Then winked.

With her insisting on paying for dinner I suggested that we ate in the downstairs café at the Royal Festival Hall, knowing the meal might not be a showstopper, but was fairly cheap and the portions reasonably generous. Raúl and Sol had known in advance that British food would not be great but had thought that at least it would be served in profusion, Spanish style. They'd have an ever-bigger shock coming when they ordered a drink in a pub and realized they'd get about a sixth of a typical Spanish measure for the same price it would cost them back home.

Afterwards we strolled back towards Embankment tube. We'd need to get the visitors back to their hotel if Elena was going to make the last train home to Dorking. Remembering what we'd talked about when she and I had been there the week before, I took out a copy of an article on London's rivers I'd brought along. "It's just something I wrote years ago; in case you get a chance to read it sometime."

She and I were now walking together. From behind we heard Raúl comment disparagingly about the Thames and how dirty it was. Elena stiffened for a second, walked on for a few minutes, then stopped and turned towards the lamplit river, which looked high, mysterious and powerful. "Tom, we don't know anything about the river. Do you? Is there anything you can tell us?"

Blocked from Raúl and Sol's view I felt her hand take my arm for a second and give it a conspiratorial squeeze.

Later we left them at their hotel. On the tube I had answered questions about London while Elena, to admiring looks from her cousin, took out the article[1] I'd given her and, intently studied the English text. She finished it just as we pulled into Edgware Road station, near where they were staying.

"Thank you for helping Sol and Raúl. They will have got more out of their visit because you came. You are a good man." She laughed, "Like we say at home, better than bread. And cleverer than wire."

"You don't have to thank me. I enjoyed it. Don't worry about your train, we should get to Waterloo with about ten minutes to spare."

"Thank you for showing me your article. It was very interesting."

"Thanks."

"There were some words I did not understand."

"That's all right, don't worry. Which ones?"

She waved her hand over the page and gave me a half embarrassed, half mischievous look. "The ones in English."

Chapter Eight

"Tom?"

"Yes, it's me. Hola. Are you at work? I thought you weren't meant to use the phone."

"I'm not. I have to be quick. Look. Can we meet Saturday? I know it's a bit sudden, but I want to say goodbye. There are problems at home. Family. I must go back to Spain. Maybe for good."

"Saturday sounds fine. Somewhere you haven't been before?"

"Um there is a little problem with that…"

Roger, surrendering to premature middle age in Marks and Spencer slacks and colour supplement shoes, waited till I put the phone down, then asked,

"Going somewhere, are we?"

"Not in this job, mate."

He waited a few minutes. "Was that the Spanish girl? What's her name again? Getting a bit serious, isn't it? You must have seen her at least 10 times now. Girlfriend is she? Thought you weren't planning on going out with anyone for a while. Bet you are going out with her."

"Yes. Elena. No. Four times. No. Correct. Incorrect." When I looked up, he was smirking. It was the number of times we'd met he had been fishing for. Bugger. I'd been tricked into giving away personal information.

He gloated briefly then piped up again. "OK, here's one for you. What's the connection between Get Carter and the Flying Squad?"

"Easy, George Sewell was in Get Carter. He was Patrick Mower's boss in Special Branch, which was the precursor to the Sweeney. In which Mower also turned up. He was Colonel Freeman in UFO, where Mower again guested. In fact, Patrick Mower had to be in every single programme on ITV in the seventies. It was the law."

Roger thought for a minute. "I'm pretty sure he was in Space 1999 too. Speaking of which, now that we're in the future don't you think it's all a bit of a disappointment. No anti-gravity boots, for example."

"I rather fancied the future according to UFO when I was little. That was meant to be 1980. Better music. Slightly less embarrassing clothes. Apart from the Nehru jackets and string vests. Not that I want to insult an integral part of your daily wardrobe."

He looked around the office. "Yes. Perhaps we could ask the receptionists to wear purple metallic wigs, though personally I think it would be better if the company was based inside an extinct volcano, with a rocket in the middle and a monorail to the coffee machine. Anyway, you're so clever, what's this the music from then?" He hummed a light tune.

"I Dream of Jeannie. Larry Hagman and Barbara somebody. Steele. No, Eden."

"No, it's not, it's Bewitched."

"No, that was more twiddly. I can't remember it, but that wasn't it."

"You're always saying things like that. If you can't remember it, how do you know that wasn't it?"

"Christ. Shut up will you. We're beginning to sound like an old married couple."

"Alright, we'll come back to that one. TV theme tunes then. I hum one, you name it, then it's your turn..."

That was us taken care of for the rest of the day.

"Hola Chico."

"Hola Chiquitita."

"I am sorry you had to come here; I wish we could be in London. But I am on late shift tomorrow and I fly Monday. If you couldn't have come, I don't know how long it would be before we could meet."

"It's alright, Dorking's not so far, and I quite like it. It's got character. I waved a bag full of wine, crisps and pork pies. "The countryside looked beautiful from the train. I don't know what you have planned, but I thought that maybe we could go for a little picnic."

"Well, I have everything ready for cooking dinner later, but yes, we could do that."

So, we did, and the countryside really was beautiful. I found the remnant of a rope hung from a tree over the River Mole and, even though it was obvious that it was too short, I had to jump for it. I just managed to close my fingertips on it, swung out over the river once, twice and then the swing ran out, well short of the bank. Leaving me hanging there. Elena wanted to try and hook me back but might have fallen in, so I had to take the manly course and order her back. Then wait till I couldn't hold on any longer and – having probably known deep down all along that it would end this way but having still failed to ignore the rope's siren call – drop six feet into the waist-deep water.

I scrambled out, checked that I hadn't lost my wallet, keys or penknife to the river and wrung out my socks. Laid out over the long grass, there was just enough sun to dry them out. If we had several hours to waste. I resigned myself to my complete loss of dignity. Elena tried to be helpful, if strangely silent. The odd strangled squeak she let out suggested why.

Though she managed to hold it in at first, she was soon doubled up laughing at the noise my size 12, waterlogged desert boots made as we walked. To make it even better for her, as we laid the picnic out a cloud of horseflies began to attack. The only way to escape them was to send her up the field and draw them off after me. Then run back as fast as I could with the aggressive little bastards pounding against my head and eyes, making for the cover of a pub at the field's edge. The sight of me at full speed in a cloud of insectile dive bombers, clutching our picnic things and shouting at her to get through the door quick, while my boots went Squish! Squish! Squish! was enough to almost incapacitate her with laughter.

That's me. Always doing the right thing. In comedy boots.

By the time we left the pub the miniature stuka storm was gone, allowing us to enjoy the woods and meadows in the thin sharp light of early winter sunshine. The sensual pleasures – smell, sight, sound – of British woodlands and the memories of days among them are one of the things that have always brought me back to this country. The walk was also an object lesson in how you develop a preternatural vision for things that you are interested in, but which are invisible to those who aren't.

I peeled off the path a couple of times when I noticed old glass among the bracken and tree roots. The third time I was rewarded with a present for Elena, a deep green, stoppered lemonade bottle that a ploughman or picnicker must have jettisoned ninety years ago. I restrained myself from exploring a half-buried pillbox that we passed within yards of without her noticing it, and decided that about the only thing missing, apart from a haunted forest pool, a cursed folly or a ruined house to explore, was a mysterious tunnel entrance. In fact, not that long afterwards I spotted the telltale overgrown concrete square of a likely World War II shelter entrance, and wondered what the chances were of getting it open with nothing more than a Swiss army knife.

Strangely it is almost impossible to completely conceal something built under the ground. There are always signs: subsidence and excavated soil, or essential features like steel doors, stairs, emergency exits and ventilators. The only way to hide what's going on beneath the surface is to take away all the things necessary to make its existence worthwhile or cover them in a carapace so deep and damage-resistant that you lose sight of what it is you are trying to protect.

If there was some kind of an emotional metaphor there, I was happy to ignore it.

It had been a frabjous day spent in watercolour pastures, but as we got nearer to her house a sadness came over Elena as she tried to hide her homesickness and her concerns about home. Whatever was worrying her was personal to her family so she would only skirt around it, but from the little she gave away it sounded like someone was in trouble, leaving their children to be looked after by Elena and the others.

We walked back to her home, passing a Nissan Pajero, which was at least good for a small laugh from her at whoever looked up hayloft in a Spanish dictionary so old that it failed to mention that pajero has had only one meaning for the last two hundred years, and that isn't it. Leaving the owners driving around in a huge car prominently badged "Wanker".

Later, after I had met her housemates, the two of us paired the unused picnic wine with dinner, which she cooked while I sat under orders to relax and not interfere: prawns cooked in garlic and olive oil. Fried salted almonds. Bocaditos – toasted slices of French bread topped with crushed tomato and sea salt – to which we added slices of Serrano ham and Manchegan cow and sheep milk cheese ("from La Mancha, near my village"). And, best of all, potato omelette. ("Tortilla

Valenciana. In La Mancha we make it plain, it is very good, but in Valencia, they make it like this, thicker, often with vegetables and chorizo sausage. It is even better.") Every Spanish woman I'd known could make tortilla, but this was the best I'd had. I told her so.

"You should try my mother's," she replied.

After dinner she put on a brave face, but she was drifting away, preoccupied. She needed to be distracted. My reporting skills were rusty, but I hadn't wholly lost the ability to get people to open up. I asked her about post-Franco Spain, a subject which led on to the 1981 military coup attempt, when a Civil Guard colonel and his accomplices stormed the Spanish parliament, and people like me wondered where to go to sign up for an International Brigade.

"We were in school," she told me, "and the teacher came in, pale like death. 'Go, don't stop to pick up anything,' he told us. 'Run to your homes and lock the doors. Don't open for anyone who isn't family. If soldiers or police come, hide.' The streets were full of tanks. And, of course, the Guardia Civiles, they were at the centre of it. For hours it looked like they would win. Those bastards. They are not so free to do what they want now but before they were like wolves, they could do anything to the poor and the weak. Anything. You do not know how much my class hates them."

The conversation shifted around. "There is one thing I'm embarrassed to admit. Your name. I still don't know if it's T-o-m, or T-o-n."

So, like most Spanish people, she wasn't sure about our shortened names. To make a familiar name they tend to add a diminutive ending or substitute a set one, rather than a true abbreviation: Juanito for Juan, Lalo for Eduardo, Moncho for Ramón, Charo for Rosario, Paco, Paqui for Francisco, Francesca, and so on.

"Tom. With M. It's short for Thomas."

"Ah! *Tomás*". From then on that's what she called me. Usually, only girlfriends ever use my full name. It gave a kind of added intimacy when she spoke.

It was probably inevitable that she would begin to talk about her mother.

"I feel so sorry for her, she has had such a miserable life. When she was little there was not enough work. They had to go to wherever a landowner needed casual labourers. She remembers when she was eight walking thirty kilometres through the night with her father. When they arrived, it was dawn, and they began work straight away. All for one day's work. Her hands are still swollen and some of her fingers don't close because splinters of wheat punctured them and festered when they were cutting the crops. And when she was twenty-one, she married my father, and married his rages and his madness. Poor Mami. She is old before her time."

It seemed like a good time to change the subject and take her mind off her worries. I leapt on a story she had told me earlier about a group of female artists she knew near her and Paco's flat in the rundown but bohemian part of old Valencia.

"I knew someone like that when I first moved to London. Jamie. Irish. About twenty years old. Of course he lived in an attic, in this Tooting tenement. Crooked landlord after crooked landlord: it would all go up in flames within a year. I used to go to visit another friend, but I would guiltily hope that he wouldn't be in, and Jamie would, because he was such a one off, and so interested in fitting in everything that his home village couldn't offer, and London could. He was usually painting in the kitchen, even though the ceiling was falling in. Literally. He'd usher me in and give me the one chair, which meant a guaranteed paint stain from the big canvas it was holding up. Then he'd root around for his cigarettes or have one of mine, getting more paint into the packets, and offer me a cup of tea from this huge old teapot he filled when he began working and kept on the lowest heat till he knocked off about 10 hours later. I only ever had the one cup from that pot. I'd rather have drunk his brush cleaner. He painted all day like that, lost in his work the way you can get lost in a book, occasionally using his spare hand to smoke or eat, Ryvita with cheese and raw onion, and grinding out the cigarettes in a hole in the cooker where one of the rings had been removed. Hundreds of butts, not very nice really, but at that age you just don't mind those things.

She looked unconvinced by that last bit.

"Anyway," I continued, "we'd decide to go out, he'd find that weeks *Time Out* or *City Limits*, read out what was on, and we'd choose something. Only it was always starting in thirty minutes, and we'd have to run down the middle of Tooting

High Street dodging through the cars, chasing the open platform of a moving bus. But we never saw what we set out to. He had always read the listing wrong, and we were a week late or a week early. We sat through bad films when we'd gone for classics, listened to jazz when we'd planned to see the Undertones and fidgeted through modern dance when we'd wanted ska. But we never just said "why don't we see what's on the telly". I only remember him putting on the TV once, for a literary adaptation he'd been talking about for weeks, and it didn't work. I don't think it ever did. It was a big seventies black and white monolith, and he used to carry it on the bus to the repairers. The conductors used to tell him to just give it the fare and put it on by itself because it had been to be fixed so many times it knew its own way. I wonder where he is now. Wherever it is, I bet he's brewing tea and planning a night out."

I managed to string the story out till it was bedtime. She guessed what I was doing, but it worked. It took her out of herself for a while.

The only place to sleep was on her bedroom floor. Faced with a vulnerable, sad, lonely, slightly drunk girl I did the decent thing and left the room while she undressed and got into bed, then returned in the dark to slip into the sleeping bag a few feet away. Very gentlemanly. Then I spent the night having ungentlemanly dreams.

The next day she gave me bocadillos (baguettes spread with olive oil and the rest of the tortilla, which tasted even better cold) to eat on the train and we walked to the station to make our goodbyes. We only needed Rachmaninov and a steam train to turn it into Brief Encounter. She looked at me like she was storing me up in her memory. We embraced clumsily, as two people will who fancy each other but know they mustn't take it any further, then she was gone.

Chapter Nine

She'd never been in my flat, yet somehow when I got home it felt empty. The only sound was one I alone could hear. The noise of a small chink appearing in emotional armour.

I'd never invited her back because of the risk that we'd have ended up in bed together. That and the fact that she would have seen the spare room.

When my former flatmate, Michael, moved out to be nearer his mother (He's half Portuguese. It must be a Latin thing) I had thought about finding someone new. But years of living in shared houses suggested that only the first generation works out. As people leave and replacements arrive things fall apart, and you move inexorably nearer to the coming of The Destroyer. Who is usually one of two types. Either the girlfriend/boyfriend of a housemate who moves in uninvited and bent on domination, or the new tenant who arrives covered in bargepole marks and before you know it the food is labelled, and the house is divided into camps. They tend to bring an over-developed sense of self-worth and a gift for malignity (appropriately enough one was into witchcraft of the Satanic kind, that last resort of the unfuckworthy). The reason I had first moved to the flat was to escape one of these. Sasha, who, as a visitor shocked by her behaviour put it, was unique in being the only woman who became uglier the more you drank. I repressed a shudder and made a mental note to give Michael a call.

So, I kept the room empty, if that is the right word. For a while I rationalised it as gaining a work area that would be handy for the freelance jobs I needed to pay the now crippling rent. Not for long though. Despite shelving all four walls it soon turned into a glorified box room, even if it probably did contain everything I wanted as a youngster – things with a history, things to impress. Except that after you stop being a teen you shouldn't need props, so I kept it closed. It held a jumble of protective headgear from various sports and pastimes; medical supplies waiting to be sent to the clinics I'd worked at during trips to South America; a gift handmade by political prisoners there and smuggled out to me; a set of neon-lit glass shelves for the best of the gloriously multicoloured antique bottles I'd dug up over the years; first aid kits for a variety of situations; Bakelite radios; tin toys; old telephones; parachuting and rifle-shooting certificates; vintage cameras; photos of my father as an achingly young man going off to face the horrors of the Japanese in World War II; records, videos; and books, books, books. Including piles of old boys' annuals picked up down Portobello for the unintentional double entendres and amusingly earnest illustrations. Mind you, I shouldn't knock them. If I hadn't read them in childhood, I'd never have come to believe that every abandoned lighthouse, ruined tower and cliff cave hid a secret passage to the headquarters of a gang of smugglers, a mad scientist or a secret U-boat base.

Without those promises of adventure, I might not have been drawn to every pillbox, castle or empty house I could find as a boy, and I wouldn't still thrill at the idea of discovering dark and lonely places. I feel the same now late at night re-reading MR James's perfect ghost stories of honest souls who, for no greater sin than curiosity and an interest in the past, are rewarded with a visit from elemental forces of madness and vengeance.

The rest of the flat-come-bedsit had been squeezed into the living room of a much larger 1930s apartment. My bedroom had space for a bed, TV, the kind of stereo I used to dream of at sixteen, and a wardrobe that groaned under the burden of the clothes I actually wore plus a mix of cold weather gear, hats, boots, overcoats, leather jackets and 1940s and 50s suits that I probably should have sold or thrown away. But probably never would (I smiled as I thought of my American cousin, whose answer would be "Hey, it's a guy thing"). The cold-water-only kitchenette was shaped to follow the slope of the roof above and had enough space for a Belling cooker. It was tiny, but fine for me and, with just a small skylight window, made an excellent darkroom. The bathroom was damp and windowless, holding just a toilet; there was a shared sink and shower one floor below.

I put the kettle on and wondered about catching up on some reading. Because I wanted Elena to have a good time, I had secretly been hitting my credit card pretty hard. Staying in a bit more would be no bad thing. Pleased to have found something good in what might otherwise have been a slightly sad event, I put on Waterloo Sunset by the Kinks, which fitted the mood somehow, and wondered when I'd hear from her.

The next few weeks passed. I had a job interview and, as usual, got to the final round, then came second. Applied for another couple of posts. Went out with friends for drinks at a student pub. They were playing Dark Side of the Moon, which had mysteriously changed from being the target of cognoscenti scorn to fashionable again. I had forgotten what a groundbreaking album it was in its time. It gave me an idea of what to do the following weekend, since I was too broke to go out. I'd risk two days of the psychedelic and progressive music that I listened to in my early teens.

I hadn't heard any played since I was in my mid-20s, by which time I found it a huge embarrassment. I would probably have given away all the records on principle, except that they had stayed in the attic at my mother's house when I first left home. It was only when she moved to a flat that I picked them up, all boxed up, preserved from that time like a fly in amber (there was even one of my once long, once much lighter hairs stuck to a record by static).

I decided to select only the ones that I hadn't heard since the seventies and those which might be the most evocative. Of course, they all had to predate their replacements, the more acceptable music strongly linked in my memory with partying and protesting in the early anti-Thatcher years: Robert Wyatt, The Jam, Elvis Costello, Moving Hearts, Trojan, Motown. In the first box I opened I found some Fairport Convention, Caravan and Curved Air. Sure, the experiment would last about five minutes, I put the first one on.

Instead, it worked. I could almost be 13 again, sitting at night in a friend's room, its blackness punctuated only by the glowing ends of our Player's Number Six cigarettes, listening to Faust, Can, The Moody Blues and Led Zeppelin on his homemade quadrophonic speakers, while outside the collapsing branches of a dead tree occasionally wind-whipped against the uncurtained window, and life seemed full of mysteries and possibilities of magic, myth and lost knowledge.

It was just as well no one from my West London stamping grounds could see me. I'd have been drummed out of the Ladbroke Grovaltineys.

I don't know what it was that reminded me of Elena, for the first time since she left, but I suddenly realized that two weeks had passed, and she hadn't phoned. I felt a slight twinge. What was that emotion? Oh yes, it must be loneliness. I'd heard of that one.

Chapter Ten

And then she did. She called, sounding secretive, as though she didn't want to be overheard. In two days' time she'd be arriving at Victoria Coach Station. If I wanted to, I could meet her there, if not, not. No problem.

Roger and I were used to covering for each other on occasions like these. With his help I invented a press conference, wore the appropriate suit and tie that morning, then left to pick her up.

She was flustered and tired after the journey. The coach station was noisy, and fume filled. We hugged and continental-kissed hello. For once I remembered to do both cheeks, meaning the next time an Englishwoman expected a peck I'd be bound to lunge embarrassingly for a second go just as she pulled her head back. As I shouldered some of the extraordinary amount of luggage that Spaniards consider normal, I got the impression she was putting off deciding where we were going next – even though she had the air of having settled some much bigger decision during her time away.

She pre-empted my question by lifting a plastic bag. "Presents for you. Spanish brandy. A *Mafalda* book, a bottle of Anis. I hope you like them."

"Lovely, thanks. Me too. I've been feeling guilty about never talking to you in English, so I got a few books for you to practise on. Kind of a mix of levels. *Just William*, it's a children's book I read when I was little. I'd forgotten how funny it was. I started flicking through it on the tube here and it made me laugh out loud. I can't remember when that last happened. And *Cider with Rosie*, it's about an English village, but it's also about the people in any village in any country. A wonderful book. Oh, and a record. Dusty Springfield. I saw it in a charity shop and thought of you. I don't think she's known in Spain, but I'm sure you'll like her."

"I don't have a record player."

"Oh, I couldn't remember whether you did or not. Never mind, I can record it if you like."

"You have one?"

48

"Yes, certainly do, back at my flat, I don't use it much though. Just..."

She cut through me: "We'd better go there then."

My shirt was on the floor, minus some buttons, and hers was on its way. Once it was off there wasn't going to be any turning back. I took my mouth from hers and wriggled back a little. "This is lovely, but I don't know if it's right. I never have affairs. I completely understand why people do, but I don't. Someone has to be cheated and I've never wanted to be a part of that..."

She looked momentarily hurt. "Paco's been with someone almost since I left. He's very sexual. He says that if it isn't love it doesn't matter. We sort of had an arrangement; we can do what we want so long as it doesn't become serious. I didn't want to tell you before. I thought that if we started something it might not stay casual." Then she shut me up.

Later. We were sharing a cigarette, naked on the bed. "I have a ticket home in one month. My English exam is in three weeks. I don't know what you think, but if you like I could stay here for the last week. We wouldn't need to tell anybody; it would be just us. Once I go back to Spain..."

She left that thought unfinished.

"Sure. Why not. Listen, are you thirsty? Yes? Wait here, I'll be back in a minute." I was wondering how the anis would taste off her skin.

"Why do you do that?"

"Do what?"

"You're walking all bent over. Stop hiding. You've got a good body; you should be proud of it. Why don't you let me see it?"

I stood up straight as I stepped over the trail of clothes from the front door. It was vaguely liberating.

"And Tomás,"

"Yes?"

"Hurry back, you funny Englishman."

We didn't surface till the next day, Friday, when I dragged myself up to phone Roger. I'd never pulled a sickie at Montressor Publishing and I knew he'd have kept quiet if I'd told him what was happening, but on this occasion I lied. I just didn't want to give away all the details of my private life as soon as they happened. Luckily, I sounded knackered and had in fact had a very mild stomach bug going for a few days, so I didn't feel too guilty.

"Don't worry," he said, "You hardly ever take sick days, and we don't want you here spreading germs. Go to bed and rest."

I was hanging up when I heard him suddenly shout "Tom, Tom, are you still there? There's something I forgot."

"Yes, I'm here, what is it?"

"Enjoy your three-day fuckfest. See you Monday."

She was bent over the stereo, wearing one of my T-shirts and humming Mockingbird from the Dusty Springfield album, which we'd almost played a hole in. Absurdly I felt a sudden nervousness about what was on the CD player. If my memory was right, it was The Andrews Sisters. In typical male style I wondered what that said about me to someone I was starting a relationship with.

It didn't matter. She was Spanish. As soon as she found the Rolling Stones albums ("¡Aja! ¡Los Rollings!") she was happy.

We consumed each other over the next few weeks, squeezing in all the time together that we could and spending much of it in bed, the meeting point for our two different sexual cultures. My British, pro-feminist, lefty background had taught that practically every inch of a woman should be kissed and caressed in a long, selfless process devoted to increasing her pleasure. Anything less than an absolute minimum of two hours' foreplay was clear proof of rampant misogyny. Elena was heir to the contrasting Spanish tradition of the hot, hard, passionate shag. When we weren't in bed we saw as much as we could of London, before I would take her to catch her train home, walking hand in hand under a Waterloo sunset.

"You haven't been to the British Museum? You must. Maybe we could fix it to spend a whole day there. You really need two, but this is a good time of year. Usually, you can't get near the displays for tourists. We could see a film afterwards. There's a friend I want you to meet, he loves cinema. Speaking of which, do you want to watch something while we eat?" I rooted around for a film that wasn't too script-heavy and came up with Laurel and Hardy's Bonnie Scotland. Then we sat through the pedestrian romantic substory for the sequence where, in kilts, they dance to 100 Pipers. I heard sobs from next to me and looked at Elena. She was rocking backwards and forwards, at first crying and then weeping with laughter.

We pressed our heads to the tube's window as the train shuddered past the deserted platform walls. "There it is," I told her. "British Museum Station, closed since 1933. It's the ghost station I'd most like to get into. There's something so deep and dark and alone about it."

I was boyishly excited at showing her the once gaslit, now soot-darkened walls outside that the rest of the carriage were oblivious to. "Don't you think it's mysterious? Like you could live down here in the old tunnels and stairways and rooms and no one would know. Oh, here we are, Holborn. We get off here for the museum. If you like I could put together a little underground history tour for you. Maybe a few more abandoned stations, the first ever platforms, some of the quirky places most people pass every day and never notice. What do you think?"

Her eyes were sparkling, and she seemed to have to pull herself back to what I'd said. She suddenly rose on tiptoe and gave me a kiss. "Of course, if you like, Tomás. Would that be easy? Do you know enough about it to fix it up so quickly?"

"Oh, I reckon I know a bit. I might have written an article or two about it a few jobs back."*

I chose to believe that her expression reflected amusement.

I've been told before by girlfriends that I sometimes become boyish when I'm excited, and that this can be strangely endearing.

It had to be that.

The alternative was that she had just decided she was in love with me.

*See appendix

Chapter Eleven

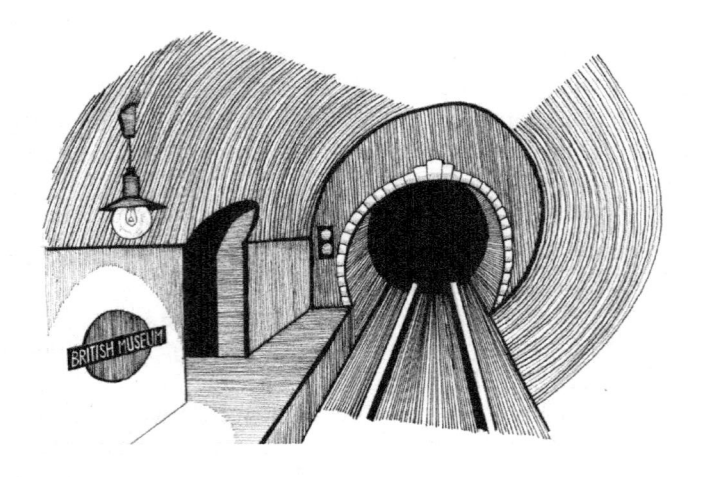

"There it is again. That was the other platform. Wouldn't it be perfect if they'd left the old British Museum station signs up and the vending machines in place? Can't you just see a ghostly gent in a top hat and frockcoat filling his cigarette case, or a lady in a bustle buying a penny bar of Fry's chocolate? Anyway, we'll change at Oxford Circus. Two stops. We're meeting Hugh at the cinema in half an hour, so we'll have to hurry, or we'll miss the beginning of the film."

"Actually, Tomás? Would you mind, perhaps if we didn't do an underground tour? Tell me the stories instead. I like that. But thank you so much for taking me to the British Museum," she held her arm across her body and waved her hand as though trying to shake water from the fingers, "It was de putamadre! I am going to have nightmares about those mummies."

The paradoxes of other people's slang. To insult a Spaniard call them a son of a whore, hijo de puta. But to say something is outstanding describe it as de putamadre. Whoremotherishly good. You shouldn't say somewhere looks like a brothel, but you can describe it as a puticlub – in other words, a brothel. Since it ends in a confusing English - ub sound, and in Spanish there's no real difference between b and v, this is pronounced pootie-cloo, which amuses me, if no

one else. We once had a conversation about childhood illnesses where Elena told me that they used to give her bick-backo-roo for bronchitis.
"What's that?"
"You know, bick-backo-roo."
"No, is it a Spanish medicine?"
"No, it's English, you must know it, it's famous. Bick. Backo. Roo."
"No. Sorry."
"I've seen it in chemists here. Listen. BICK. BACKO. ROO. In a little blue jar, you rub it on your chest."
"O-h-h, *Vick's VapoRub.*"
"Yes. Dios mío. That's what I said, isn't it! Bick-backo-roo."

I knew that to show real contempt for someone you said me cago en su putissima madre, I shit myself on his very whorish mother, but would have to fight to keep a straight face when Elena expressed exasperation or surprise with "I shit in the sea" or "I shit in the milk". A measure of her father's bluster and deliberate provocation, she explained, was to threaten to shit on God, back in the village, where such blasphemies were not normally spoken aloud, let alone shouted.

"Hugh, Elena, Elena, Hugh. Sorry we're late." He already had the tickets, and we went straight in, fumbling our way to our seats in the dark. The film was What Have I Done to Deserve This, part of a Pedro Almodóvar retrospective. At regular intervals it elicited delighted comments from Elena: "¡Ay que escándalo!" and "¡Ay, ay, ay!" This was mildly embarrassing, but I consoled myself with the fact that at least it confounded those Londoners who go to every Spanish-speaking film and rush to laugh uproariously at the unfunniest joke so that they can be seen to have understood it before it is shown on the subtitles.

Afterwards we went to a pub, choosing one with its Victorian fittings intact, all brass and acid-etched glass, mahogany booths and snob screens. We showed her how, when most pubs had first, second and sometimes third classrooms, these could be used by gentlemen to obscure the sight of the lower orders drinking porter, spitting and smoking their clay pipes in the Public Bar. I ordered my usual cider; Hugh had a murky guest bitter called something like Old Scrote and Elena a Bailey's. By the time I'd carried the drinks back to the table and dropped the bags of crisps and peanuts I'd been holding in my teeth, they were getting on famously, though that they would have never been in doubt. I'd known him since we were both volunteers at CND, the Campaign for Nuclear Disarmament, in the 1980s, and he had remained one of the most decent blokes I've met. You couldn't help but like him. He didn't say pretentious things when leaving a cinema and could talk enthusiastically about film, television and books. And he never missed a cultural or political reference, so you weren't left talking to someone who suddenly looked stupefied, the way younger work colleagues did when I mentioned something that hadn't been covered in their Media Studies degrees.

We were careful to keep the conversation on topics that Elena would know and want to chat about. When she wasn't saying anything, Hugh talked, and was interesting, or listened and was interested. We briefly deviated from this when Elena mentioned that our television had been a bit of a disappointment. She'd heard Brits boasting about how it was the best in the world, yet when she got here it was little different from what they had in Spain. In response Hugh and I mourned the passing of weekly foreign films and brave and innovative programmes like The Singing Detective, A Very British Coup and Edge of Darkness. Or dramas such as I, Claudius, which had dragged us in as pre-pubescents with its promise of glimpsed nudity, then captivated and educated us with plot and history and acting.

We were trying to explain how even a series like the long-gone Fall and Rise of Reggie Perrin had been gently subversive in its sniping at the once prevalent job-for-life work ethic, when Elena mentioned something she had seen at work. "Some of the old people like to see it. Oh, it is called what, oh, yes, Dad's Army."

At that point, with an evangelist's feverish enthusiasm. Hugh rushed to extoll the sophistication of its different levels, from the simple comedy to its examination of the class warfare between the meritocratic stuffed shirt Mainwaring and the languid, undermining, aristocratic Wilson, secret father of Private Pike.

I was convinced. I'm not sure she was.

As the evening ended, he was looking at me with a gleam in his eye and a poorly concealed smile. On the way out he leaned over and whispered: "She's a bit special. Are you sure you're really going to let her go?"

He'd known me a long time. He could see that this relationship was different from the kind I normally had. Even I knew it by then.

We said goodbye to him and went back to my flat. Elena's back was hurting from moving patients at work, so I bearhug-lifted her till it cracked itself better. With her feet back on the ground she put her arms round me and turned her head on my chest, eyes closed, her hair just tickling my chin. There was no Terry-Thomas moment ("Hello, hello, hello-o-o, where did you find this lovely creature?"). I just broke the habit of a lifetime and told her I loved her.

How easy it is to say it, especially in another language, when it happens for the first time.

She sighed with relief. Naming what had been developing unspoken between us was liberating, like unshouldering a heavy load, or inviting the ghost at the feast to make himself at home and tuck in. I soon found myself using the simple but previously forbidden phrase almost as much as she did back to me. It was the only thing that had been missing. Over the next days we seemed to be moving in a warm vague haze of happiness.

But no matter how we felt about each other winter was closing in and with it her departure. Our time together was running out. That she had to go was a fact that could not be questioned.

Or could it? What would asking her to stay do to her normal life back in Spain? Wreck it. But would doing the decent thing and letting her go ensure her happiness, or would these days together always secretly eat away at her relationship with Paco? Should I just continue trying to make her time here as unforgettable as possible, so that for the rest of our lives we'd have the memory of these months to look back on ("We'll always have Harlesden"), or should I be planning ahead for a time when seeds of romance and perhaps discontent sown here might take root and grow over there?

What was not in doubt was that we had almost reached the final week. She took her English exam (she would fail) and phoned me after finishing her last shift. "I'm packed and ready to leave the house, it feels a little sad, but I can't wait to get to you. A friend is giving me a lift to the station. I have more things here than I realised. Some I have given to my flatmates, some we are going to drop off at the Oxfam shop, a few things perhaps if you don't mind, I will leave at your flat and you can use them or send them on later. Is there anything I may have forgotten that you want me to bring?"

"Nope, just you. I'll go straight from work to meet you at Waterloo and give you a hand."

"You're an angel without wings. Gracias. That will be a help. Are you sure there is nothing you want me to bring with me?"

I shouldn't really.

But what the hell. "Your nurse's uniform?"

Chapter Twelve

I never knew a week could go so fast. Like a fortnight's holiday, where the first week seems endless and the second flies by. Or maybe like starting a fire. The kindling doesn't take at first then there's a flash of flame, colour and heat, and next thing your carefully constructed little kingdom of twigs is embers.

How did we spend it? We went to Portobello, of course, stocking up on Spanish food (Elena insisted on cooking most of the meals and I put on almost half a stone) and did some Christmas shopping, buying presents for her family and myriad nieces and nephews, at least some of whom were going to get promotional toy lorries courtesy of *World Transport Industry News* magazine. We made only a few day trips. One was to Kensal Green Cemetery and its magnificent record in stone of eminent Victorians' struggle to challenge not so much death as death's forgetting.

I managed to persuade Elena underground, after all, choosing the dark chalk tunnels of Chislehurst Caves in Kent, where we kept peeling off from the end of the tour to explore side passages and decaying relics of the huge air raid shelter it once housed, before rushing back to the group just before the guide counted heads. As we came out into the fresh air, I saw that the lamplight below hadn't lied: she was flushed and glowing with excitement, the way she became sometimes when talking about the best of her family memories.

Our final visit was to the Tower of London, where she was bad tempered throughout because of the cold, to which I was oblivious. After that we stayed at home, where the new intensity to our time together was most obvious, and where the grey skies and nights closing in for the end of the year were a less obvious counterpoint to where our relationship was headed.

"Look at your flat," she said, "why do we need to go out?"

She loved the place, like a child who has discovered a secret museum and then been told that every exhibit was there just for her to play with. I imagined the novelty might wear off if she ever had to compete with the artifacts for living space, but in the meantime, she amused herself by feeding the money banks with foreign coins, having dialling races with the lines of phones, setting the tin robots marching, and buying aged packets of 10 Navy Cut from the old cigarette machine for thruppence.

And of course we talked. And she talked. Most often about her family, her childhood, and the village. Sometimes unhappily – the shortage of food, the absence of sweets, treats, or a single birthday or Christmas present ever – but more often with genuine affection. Especially when it came to her mother. Or the childhood summers when, to relieve the overcrowding in the flat in Valencia, she was sent to stay with her eccentric spinster Aunt Marisol in the village, living off eggs from the chickens that ran wild in the yard, cooked (and then eaten from the pan) on an open fire in the dirt-floored kitchen.

And we watched videos. O! Lucky Man (she liked the music so much I bought her an Alan Price CD), Stand by Me,

The Odd Couple, Kes (she cried), The Red Shoes (she cried), City Lights (we both cried), and Sons of the Desert (she cried with laughter.) We spent two days singing Honolulu Baby to each other after that one.
And we listened to music.
She had painstakingly recorded several cassettes of Spanish music for me, including a collection of coplas, a class of antique popular songs that was new to me. I already knew something about flamenco, that extemporized expression of despair and suffering that in its deepest form reflects possession by tragedy and duende, the spirit of ill fortune.
I'd have to admit that I've never sat down and thought, let's listen to something relaxing. I know, I'll put some flamenco on, I just feel like an extemporized expression of despair and suffering, but many of the coplas included the same astonishing vocal feats and rhythmic wizardry. Just as I was making this discovery Elena brought in jotas and fandangos, which were recognisable as the parents of the rather formal cueca, the national dance I'd seen in Chile, but which were revealed in their birthplace as capable of being a spontaneous celebration and momentary resistance in the face of the grinding poverty of peasant life. The styles ranged from a slow and elegant form to one of almost sensual abandon.
"Flamenco is pure Gypsy," she explained. "More aggressive than other dances, more internalised. The hand gestures are very important and there is this fast, tight stamping of the feet." She would show me a few of the moves, like any woman from her country able to instantly drop into the pose, fierce-faced, furrowed-forehead, hands describing arcs and feet ready to blur. "Sevillanas are similar but gentler, two people can dance together; at weddings even young people might dance paso dobles or jotas. They're still quite trendy. It's normal to use castañuelas, that's castanets to you, to accompany the music. Where I come from, we also use sticks, like that English dancing you're so embarrassed about, what's it called? Yes, that, Morris. A bit livelier though, with a hint of something old and violent. Oh, and there are fandangos, boleros, malagueñas, a hundred different kinds of music and dance."
With incredible self-control I refrained from asking where Baccara fitted in.

When the music was on and I was out of the room I'd sometimes catch her making the jaleo accompaniment, that incredible fast clapping, or snapping her fingers like castanets and adding "Olés". She'd stop, slightly embarrassed, when I came in, even though I found the speed and sound of the clapping quite astonishing and always wanted to see more.

Then it was the last night. Elena cooked tortilla, talking me through it step by step while I wrote down the recipe. And with it tomato salad, green beans fried with nuggets of ham and garlic, and bocaditos topped with red pepper and cheese in olive oil. I got out a pair of old painter's trestles, put a square of MDF on top and finished it off with a tablecloth, candles and flowers. Et voila, instant romantic table for two. So long as you remembered not to lean on it.

We went over when we would have to leave the next day to make it to Heathrow in good time.

There was a pause.

I broke it.

"Paco was first."

"Yes, Paco was first."

"But if things don't work out when you get back, phone me and I'll take a plane and come for you. And if you ever change your mind, I'll be waiting. If it happens suddenly then I can't promise that I might not be going out with someone, but if I am I will disengage in a way that I hope doesn't hurt her, whoever she is. Don't forget that. Or in the months or years to come, if you want us to be together again, then I do too."

Once this had been said and was out of the way the atmosphere was almost light. It felt like her returning to Paco, family and Spain was the right thing, the just thing, if not the easy one. But I did not believe she was going for ever, and I'm not sure she did either.

For dessert she had cooked pears in rioja.

I hadn't drunk wine with the meal because I wanted a clear head the next morning, but we permitted ourselves a glass of Spanish brandy each. At times like that I always wished I'd learned to enjoy cigars. We sat in the comfortable silence that is a mark of the best friendships and relationships. The room glowed in the candlelight, the loudest noise was the rain driving against the windows, and the only thing missing was an open fire.

She snuggled up to me. "Well? Was the dinner good?"

"Whoremotherishly good."

Chapter Thirteen

Unusually, the Tube worked, and we arrived at Heathrow early to find that the flight to Valencia was running late. Which made things worse. I didn't want to go before Elena's plane was due, but by arriving at the terminal we had entered airport time. Unless you're on your own with a book there is nothing you can do to make it move at its normal outside speed. You can shuttle from seat to café and back again and fill yourself to bursting with teas, coffees and sandwiches but you cannot dent by more than minutes the hours still left to drag themselves around to the departure time. Time's moving finger writes, and, having writ, moves on, but in airports it slopes off and plays a lot of Tetris first.

Elena was controlled, tight, inside herself. Making I don't know what projections of the future and examinations of the recent past. To my shame I turned into a big wet heap, unable to stop tears spilling down my face.

In times of crisis, I usually maintain emotional self-control. (I can think of giving first aid in some fairly horrific situations where I was visibly in command even though secretly terrified I would screw up and have someone die in my arms. Only later, with the release of tension, would I allow myself the luxury of tears. The most notable example being when, closely watched by the population of a South American shantytown, I cradled the head of an accident victim and felt my fingers sink deep into his brain. He lived. I cried – later.)

So, I was unprepared for what was happening here. Is it always this way during farewells, one partner closed off, the other the unexpectedly helpless cry-baby? I thought how lucky our generation has been in its wars. How do soldiers bear the repeated partings, the waving goodbye to their partners and children, and vice versa?

Finally, finally, the time dragged itself around to where it wouldn't be indecently hasty for her to go into the departures area.

And so, she walked away, passed the security checks and kept on walking. I could see her all the way through the long hall, but she forgot or didn't think to turn for the last backward look and wave I'd been expecting. So, I waited and waited, while the security guard watched this big sodden bloke hanging around for 20 minutes, hoping that she'd realise and come back near enough to the windows to be seen.

She didn't, of course. I'm not sure you even can.

Chapter Fourteen

The tears were replaced by an ache, just below consciousness, that would flare up into sadness when the right emotional nerve was unwittingly touched. For some reason Sundays were the worst, a succession of grey, rainy days. Luckily Christmas was coming and would provide a break from my moping. But first there was the Montressor Publishing Christmas party to get through.

We shuffled down to the local Greek restaurant, with its claustrophobically low ceiling and windowless walls, all covered in sculpted Artex waves, giving the impression you were inside a badly lit wedding cake. The publishing director heaped a dish with vol au vents, lined up his drinks, then sat by the door so he could catch anyone trying to leave. The managing director stood on a chair and delivered a speech ridiculing some of the worst performing salesmen, congratulating himself on spotting the business opportunities that he expected us to make the most of in the coming year, and warning us that only the first drink was free.

Some of the younger admen headed to the toilets for the cocaine that was their essential sales aid, while their middle-aged, jobs-in-jeopardy colleagues milled nervously, trying to avoid the eye of the MD. He, in turn, was abusing one of the young foreign bar staff who had got his drinks order wrong. "I said a pint. PINT. Of BEER. What's the matter, don't you speak-a da English?"

It was hot, cramped and ugly. After 10 minutes I went through the kitchens, out the back door and over the fence, then headed for the pub to await other escapees.

Roger came unsteadily out of the toilets.
"You alright? You were in there ages."
"Yeah, sorry," He waved a hand at his cotton slacks. "Piss-magnet trousers. Forgot. Shouldn't have worn boxers. Had to stand under the hand drier."

He squeezed into his seat. We'd been discussing The Monocled Mutineer and how its hero sounded like a service a prostitute would offer "Percy Topless? That'll be fifteen quid extra". However, it appeared to be time for our traditional Xmas lifestyle argument, with points to be removed for rationality. Roger was drunker than me, so he got it under way by jumping straight in: "All these martial arts and exploring rubbish you do is just cowardice. You're afraid to face up to the fact that all you want to do is settle down and have a quiet life."

"Oh yeah, that'll be right. Listen, if I had the time and money I'd be doing a lot more of that kind of thing. Not pissing my life away here."

"Here? What's wrong with here? It's a perfectly good job you've got, reporting the fast-moving world of the transport industry. All the little model buses and trucks you could want. What could possibly be more interesting to write about?"

"Ooh that's difficult. Let me see. History? News? Politics? Gunpowder, treason and plot? Tales of drunkenness and cruelty?"

"Who do you think you are? Peter Pan? It's time you grew up, Tom. I tell you something, I wouldn't swap one minute of my life for a month of yours."

"Well thank fuck for that. Keep it that way, will you. Please. I don't want your Bob and Thelma existence. A house in Hertfordshire and nothing to look forward to except royal weddings and a bit of wife-swapping with Margo and Jerry Leadbetter next door."

"*My* life?" His voice went shrill with indignation. "It's not *my* life we're discussing. There's nothing wrong there. *I'm* not the one who has to keep putting it at risk. *You* haven't got the guts to admit that what you really want is a life like mine."

"Yeah. I really, really wish I'd worked for the same trade publisher for the last fifteen years. I'd write a book about it. *Rough Trade*, I'd call it. The autobiography of someone who got old without ever having been young. Whose gravestone, when it comes, will read simply 'Was That It?'."

He began an almost helium-voiced reply, then noticed that his glass was empty and moved his head down to with six inches of it to confirm this. "Oh. My round. Another cider?"

"Um, just a half, ta. Got the train home to catch."

I was glad that Christmas was coming and knew exactly what shape it would take. My mother would bustle around, my brother would surprise me by remembering childhood events

I'd forgotten, and I'd do the same back to him. There'd be about five films that I wanted to see – probably including Great Expectations and Scrooge, but they'd all clash with lunch or something. Instead, I'd tune into Jason and the Argonauts for the skeletons and turn on The Ipcress File sometime after midnight just to listen to the typically brilliant John Barry soundtrack, then end up watching it all. I would not for even one second think about work. All cosy and familiar. The problem was that a week later I'd be climbing those Montressor Publishing stairs, hating myself for once again beginning a new year there.

A week later I climbed the stairs and hated myself.

The job, once a bolthole to help me begin to pay back the debts run up during years of working for free for good causes, felt that day like a sinking ship from which I was desperate to jump. It paid the rent, of course, but at the price of a slow loss of self-respect. Despite my previous work and the new qualifications I kept taking in my spare time, I was always the also-ran at interviews for jobs in news or charity journalism. Nothing would be easier than to get headhunted by a rival trade magazine, but that wasn't what I wanted, and I was too tied down by the flat to jack it all in and hope something better would turn up.

Trade journalism is for people starting a career who are determined to learn what they can in one year and get out, or professionals with a love for (and a certainty they are serving) a particular industry. I didn't fit the first category, and the second was being squeezed out of Montressor as too expensive and inflexible.

Bob Duff, a stout, unattractive, middle-aged fantasist known to us as Duff the Tragic Adman, sidled up to our desks.

"Have a good Christmas?" He asked, then, without waiting for a reply, launched straight into one of his unbelievable stories. "I did. Mind you, best Christmas I ever had was in 1975. Me and my mates used to rent a big cabin cruiser down the coast, and we'd sit on the deck and sunbathe and get pissed. It was really warm that year. Well these birds came along the beach and saw us and called over to send a boat and pick them up so we said yeah you can come aboard, but you have to swim, so they took their clothes off and swam over, and then we shagged 'em soppy, and after we said alright you can get off now and they said what, you just shagged us, you're not going to send us back are you and we said yeah, get off or we'll throw you off, so they had to, phew you should have heard the language they used. Best Christmas I ever had."

He chortled at his ridiculous tale, which he had told so many times that he, uniquely, actually believed it. "Shagged 'em soppy". For fuck's sake. This place couldn't get any worse, could it?

Then he looked critically at my clothes. The ad sales staff expected editors to be scruffy and unpunctual, and I did my best not to disappoint them.

"Would've thought you'd have made a bit more effort today," he said.

"Eh?"

"The presentations. You know. You're giving a talk on the future of your magazine. You had the Christmas holiday to prepare it."

The company boasted two yes men of unusual dedication, David and Tony. Both capable of having children just so they could name them after the managing director, Darren George. They had sold their souls for little reward. In a rare flash of insight, he had given them paper titles and put them in an office together, where they were kept in a ferment of activity by the fear that the other would come up with a better means of ingratiating himself. It might have been a shrewd move if it weren't for the fact that their souls ached and their minds laboured to come up with rival-topping schemes that would appeal to the managing director's vanity, rather than actually do the company any good. Tony's latest great idea was the editors' presentations, where we'd explain our plans for relaunches and circulation boosts to our bored colleagues, who knew the real audience was the MD and David.

Roger had remembered to write a presentation so could relax while I tried to throw one together. Thanks to Christmas gift tokens he was also appropriately dressed in a shirt, tie and a pair of shoes he must have wrestled from the hands of a pensioner at the M&S checkout. He sat back, hands behind his head, watching me and singing: "You can stand it with

Bandit. You can stand it with Bandit. What was the next line?"

"You can stand it with Bandit, get your chin off the floor, you can stand it with Bandit, it's as big as a door."

"Get your chin off the floor? No! That's ridiculous."

"I think that was it. However, could we perhaps not pursue it now? For one thing I have one hour left in which to prepare something. For another I suggest we don't go down the lost confectionery route. You start with Wagon Wheels getting smaller and whatever happened to Spangles, and you end up with how The Magic Roundabout was supposedly full of drug references. At that point I may have to kill you."

Tony walked by. "Everyone to the meeting room. Editors' presentations have been brought forward an hour." He made it sound as though the whole exercise was all some tiresome order from above that had nothing to do with him.

Roger drummed a tom-tom beat on the desk. "Anything can happen in the next half hour."

"When do we live? That's what I want to know."

We shuffled in and took our places, all avoiding the front row. Darren George stumped in. A small man with a big chip on his shoulder, always thrusting his chin forward pugnaciously then jerking it back, since, despite his bullying, he was a physical coward and lived in justified fear of being punched. He had a Burt Reynolds moustache and a younger man's hair, which was styled into an ill-advised Purdey cut. His angry potato face looked from the empty row to the rest of us and growled, "Who shat on the chairs?"

The cheaper the crook the gaudier the patter.

Thankfully he soon got bored and left, to Tony's disappointment and David's delight. The rest of us barely went through the motions, ad libbing to an early finish.

David, emboldened by Tony's flop and wanting to sound decisive within earshot of the MD's office, tried to hurry us back to work. "Come on. What are you all dawdling for? You can run, you know."

If we were going to be ordered to run, it seemed reasonable to me to want to know why. If it were an emergency, fine. But this wasn't. I slowed my pace to a crawl and dawdled back to my desk. Today it was time to do my own running.

At lunchtime I reviewed my options. I had a few hundred pounds in an investment account that, no matter how broke I was, I never touched, thanks to the compulsory three-month notice period. It swung between being the beginning of the deposit for the flat I would never be able to buy and the down payment for a VW Karmann Ghia, a vehicle that is practically compulsory in Ladbroke Grove (a Citroen DS19 being the only acceptable alternative), but one I still wanted, despite the cliché. The bank was always extending the limit of my credit card, so there was potentially a good bit there. Put together it would buy a few months out of the Montressor Publishing rut, giving space to maybe research a couple of big feature articles that would prove I could still write, plus time to hawk them around and try for a new job. The biggest part of the money would go on rent for the flat, but there would be enough to live somewhere cheap for a while. Like – oh, for no particular reason, it wasn't as if I knew anyone there – Valencia.

After lunch I went in to see the publishing director and said I'd like a couple of months leave, unpaid of course, to do some travelling. Naturally I wouldn't rush off, I'd build up some articles to use while I was away. How about if I went after, oh, let's say, three months? He sucked his teeth and looked off into the distance, calculating how much it would cost to replace me if he said no and I went anyway. There'd be the price of a job advert. There'd be the time it would take to get a replacement up to speed. After less than a minute he said yes. Never even asked where I was going.

I spent the rest of the afternoon doing sums and making plans, then it was five thirty and I was a man again.

Chapter Fifteen

When I got home there were three letters from Elena waiting for me, each posted a few days apart. I opened them in order. They were sad, but reassuringly passionate. She spoke of how difficult it was to re-enter her former life and relationship while maintaining the outward appearance of joy at being back in Spain. The first letter was a heartbreaker. If it had come when it should, instead of a week late, I might have got on a plane straight away. The second rushed to reassure me that this wasn't necessary, that she was putting a brave face on things. The third was still wistful for times past, but happier to be seeing her family again.

I spent the evening writing a long letter back, checking spelling against the dictionary and the use of the conditional tense against a grammar guide. It was bedtime before I knew it. If only all days could be like this.

On the Wednesday I went to martial arts and received the kicking I deserved for missing so many recent classes. It's a funny thing with exercising after work. Go every week and it's a doddle, miss even one and it's so difficult to find the energy to restart. Yet when you do, no matter how tired you go in, you come out feeling fit and fine, bruised but buzzing. The class was in Krav Maga, a fast, inelegant fighting system with a good reputation for being brutal but effective. Instead of stylish throws and manoeuvres we learnt short, vicious moves based on the body's reflex reactions to an attack, with a strong element of just going in hard and fast and ugly and throwing in as many punches, kicks, knees, headbutts and elbows as possible.

Its drawback was that as a pure combat technique it had no sport element, so sparring was forbidden, meaning that I wouldn't know till I needed it if I would remember what to do. I wasn't wholly confident but hoped that if I practised enough then instinct would kick in when needed. In the meantime, with the exception of a couple of fairly serious knee injuries, I treated the bruises and black eyes I built up as character-strengthening and useful practice in keeping my head if I ever did get walloped unexpectedly.

Our instructor, Sue, was a lovely woman who assured us that if the time came, we would piss all over our opponents (She may not have used those exact words) and that the experience of students who had defended themselves was how fast it was over: before they knew it the attacker was downed or running away, and they were left wondering when the real fight was going to begin.

As well as fighting techniques we also practised all-round awareness – using peripheral vision, knowing what you're walking into, who's close and who's coming closer. I couldn't pretend to have it switched on all the time, but it was always interesting when I did, and I supplemented it with a personal habit of watching for patterns of movement. Why did two separate people in that crowd divert from their paths at the same time? Why did those three apparent strangers just exchange quick, secretive, confirmatory glances before moving into the tube train? Less easy, because it was more counter-intuitive, was what we were advised to do in times of serious trouble – react immediately with maximum force.

The example we were given was an attempted abduction. Novels taught us that by sangfroid and split-second timing the fictional hero would sooner or later be faced with a moment when he could loosen the ropes/feign illness/distract the crook. We were told the opposite. It is likely to be that first moment that the perpetrator can least control. When the public is around. When you're on your own territory. When he has to keep a weapon concealed. Go with him, hoping for a better opportunity, and you're going to where he has a friend, or restraints and a gag waiting for you. And then, literally or metaphorically, you're fucked.

Unlike in my twenties, when it would have been a useful survival skill that complemented rather more dangerous activities, Krav Maga had recently become about the riskiest thing that I did on a regular basis, but I could live with that.

When I was little everything from the comics I read to films and essential television such as The Avengers promised a life of espionage, suspense and fist fights, often accompanied by whisky in a cut-glass tumbler, an E-Type Jaguar and a cool jazz-inspired score.

I'd grown up enough to realise that the scenarios I took for granted in childhood were not going to be realised. I'd never walk on the moon, order my men to fire five rounds rapid at alien shape changers, commute to work by jetpack or swap quips with Emma Peel after defeating a kitsch menace that had been bumping off barmy British eccentrics. I accepted this. This was a sign of realism and adulthood, I told myself.

It was a shame about the E-Type though.

I cruised through the week, the feeling that I might find a new job making me impervious to any petty annoyances at work. A letter asking if I could see her if I happened to be visiting Spain got an enthusiastic yes from Elena. We were unusually busy at work, so I put off beginning to make some proper plans till the weekend. On the Friday I met Karl, my oldest friend, who was on one of his rare, all-too-brief trips home from his work as a travel courier in Latin America. For years when we met up, we had compared adventures, with him pulling ahead the last few times with his stories of gunplay and romantic liaisons. (Unthinkingly I had introduced him to Roger once when we met straight after a London press conference. They had got on like a house on fire – that is, heat, drama and a lot of raised voices.)

We filled each other in on what we had been up to, with him confessing to a certain nostalgia for dark beer and policemen you didn't have to bribe, and expressing disbelief that I was still in the same job. "Yeah, well, If I'm still working there when you next come back in a year's time, I think I might have to kill myself," I told him.

"If you are then maybe you should," he said, not joking.

The next day it was time to think ahead. I bought four shorthand reporter's notebooks and laid them out on the desk in the spare bedroom. Two or three months, more than enough time for a minimum of four or five really good articles or photo essays. I'd need to choose topics I could research and do many of the interviews for in the UK, then write up later in Spain. Stuff that would be interesting to spend a lot of time on. Call me old-fashioned but I wanted to write articles that were meticulously researched. The rare kind where you know that the author has put in more background work than the freelance fee will pay for because they are interested and want to share that interest.

What were the options?

I wrote "Film? History? Spain x3?". Under the first of these I put "Article on individual film. Synopsis, history, makers. Needs to be something due for new print re-release. Check with BFI. Not sellable if nothing coming up".

Then

"British horror films, explosion of during golden age, 1960s and 70s. Hammer, Amicus, Tigon, Tyburn, British Lion etc". I decided not to include their skewed effects on avid prepubescent TV viewers eager to learn what sex was all about, even though this would seriously limit any truthful discussion of The Wicker Man's popularity. Which took me back to age 14 and the last film that had ever frightened me, the morally flawed but at the time dangerously exciting Blood on Satan's Claw. Then I remembered seeing it referred to in a lovingly written recent article on just this subject. I scratched "Horror" off the list and replaced it with "Underground Cinema".

If you're below the ground, you're in an almost monochrome world of Caligarian light and darkness. There is what is in the beam of your torch and there is blackness. Carol Reed realised it in The Third Man, using sound and almost German Expressionist lighting contrasts in the sewer scenes as readily as he did above (think of where Harry Lime is seen for the first time, his face leaping into the light and into the film). The thought of the scene with Lime's fingers stretching through a grating in search of escape from the sewers and death, even though we can see that all above is wind and dark and cold and corruption, almost sent me running to the video.

Both the cinematic and subterranean worlds involve a journey through an essentially linear progression of undiscovered settings, all illuminated by a flickering light in the darkness, yet there are few great films set below ground. Apart from The Third Man I could only think of Kanal and the studio-bound but scenically brilliant 1925 Phantom of the Opera. And what about the London Underground? How can you put that in a film and not make it exciting? (When I was two or three, I'd look from the platform into the tunnel entrances and the blackness, which seemed to have a velvety texture and quality of darkness that existed nowhere else. I believed that dragons lived in there.)

There is only one film that lets the below-the-surface menace of the Tube come out, and that's Quatermass and the Pit. The scenes in the otherwise good fun An American Werewolf in London come nowhere near, not to mention the complete failure to frighten of Deathline, with its troglodyte cannibal hunting the platforms, mindlessly mouthing the only words he knows: "Mind the Doors".

If there were any upcoming film partly shot on the London Underground, then it could be used as a hook to hang a sellable article on. All I'd need to do would be to add something on tube locations (usually Aldwych AKA Strand) and a text box on films made there. Decision made. Across the front of the first notebook, I wrote "Underground Film".

One down, four to go. As a reward I cracked open a Diet Coke and poured it into one of the whisky glasses that went with the chipped crystal decanter I kept for visitors and occasions like this. And because having one made me feel a bit like John Steed. On the shelf near it there was a 1960s Dinky Toys E-Type.

After all, there's always hope.

Chapter Sixteen

History next. The choices were endless; there are so many places where the past overlaps the present.

One strong contender was a place I had researched when writing a previous article on the dark history of the Thames – of the "Found Drowned", the corpses of the countless suicides, the drunks and murder victims once dragged from its waters; of the criminals and beggars who lived off it; and the toshermen who searched among the poisoned excrement of the sewers which emptied into it for dropped coins and recyclables.

The contender was Jacob's Island, that rotting tooth in mighty Britannia's smile. A location that for a period in the nineteenth century could equal anywhere in the capital for poverty, and almost match Seven Dials and the Fleet Valley for criminality. It was probably the worst single place in South London, at a time when that half of the capital was still remembered as being part of the Without. That is – like a green hill far away – outside the protection of a city wall, and outside its rule of law too. Where all that was illegal in the City of London had, since mediaeval times, been laid on if money could be made from it. Theatres, brothels, child prostitution, cockfights, dogfights, the setting of rats on dogs, and dogs on tethered bulls and bears. While, for those who could pay, worse things could be organised in private.

In a box file of old research, I found an article by Henry Mayhew, one of seventeen children, a public schoolboy who ran away to sea to avoid working with his solicitor father, then came back and did just that, co-founded *Punch*, went bankrupt and fled abroad. All before finally finding his niche as a campaigning journalist who rocked Victorian sensibilities by showing what was happening under the complacent noses of the citizens at the heart of the world's greatest empire. He began with a description in *The Morning Chronicle* of conditions in a Bermondsey backwater, enclosed by river and sewers, that was named on no map but, to those who knew it, was a byword for filth, disease and despair. The four hundred square yards of misery that was Jacob's Island.

It was brilliantly written, a journey into a dense, dark plague-sore that reached a hellish nadir lasting decades before the catalyst of cholera led to it being razed and rebuilt in the 1860s. An "island" boxed in by Folly Ditch – named after a long-gone pleasure garden – a watercourse originally cut to harness the power of the Neckinger river and the tidal Thames. Eight feet deep and twenty feet wide at high tide, crossed by six rickety, rotting bridges within just a few hundred yards, giving slippery access to a catacomb labyrinth of dripping, dank alleys and courts. Festering Folly Ditch: an open sewer, poisoned by the lead mills built on its banks, thickened by the outpourings of the nearby glue factory, corrupted by the acidic wastes of the tanneries, made vile by dead dogs, cats and rats, filthened by human excrement, and the sole source of drinking water for hundreds of people.

Mayhew described the graveyard smell of the air and the scum-covered water, prismatic with grease, to whose surface bubbles would rise and pop, releasing the stink of decomposition. Among the "swollen carcasses of dead animals, almost bursting with the gases of putrefaction", children bathed, and pails were lowered on ropes to dip for drinking water, even as just next to them a bucketload of excrement slapped into the water. And overhanging all this were the teetering, falling houses, some already collapsed into the creek, some accessible only by planks and aerial walkways, and all "with the stench of death rising through the boards".

Now, on the "Island" the hovels that overhung the creek have gone, some revealing smugglers' cellars and crooks' escape tunnels when demolished, but the main thoroughfares remain. Walk down Wolseley Street and you walk over lost London Street, Water Lane and filled-in Folly Ditch. Jacob Street and George Row are still there, while Mill Street has followed the same route for three centuries, only now it's a warehouse-flanked roadway, not a lane bordered by a festering waterway.

The other one-time bywords for infamy or poverty, like Clerkenwell, Covent Garden and Shoreditch, have all been turned into media land, full of bijou apartments and chi chi brasseries, but not Bermondsey. Despite the estate agents branding the area by the name that once would have created bafflement or revulsion, the makeover of Jacob's Island is ribbon deep. The converted warehouses contain luxury offices and flats, but only up to Dockhead and Jamaica Road. Cross them and you're in the council estates that replaced the borough's notorious slums. There's a whiff of economic apartheid. On one side riverside views and underground car parks, and on the other side traditional Bermondsey: a good place for a mugging.

Which would be an angle to explore. I could talk to the locals of both sides, try and find anyone who remembered how it used to be, but who hadn't managed to move out to Kent, Croydon, Mitcham or Streatham. And talk to the incomers, who had broken the patterns of centuries and chosen to live in Bermondsey, rather than to escape from it.

That one then. Another decision made. Even beginning a little research had dulled the ache of Elena's absence and quietened the internal voice telling me that I had lost her for ever, replacing it with a feeling that I was doing something concrete to keep our relationship alive. So, what to do about her country?

Spain. There's an extraordinary story there. A nation that never had a reformation, never even really had an industrial revolution, has been transformed since Franco's death in 1975. A Catholic country, whose traditionally church-schooled people have the world's lowest birth rate. Until recently, one of Europe's most backward nations, a post-imperial backwater that is now throwing up science parks and sports centres and running ultra-modern trains that shame their British equivalents. A priest-ruled dictatorship that became a ferment of arts and culture.

I could go on like that for a while. If I wasn't careful, I'd end up with a Spain, Land of Contrasts piece. Or one of those Sunday paper features on Undiscovered Spain: the Places the Tourists Don't Know. (Are you a traveller, not a tourist? Then visit these secret places known only to several hundred thousand other *Sunday Times* readers. Want to leave the herd behind and strike out on your own? Then let *Lonely Planet* guide you to a remote mountain hideaway packed with hundreds of their other readers, including a large group of Australians having an all-night drinking and belching competition.)

Perhaps I should set aside one article to be decided by political or social events happening when I was there and choose another topic that I could at least begin in London.

The subject I knew most about, in almost unhealthy detail, was the Spanish Civil War – ever since reading *Homage to Catalonia* during an Orwell frenzy that began when we studied *Animal Farm* at school. The problem was that excellent historians had surely covered everything there was to write on the subject. Looking for ideas I got up and played the tape of coplas and flamenco that Elena had given me. Then dug out an old record of Spanish Civil War songs. It began with ¡Ay, Carmela!, the most unstuffy and rousing of them all:

Long live the Fifth Brigade,
who are going to cover us with glory...

Maybe there *was* something I could write. The question of whether the struggle against Franco and his fascist allies was even worth fighting. Whether it was doomed the day the Republic first had to accept help from the USSR. Or how the war is still almost a secret in Spain. How foreigners attracted to its apparently black and white, good versus bad nature tend to know more about its history, albeit through a romantic prism, than most Spaniards born after it.

¡Ay, Carmela! ¡Ay, Carmela!

Because civil wars are the most painful. You can't pretend that the enemy are inhuman militaristic foreigners when they are your cousins, brothers and sisters. Yes, there were outsiders guilty of atrocities – the Germans and Italians bombing defenceless civilians; the Soviets torturing and murdering thousands of their anti-fascist allies; the Moroccans raping their way across Spain – but it was the native leaders of both sides who let them in.

We fight against the Moors,
mercenaries and fascists...

So, Spain has created a collective amnesia, which blanks out the horror of what Spaniards did to Spaniards, and what they allowed foreigners to do to their own kin.

¡Ay, Carmela! ¡Ay, Carmela!

Meaning that there are relatively few books or films about it written or made by Spaniards, and an average Spanish student will know more about the wars against the Moors in

the fifteenth century than they will about what happened in 1936.
The traitors let loose their airplanes,
but bombs can't overcome our hearts...
Yet to write something on that deliberate loss of memory felt rude, like telling everyone about some private weakness you discovered about your host when staying at his house. Was there something else about the war or its aftereffects that hadn't been written about? I didn't think so, until I remembered,
¡Ay, Carmela! ¡Ay, Carmela!
Nathan.

Chapter Seventeen

George Nathan. Or, more correctly, Major George Montague Nathan, first commanding officer of the British Number 1 Company of anti-fascist volunteers. A languid International Brigader who dressed like he was still what he had been in the First World War, a member of the Brigade of Guards. Even while advancing on the falangist lines nonchalantly twirling a swagger stick. Ex-intelligence officer, ex-pauper and tramp, maybe an ex-Black and Tan too, maybe gay. And no maybe about him being an authentic bloody hero.

In the ragged Republican army and militias, where most combatants thought themselves lucky if they got overalls and espadrilles, at a time when it could be dangerous to dress in anything other than an exaggeratedly proletarian manner, Nathan wore what he would have in the British Army. He sauntered towards the enemy in immaculate tunic, breeches, peaked cap and highly polished riding boots. And his men loved him for it. There's a story of them leaping out of their lorries under aerial attack and him telling them to get back in and wait for his order to dismount and take cover. Which they willingly did, fired by his knowledge of soldiering, at a time when many high command officers were communist placemen, installed for their loyalty to the party, and more dangerous to their own men than they were to the enemy.

Born in an East End Jewish family, he was fearless and utterly professional. When men were losing hope Nathan would appear, strolling in full view of the enemy, smoking his pipe, apparently invulnerable, bullets crashing around him, to urge them on: "Cheer, cheer, shout and cheer, my hearties. Give them something to fear!" No wonder they'd follow him anywhere. Then in 1937 at Brunete his luck ran out and a bomb fragment pierced his chest. They couldn't bury him in daylight; the enemy owned the skies. Instead, crying, they laid him down by night among the same hard, unforgiving rocks that had denied him shelter when he reluctantly took cover from the attacking planes.

If anyone deserved a biography it was him.

If he could reinvent himself, moving on from failure, remaking his destiny, and taking all that he had learned with him, couldn't others? Could we all? Could I? Maybe. Maybe not. But you have to try.

An interim period began, in which Elena and I wrote long weekly letters to each other and Montressor became strangely tolerable. It must be how it feels to work out your notice before moving to a better but more challenging job. Like everything was going to improve but no reciprocal effort was yet required.

Roger, meanwhile, was doing his best to convince me I'd never go.

"Good weekend?"

"Yes, fine thanks. I managed to get into the cellars of one of the old River Fleet prisons. They survived when it was knocked down and were used as an air raid shelter in the war. That's how I found a way in. One of the ventilation fans has been removed, probably nicked for scrap, so there's a small aperture. It's a real mess of course, rubble everywhere, but you can see what a grim bloody hellhole it must have been. The cold from the river comes through the walls at you. If you were locked up there, you'd soon be screaming for daylight."

"It sounds incredibly dangerous."

"Nah. Not really," (Though secretly I was glad he thought so.) "The air raid shelter was good. No one's got in and graffitied it yet. But the most interesting thing was the remaining bits of the prison cellars. The laundry and the punishment cells. They've pretty well collapsed, but you can still just make out the foundations of the treadmill."

"Treadmill?" Roger asked, with a suspicious, what-am-I-letting-myself-in-for sigh.

"You know. Nineteenth century prison fitting. A great wooden wheel on which prisoners had to stride uselessly for hours at a time. Unstopping, unable to slow or rest without being pitched over by its momentum. Like walking up a steep hill for five hours without missing a single step. The idea was to break them down, deprive them of their criminal individuality so that they could be remade as honest Christians."

I began to get enthusiastic, "In a funny way it was the beginning of the idea of rehabilitation. In its time that place would have been the face of prison reform. The treadmill had no other purpose; it didn't power grindstones or pump water or anything. To provide resistance it just turned big sails up on the prison roof. 'Treading the wind' the prisoners called it. A pointless, repetitive, soul-destroying daily grind." I looked up at Roger, who was slowly squeezing out a feature article on warehouse shelving. "Does that sound familiar?"

Refusing the bait, he looked at me with something approaching disgust. "Jesus Christ, welcome to Tom's junkshop mind. What was it you were banging on about last week? Oh yes. How the dangerous animals at London Zoo had to be shot in 1939 in case it was bombed and they escaped, and they were going to get marksmen to kill them, but the keepers insisted on doing it themselves out of respect for the animals they'd spent years looking after, and how would that feel?"

He put on an old man's voice and tugged at imaginary fingerless woollen gloves. "No? That wasn't what you were looking for, sir? Never mind, let's have a look behind this old cupboard, and see what else we can find. How about this? An authentic china po. No? Let me just blow the dust off this then. Ah, yes, the derivation of the phrase "treading the wind". That'll interest you, sir..." Rolling his eyes he turned back to his computer.

He had a point. I shut up and went back to hiding film quotes in what I was writing.

Work provided a useful place to write up the notes of the research I was doing during the evenings (along with a bit of weights of course; no point in going if I didn't look OK when I got there). The fact that my escape plans were being made in company time gave me additional satisfaction. The only risk was detection by anyone whose interest was aroused by my newfound dedication to typing at my Mac for long stretches.

Essentially there were two Spanish Civil wars. Ours – in which international volunteers went to stand, fight and die alongside their Spanish brothers and sisters, marking the first line against fascism in the sand with their own blood – and the real one. That was a war with roots sunk deep in Spanish history, fought almost wholly by Spaniards, and lost and won by Spaniards, half a million of whom died, most of them in massacres and political killings far behind the lines.

It was the fourth civil war in a century, born of fear that reform would succeed and fear that it would fail; of the dashed hopes that the five-year old republic would deliver on its promises of prosperity and education for all; of the left taking right-wingers for a paseo – a bullet in the neck in a nighttime cemetery, and the right doing the same; of Basque and Catalan nationalism, then as now tearing the nation apart; of fear of anticlericalism and modernity; of poverty and feudalism and a corrupt church and of the unquenchable desire for a piece of land to farm...

"Well?" Interrupted Roger.

"Well, what?" There was a moment of disorientation as I pulled my mind out of the 1930s and back to Montressor.

"We were meant to be discussing 1970s music, if you remember. Buzzcocks: good band?"

"Buzzcocks: good band. Great single."

"Plastic Bertrand?"

"So far beyond our concepts of good or bad it would make my head hurt trying to decide. Let's just say ripe for post-ironic re-evaluation. By someone who's not trying to do some writing. Like I am."

He mused. "What would you call the Boomtown Rats? Punk or post-punk?"

"Neither."

"What would you call them, then?"

"I'd call them shit. Obviously."

...our Spanish Civil war is one of icons and gilded youth, of Homage to Catalonia and the poet John Cornford, killed on his 21st birthday, of Robert Capa's faked photo of a shot militiaman falling as though crucified, dying for all our sins. In reality the International Brigades – tens of thousands compared to the Spanish millions – were repeatedly thrown away in needless attempts to try and plug the gaps caused by their commanders' incompetence.

To be eleven years old and first reading about that war was to feel a regret that is close to shame that you couldn't be one of those who fought. Later, knowledge blunts that regret, throwing up the question of whether it was worth enduring the shockingly high International Brigade casualty rates, only to risk arrest and execution by order of Stalin's psychotic appointees. Even Jarama, the Brigade's proudest victory, was militarily a farce, with three quarters of Nathan's troops never having held a gun before.

For months they'd pleaded for military instruction and instead received endless lectures about how many tractors the USSR produced. They saved the battle, but untrained, under-armed and unsupported, they were scythed down.

The same thing happened at Brunete, another monumental fuck up, where Nathan died. Pinned down by murderous artillery and rifle fire, the troops were desperate for food, water, ammunition and shelter. In response the communists called a political meeting where sixteen of those attending were quickly picked off by snipers. The British, some of the finest fighters in the International Brigades, had to retreat, leaving their comrades behind, lying holding their guts in and begging for help as the merciless Moroccans, Franco's torturing terror troops, advanced, their knives unsheathed, ready to castrate and mutilate. Again, and again the Republicans left behind their wounded. The Moors would kill them all and any doctors who stayed with them.

It was not so glorious as we want to think.

There was no poetry here.

I paused for a quick look around to see if anyone had observed my unaccustomed work rate, and noticed Roger shift slightly as he detected the change. I tried to resume typing before he could deliberately break my concentration, but he was too fast for me.

"Coffee?"

"No thanks," I told him, "I've used up my ration." Darren George had had kettles removed from the kitchens and replaced with coffee machines, for which we were each issued with a swipe card entitling us to two cups a day. More than that you had to pay for, unless you were management level, in which case you got an unrestricted card. Roger had one of these he had found in the toilets, and he now dangled this in front of me. "You want a coffee; I want a coffee. What say we have a little wager? A test of musical knowledge. Which lyrics belong to which song. The loser gets the coffees in with a forfeit of, say, collecting them from the machine doing the Adam Ant Prince Charming walk." Then, as if it were an afterthought, he added, "My card, so I get to choose the topic."

That did it. If it was Bowie lyrics or British hits of the sixties, I could probably take him, but if he got to choose, he'd go for the New Romantics, and I'd lose. The last time that happened I'd had to pass the sales floor doing the Shadows' walk. One step forward, one step back. It took forever.

"Roger, if you want to get a coffee get one. If you want to get me one at the same time fine. Great in fact. But till then can you shut up for a while. I've got work to do."

He said nothing, just raised an eyebrow.

"Yeah, well, when I say *work*..."

Imagine you know the history of what happened and are spirited back to 1936 to decide what to do as the army revolt begins. Would you now tell the combatants to resist; sentence the Spanish people again to that horrific mass sacrifice? Take some of the bravest and best foreigners and send them to fight a losing war? Or would it be better to let the insurrection succeed, see Franco and the Falange Party, deprived of a war, sidelined in a repressive coalition government whose unresisted accession to power might reduce the bloodlust that followed their actual victory?

Was resistance worthwhile? Who profited from it? Ernest Hemingway, given material for his novels and the chance to indulge his fantasies of military expertise while safely quaffing fine brandy in hotel suites? The Nobel-winning Chilean poet Pablo Neruda, who found early fame by organising a communist front conference of intellectuals and authors for Spain, all chauffeured from dinner to lavish dinner in luxury limousines while the Republic's fighters survived on acorn coffee and left their wounded behind in ambulances whose petrol had run out? Or Stalin, cementing his control? Maybe. The Nazis, certainly, who went into Spain with biplanes and came out with the Stuka and the Messerschmitt 109. The scientists of death, they tested their weapons and tactics and built a cadre of battle-hardened veterans schooled in the Blitzkrieg warfare they alone took as their lesson from Spain.

Roger interrupted again. "I really don't know why you bother with that. There's no way out. You'd do better try to make the best of it here."

"I don't know. You have to fight back a bit, don't you? 'It's better to die on your feet then live on your knees'. Course living on your feet and lying down for a bit of a kip now and then has to be the ideal."

I didn't tell him that it was also partly about proving to myself that I was worthy of Elena.

"Haven't you learned yet?" He made his voice harsh and Dalek-like, "Resistance is useless."

Chapter Eighteen

We were singing the old Thunderbirds song Oh Parker, Well Done. Me as Parker, Roger as Jeff Tracey and Lady Penelope. And doing pretty well too, I reckoned. Right up to the line: "Hi, Penny, Jeff here, we've got a hot one for you." At this point Roger would become so incapacitated with laughter that he was unable to stutter his way through to her reply, "Ready and waiting, Jeff," no matter how desperate he was to deliver it. In the end I got up and went to the toilet in order to re-read in peace the latest letter from Elena.

He was wiping a tear from the corner of one eye when I came back. He saw me and became serious: "You do realise, don't you, that if you ever get the job you want saving the world, you will never work again with someone who knows that song? Or be able to talk about 1970s cop shows without being told you're being sexist? That's if anyone you work with even knows what a 70s cop show was."

"Thank you, Nostradamus. Can you point to where in your book of prophecies about my life it says that this is such a bad thing?"

"No, I can't," he told me. "But it doesn't matter, does it. Because we both know it's not going to happen anyway."

I think he won that one on points.

He began to apply himself to opening the post, reading out the first line of each press release before binning it or sticking it to one side. Invitations to factory visits, lunches and product launches received the same treatment. Some we went to in order to maintain the magazine's profile in the industry. Others might occasionally be of genuine interest, or simply fall on a day when we'd be glad to come out of an event in the early afternoon and know we didn't have to go back to the office. He waved one of these in front of me. A company seminar. Looked dull.

"Bin?" He asked.

"Bin. No, hold on. Isn't that near the family records centre?"

We broke off for a discussion on the 1966 World Cup, and how it seemed a beacon of fair play and decency. We mourned an era when the only marketing was cardboard periscopes and little toys of the tournament's mascot.

"I've got a terrible case of World Cup Willy," Roger told me. Repeatedly.

I returned to my research notes on Nathan. Roger was unable to bear the silence.

"Lyrics battle?"

"OK."

"Artist?"

"God, don't know. We could try first album, last album. Songs from the first one you or I ever bought, then the most recent."

"Worth a try. What was your first LP then?"

"David Bowie, Hunky Dory. You?"

Proudly, he told me: "Supertramp, Breakfast in America. And funnily enough the last album I bought was a box set of their greatest hits."

After all the time we'd worked together, he could still surprise me. I put on my most sympathetic voice. "Roger. Why aren't you a chemistry teacher? You dress like one. You get about as much sex as one. And now you turn out to have the musical tastes of one."

"Oi!" His outrage was genuine. "Don't diss The Tramp! If you don't know enough not to insult such a groundbreaking band, then the game is off."

He lowered his head sulkily.

"Suit yourself. Oh, Roger…" He looked moodily up.

"…your Bunsen burner's gone out.."

We were writing product supplements, which involved days of heavy work to very tight deadlines. I was alternating between remembering days spent with Elena and trying to conceal the line about quiet desperation being the English way by spelling it out in the first letter of each write-up. I'm not sure what tactic Roger was using to get him through the task. It didn't take much to persuade him to listen to me talk about Nathan.

"The best descriptions are by the people who fought with him," I told him. "This is from a book called *The Armed Rehearsal*, by Peter Elstrob. Amazing bloke, by the way.

Wish I'd done half in my life what he has in his. Listen: *"[Nathan] looked so much like a film British officer that he almost seemed to be playing a part. He was tall, thin, long nosed and wore the toothbrush moustache of the British Officer of the World War. He carried a riding crop, smoked a pipe and seemed almost too typical to be true, but he proved to be a soldier to his fingertips.*

"He despised the slovenliness of the French sentries and made sure that his own men looked smart. 'That's not George Nathan's way, my lad,' he would say if he saw something that displeased him."

Then later, this: *"We might have run if the Major hadn't got a grip on us...he stood up with all this shit flying around and yelled in that parade ground voice of his, 'dress your files! Retire in proper formation!' He kept on like that until we stopped and turned and fired back."*

I flicked ahead in my notebook, looking for another quote I'd copied out.

"This was how Fred Copeman, a pretty nasty piece of work, described him: *"Outstanding...efficient, capable, with loads of courage; above all the typical British officer...I shall never forget that on the third day of the battle of Jarama, among the chaos and slaughter, with his fine boots and his batman he stood out as the most capable officer. He never failed to hold that position in my mind whenever I saw him, right up to the time when he died at Brunetti, with a wound that almost cut him in half."*

Despite himself Roger looked interested. "So why haven't you written it up and sold it?"

"Because I've got more research to do."

"Why?" He asked, genuinely puzzled. "How many books have you read just for this one article?"

"God, I don't know." I had to tot them up. "Um, eight that I already had I, think. No, nine. No, ten. Then there are seven or eight more I've bought recently. Three I skimmed through in museums. There's some other out of print ones that I've got book searches out on, but to be honest I couldn't afford them at the moment anyway. I'll get them later."

He was giving me that look of mixed frustration and incomprehension. "I've seen that paper you read and that's more than enough for one of their features. So, stick the bits you've copied out together, bang in a photo and sell it to them. Ka-ching. Couple of hundred quid in your pocket and you're famous for a day."

"But I don't want to. That way if one person has made a mistake then it just gets perpetuated. And later becomes a truth in itself." I struggled to explain. "I once wrote an article on lost London rivers. Well, there's a kind of standard book on the subject but it came out years back, and there's a lot of material that has turned up since then. So, some of the book is going to be out of date, for very understandable reasons.

"Yet you see those errors turn up in much later histories that have used it. When I did my research, I didn't read it because it would have been too easy just to lift information. I preferred to work from old maps and documents and begin by walking the routes of the rivers so I could check that what I was writing was reasonably correct." (I felt a sudden nostalgia for those Thameside explorations, and heard it reflected in my voice.) "Even though it meant wading through shit and making sure I didn't get trapped in a sewer entrance by the rising tide."

At this last sentence Roger sighed, then lowered his head and began to hit it gently against his desk.

It must have been nagging at him, because an hour later he sat back from his keyboard and raised the subject again. "Didn't you say that you wanted to visit the places in Spain where this character fought? Do you ever think that you might be poking your nose in where it's not wanted? Or where it's dangerous? You know, like that thing you do where as soon as you read about a haunted house or hilltop where no one can spend a night without fleeing in terror you run off and prove that you can. Thereby pissing off all the locals who had said if you went up there, you'd never be seen again."

"Probably. But to be honest I don't think I can help it. I just notice things and want to find out more. If I dig up something labelled 'A warning to the curious' I can only see the last three words and think 'To the curious'. Oh, that'll be for me then."

"I'll remember that" he told me. "It'll look good on your gravestone."

Chapter Nineteen

The next day I woke up with a temperature of 102 degrees. I had succumbed to the twenty-four-hour bug that was going around the office. Excellent news. I tilted myself out of bed and walked on rubbery legs to the phone to huskily call in sick. Then took a couple of paracetamols and set my alarm clock for a few hours extra sleep, before getting up and heading happily off to the International Brigade archives at the Marx Memorial Library, occasionally bumping into a lamppost on the way, my balance gone.

With my three-month break coming up this was the last day I could take off for research. Even though the desire to find out more was constantly eating at me. I'd got the bug. Arriving home each evening I'd wander around frustratedly, dissatisfied that I didn't have access to any new historical materials.

As usual I was broke. Saturdays found me in record offices or staying in, writing long and carefully crafted letters to Elena and then treating myself to a film.

I put A Matter of Life and Death in the video. David Niven was Peter, a young pilot flying a shattered and burning bomber towards nighttime England, his dead radio operator at his side. Kim Hunter was June, a young American ground controller on the other end of the radio, trying to talk him home. Except, he explains, there isn't any point. He can't land. His undercarriage is gone and the flames are getting nearer.

Is he wounded, is he going to bail out, she asks?

"Yes, June, I'm bailing out, but there's a catch. I've got no parachute." He's going to have to jump to his death to escape the agony of being burned alive.

He apologises for frightening her and asks her to let his mother know he loves her.

"I'm not frightened," she tells him, holding back tears.

In those last minutes left to them they forge a relationship, June desperately trying to find a way to save him, Peter clinging to the unattainable promise of her voice.

"You've got guts," he tells her. "It's funny. I've known dozens of girls...but it's an American girl whom I've never seen and never shall see who'll hear my last words."

Then it's time to go, and he signs off with, "June, if you're around when they pick me up, turn your head away..."

Tears trickled from the outside corners of my eyes. I wiped them away. I didn't have a girlfriend, so I didn't need to hide them. There are good things about being single.

Which may be why I didn't notice that I hadn't received a letter from Elena that week.

Suddenly I was losing her. A message arrived complaining about me sending letters about us and what we'd been together. She was sorry, but I had agreed to her going and remaking her life with Paco, and I was making it doubly difficult. If I couldn't write as just a friend, then it would be better if I didn't write at all. The underlying message was plain – it was time to stop altogether.

I could have written to apologise and promised to be less romantic, but in my gut I was sure that to do so would mean the end of everything. Instead, I took what seemed to me the appalling risk of replying that while I was sorry that my Spanish was not as good as it might be and obviously open to different interpretations, I thought her reading all these hidden meanings into perfectly normal letters was, one, inexplicable and, two, more her fault than mine.

Unbelievably, it worked. She actually wrote and apologised for the misunderstanding. Guilty but relieved, I committed myself to spending even more time planning and double checking what I wrote and only sending notes that she (hopefully) would look forward to receiving but that were safely neutral.

At least for the immediate future.

It was a close thing that revealed how quickly a trapdoor can open beneath you and your plans.

I continued pushing the limits of what's fair in love and war. I spent money I didn't have buying a set of highly flattering flight overalls I'd never wear again, having a costly haircut and going parachuting. Then I paid an out-of-work photographer friend to take some moody black and white shots of me on the airfield.

I was undoubtedly the best dressed, best haircutted person sleeping in an open shack in the freezing countryside that weekend, since there was no money left over for accommodation. Which, did, however, help me achieve the gaunt, lean, deeply-cheekboned look I wanted in the photo I sent to Elena in a seemingly routine newsy letter whose hidden message was (I hoped) that this was the kind of way we could be spending our days if we were together.

Similarly, I was assiduous in forwarding the regards of mutual friends, never forgetting to add at which film, club or pub they'd passed on their greetings to her.

Outside work almost all my time was now spent on either these kinds of tactics or on research, but I knew that the time was coming closer when I'd have to move the campaign to win back Elena up a gear and leave behind the comfort and interest of historical books and documents.

It would have been an act of folly I couldn't have permitted myself if I hadn't known I was going to see her again, but one night, in a moment of sadness, I took out the raincoat she had left behind, in order to smell her perfume on it. It brought back a pitiful childhood memory. Of me as a boy checking my Dad's clothes in the hope that some olfactory proof of his existence remained. Only then it hadn't occurred to me to do it till weeks after his death, and no scent of him lingered, no matter how desperately I went from jacket to coat to shirt.

I thought about him then, but then I did most days. I did it in different ways: sometimes trying to revisit all my memories of him in case, unused, they faded away beyond recapture; sometimes in the dreams where he returned to life; sometimes in a fantasy in which I travelled back in time to warn him how to prevent his death, proving who I was by telling him "you may not believe me, but here's the proof. The World Cup final is going to be between England and West Germany, and you might want to put some money on the score being..." And sometimes guiltily, wondering what he would have thought of what I had and hadn't made of my life. Born with all the advantages he lacked but without the ambition to succeed that drove him from a dirt-poor Scottish coal mining village to Fleet Street. He wouldn't have tolerated more than a day at Montressor, I knew that much.

He had been a reserved man of quiet power, who came from a time and a loveless "Wee Free" Presbyterian background that precluded displays of affection for his children. He was, I knew, intelligent, brave, quietly patient and protective. He hadn't been allowed tears as a child, and this limited his tolerance of mine and my brother's. As a result, I always felt that I didn't quite live up to his standards, even though years later my mother would tell me that he had brimmed with a pride in me that his upbringing had given him no means to express.

The resulting paradox was that while feeling less than the man I should have been as his son, I had always tested myself against pain and fears, developing a sometimes-fierce willpower to overcome them that, for me, would never seem quite enough.

Ah well, we're all soft compared to that generation. At least with age came more understanding. That he must have had his own fears and frustrations and would surely have valued the positive things I had achieved. Even if I had squandered my teens in drugs and indolence and rebellion, I had done some worthwhile stuff since.

I could only dream of talking with him man-to-man. Instead, I had to be content with memories of the father-son talks we had when walking in the countryside on holiday. Or on Saturdays, when we'd go to a distant newsagent to buy the newspaper he picked up from the much closer-to-home shop all the other days of the week, and he'd give me and my brother a little pocket money to spend in the tiny toy shop next door. (Jesus, I've only just now realised that that was his way of spending time with us.)

The war was the most common topic, with amusing anecdotes to the fore. Only occasionally did he forget our age and let slip little glimpses that I'd never be able to follow up. Of learning how to live and fight in the jungle. Of the horrors endured by his comrades who'd been in the Japanese prisoner of war camps. Of taking out one of his first patrols, a boy in grown up clothing, to try and find a Burmese tribesman who had helped the British and been kidnapped by the Japanese for it. Knowing that they'd never find him alive, but that they had to look. Discovering him dead, of course, hung in a noose of barbed wire, and bayoneted to death up the rectum. I think

I could just about keep a brave face on finding that now, but how did he and others like him manage it when so grievously young, then do what had to be done and return to a disease- and scorpion-ridden camp for years more of it?

It reminded me of something a colleague had once told me about how, in 1943 in North Africa his father, aged nineteen, had been caught in the open by a German fighter. With no cover near he'd stood firing his Sten gun at the raider as it opened up its guns on him. And for only one second as it roared over him, almost at ground level, both he and the pilot locked eyes, two youngsters, almost near enough to touch, both putting their whole being into trying to kill the other.

I thought of Dad on his nineteenth birthday – sick with dysentery, refusing to report to the doctor because there were people relying on him, lying vomiting onto his sweat-sodden camp bed, unable to take his boots off because his feet would swell, and he wouldn't get them on again if the Japanese attacked. Maybe thinking about when it would all be over and what the future would hold and vowing that it wouldn't be returning to a grindingly poor and blinkered existence in a remote, puritanical Scots village. Nineteen. Nine bloody teen.

Christ, I could hardly get out of bed at that age.

He'd have liked Elena though.

Then it was time to put away the bookish pursuits, stop treading the wind, and get out and do something.

Chapter Twenty

The last day arrived. For three months anyway.

Our first job was to decide what form of brain yoga would get us through it, and we quickly agreed on a hidden lyric battle. In an example of the subconscious enthusiastically bypassing the conscious I had entered the office singing We've Got to Get Out of This Place. Roger, a symphony in brown corduroy (the *Daily Telegraph* must have been running a reader offer), was, perhaps for the same reasons, humming the theme from Terry and June. Even he realised the futility of roleplaying the boss unexpectedly coming to dinner all day, so we committed ourselves to trying to get lines sung by British R&B groups past each other instead.

Inevitably, time's winged chariot dragged even more slowly than usual. Possibly it was using the Central Line. Deciding I'd never make it to five-thirty, at five I pushed my chair back and got ready to sneak for the door.

"Well, that's it, mate. I've done all my work for today. It's time for me to leave off being one of Darren George's winged monkeys for a while".

Roger didn't turn round, just told me: "You think you can get what you want, but you can't."

It seemed an odd way of saying goodbye. Before I could answer he continued: "Just wait and see, you'll come running back."

I was about to tell him that when I came back it wouldn't be running when I realised which band he was quoting. The bugger had almost trumped me in the last minute. I had a second to reply in the same style before he would make a klaxon noise and accuse me of hesitation. I had to show him that when you play with me you play with fire. "Yeah well, you know me, any time I see a red door I want it painted black."

He still kept his back to me. "Time is on *my* side. You'll come running back."

"Maybe I will, but not till I've tried to do something different. And not," I lowered my voice, "for long. I hope."

"Time is on my side. Yes, it is…"

"See you in three months then."

"…yes, it is."

Chapter Twenty-One

It worked every time. The plane door cracked open, the air – with its signature smell, heat and density – flooded in and I thought *Spain*. It was a place that, in the first moment of contact, could still puncture the slight staleness born of too much travel and too many one-blurring-into-another press trips.

The air still felt as different as it did when I first came here on holiday, aged 13, and I was pleased to see that Alicante airport, with its undersized luggage carousels and gloomy 1970s patina, hadn't changed much since then. Yet they were the only things that hadn't. Everywhere I looked there seemed to be new apartment blocks, holiday homes, science parks, swimming pools, playgrounds, stadia, sports centres and opera houses. Yet it was only two years since I'd last visited. It was a little like the 1960s in Britain, that same rush to build, only in Spain it's funded by the nation's newfound economic self-confidence, by a booming black economy, and of course, by the European Union.

I picked up my rucksack and headed for the connecting train that the young, posh Spanish travel representative in London had told me would be leaving shortly, even though I was arriving in the early hours of the morning. Despite her tone making clear she had other far more important things to do, she had somehow found time to assure me that the station was just a few minutes' walk away, but if I preferred there were frequent all-night buses to take me to the all-night trains that would carry me to Valencia in time to meet Elena before she went to work.

It became evident that the Spanish can run modern, punctual, non-vandalised, air-conditioned trains that even display the outside temperature, but they haven't yet eradicated enchufe, the influence that puts the well-connected and their children in cushy jobs, like embassies, cultural centres and international travel inquiries, where they are safely unsackable. Meaning they can invent non-existent train times and bus services and move a station miles in order to get rid of an irritating caller like me, rather than just actually looking in the timetable it is their job to possess.

So, I arrived at Valencia Nord Station hours after I was due to be met by Elena. There was nothing for it but to call her at home. It was Paco who answered. I stumblingly explained that I was an English friend on a visit, and I had been due to meet his girlfriend. She wasn't there, he told me, but he'd pass my message on. He sounded helpful and sincere. I felt a complete shit. I wasn't quite trying to take her away from him, but I was hoping that their relationship had at most only a few years to last, and wanted to make sure that Elena remembered that I would be there if it fell apart. Two hours later, when I'd admired as much of the art nouveau glory of the station as I could through my nerves, I saw her coming quickly across the marble floor.

I had mentally rehearsed this moment so many times. I knew that we would hug and kiss, but on the lips, or on the cheeks? Or would the meeting be so joyous that I could get away with putting my hands under her arms and lifting her high into the air?

Her face was cold, but her eyes were simmering. She was thinner, tenser, exhausted looking. Before I could say hello, I had to tell her that I'd called her flat. She looked down, groaned, and answered: "What are you doing here anyway?"

It was so far from what I'd expected that I didn't know what to tell her. All my artifice fell away. "I've missed you. I still hope that one day we can be together again, but until then, I don't know, I'll take whatever I can get. I just wanted to see you. We always said that I'd visit."

She was barely restraining her anger. "Didn't you read my last letter? I didn't want to see you again. It's over between us. You agreed to that. You had a chance to keep me, but you didn't and that's why I'm back here with Paco. It hasn't been easy. Now you're making it worse."

I could, with honesty, tell her that I hadn't received any letter before I left that said she didn't want me to come (it was probably still stuck in the Spanish postal system). With equal truthfulness I tried desperately to assure her that I had wanted to see her, without conditions, without expectations, as she had suggested in our last days together, and we had planned since.

It mollified her enough for us to go to a café where I continued to try and reassure her. I gulped two coffees without tasting them and only later realised I had burnt my mouth. I did notice that my hands were shaking, something it's hard to disguise when drinking espresso from a rattling cup and saucer. Her hostility eased only fractionally. I think her sense of justice helped. It was true, she was the one who had first suggested that I visit. I had not, as she appeared to have thought, knowingly disobeyed an instruction not to come. But for the first time in her I had seen the implacability of Spanish pride in action.

I was learning that it was part of going out with a Spaniard. Welcome the passion, warmth and sensuality and you must also accept (and risk) the wildness, the fire, the unpredictability that goes with them.

She left after just twenty minutes, having directed me towards the budget hotel I'd booked, where she told me she'd phone when (if?) it was convenient for us to meet.

It would be a lonely few days before that happened. I did what I could to enjoy the town but didn't want to be too far from the front desk if she called, in case the hotel staff lost the message. When a call came it was from an English guy who was staying with friends of Elena. She had fixed it up for them to take me out but wouldn't be there herself. Still, it was progress of a sort.

We met at a heaving street in the old town that was lined with bars, whose customers were spilled out onto the pavements outside, where they drank a little, talked a lot, and admired each other and each others' scooters. The group I was with moved from one place to another, here to buy cigarettes, there for one drink, somewhere else to sit at a table without ordering anything or to talk to a friend. They had fun and consumed little, leaving me and the other Englishman, Tony, feeling self-conscious about how relatively quickly we were emptying our glasses, even though we were drinking only moderately. I tentatively but repeatedly tried to raise the subject of how they knew Elena, hoping for any information about her, but only one of them did, the rest were friends of friends.

By two AM there must have been perhaps a thousand people in the street, and I realised that after five hours there I had seen not one person throw up and not a single fight. Then one of the girls said she couldn't live without dancing, and we all packed into a taxi that took us to a club by the beach. Or on the beach, since much of it was on wooden mats laid on the sand.

There we danced (something, to be honest, that I am more self-conscious doing with each year I travel past thirty) until four, when they finally had to reluctantly declare that it would soon be time to go home, since they all started work at eight. My danger radar was off, but it clicked in when I picked out the aggressive posture and non-Spanish colouring of one of the dancers in the shadows. He was about my age, German, and equipped with eyes so psychotic that even in the darkness they signalled how dangerous he was. He was with a six-foot teen girlfriend wearing a minuscule leather top, skirt and boots, who didn't look old enough to have legally had a large, downward-pointing arrow tattooed just above her bum cleft.

She was saying something placatory to him when he hissed a reply, shoved her away and strode between the tables, jostling people and spilling their drinks, before stopping to glare at them, willing them to say something back. He finished with a kick to a drink-laden table, then went to retrieve the girl, who rushed to embrace him and coo endearments to him in German while he grabbed her arm and pushed her out.

There was a collective sigh of relief round the dancefloor. Faced with a display of drunkenness and mindless violence that had nearly spoiled everyone's night out, they came to the same conclusion, and all around us you could hear people turn to each other and say "Inglés". English.

It took us another hour to collect ourselves together and head for our respective homes or hotels, Tony refusing an invitation from one girl who was a flight attendant and had been chatting him up all night, and me, surprised, politely declining another. Maybe Elena would have been relieved if I had accepted, or maybe she wouldn't have cared either way, but it just wasn't what I was there for.

It turned out to be just as well anyway, as early the next day there was a call for me from Elena, saying that she'd pick me up and take me to the beach that afternoon.

She arrived in a beaten-up Renault 5 I didn't know she had. Her mood was distant. I guessed that the outing was less for me than it was one of those things you just had to do when a foreigner visited. While she drove, I hid the fact that I was watching her out of the corner of my eye. Not for salacious reasons, just because, driving, she seemed a different person. Not the small, slightly vulnerable young woman I'd known in London, but someone in control, in her own city and country. With her concentrating on the way and guiding the decrepit car we didn't talk till we arrived, and maybe that was a good thing. When we did, she was more relaxed. Probably it was the beach, that integral part of Spanish coastal culture, working its magic, doing to her what a visit to an idyllic bit of countryside might to a British person.

The sand was empty of people, and she busied herself with laying out an expedition's-worth of towels, sun cream, bottles of water, apples and the inevitable bocadillo sandwiches wrapped in silver foil. I was strangely saddened to see that hers was tortilla and mine was ham and cheese. She'd forgotten how much I'd loved the tortillas she'd cooked me in England.

After eating and guessing that she was probably uncomfortable in the clothes she didn't want to take off in front of me, I stripped down to my trunks and went to swim. When I looked back, she was lying sunbathing in her bikini.

I'd have to admit that when I finished, I did not feel half bad about the fact that she had happened to look my way as I stepped out of the water, relaxed from the exercise and a little leaner and more muscled-up than I'd been when we were together in England. I'd even laid off the cigarettes and alcohol for the last month so that my skin would look good, and on impulse bought the first ever pair of flash sunglasses in my life at the airport with the last few quid left on my Visa card. Feeling relaxed in my own skin gave me a little bit of the confidence I needed to deal with the stress of the meeting. I'm not sure that she felt as good about herself: she looked vulnerably skinny in her bikini; nerves or the worries of return having made her much thinner than before. To me, though, looking through the eyes of love, she was beautiful. I had to hide that fact, however.

If there's no one spoiling the atmosphere, it's not too hot and the sand hasn't got into all your things then it's as difficult to stay tense while lying in the sun on a good beach as it is in a sauna. We talked little, the obvious topics – our times in London and Dorking – prohibited, but gradually the frostiness between us thawed. In time she even relaxed enough to allow me to take photos of her and us and the beach.

Then we idled the afternoon away until it was time for her to drop me off at the hotel. We weren't what we had been, but a certain fragile naturalness and familiarity had returned between us.

I think we were friends again.

Chapter Twenty-Two

She rang. "How's the research going?"
(Christ, what research, I'd hardly left the hotel in case she phoned) "Oh fine, fine, I haven't done as much as I planned…" (by now I should've gone to Alabacete, where the fortress walls were reportedly still marked with the International Brigades' increasingly disillusioned graffiti, in the hope there might be something by Nathan. If I were on a proper timetable, I would be on my way to Belchite, where the battle-ruined streets were never reoccupied, leaving them as a crumbling testament to the war. Plus, there was the Valley of the Fallen, where tens of thousands of Republican prisoners of war slave-laboured to build a vast monument to the winning side. Not forgetting Franco's birthplace in Galicia, to see if it was true that he was still admired as a local boy made good. And there was the place that I was keeping until last. Brunete. Where I hoped to maybe get some casual work for a few weeks while I trusted to the skills learned searching for lost habitations and their refuse sites. I wanted to at least try and find Nathan's burial place. I could ensure that it got a marker. He deserved so much more.) "…but I did get to Teruel." (Where the Republic scored a rare, short-lived victory in temperatures of -20 degrees and the troops' horses froze so solidly to death that the soldiers blunted their saws and axes trying to cut meat from them for food.)

"Oh yes, I know it. In the mountains. Every year it has the record as the coldest town in Spain," She struggled for the phrase in English, "Bleeding freezing. How was it?"

"Bleeding freezing. There was a snowstorm half an hour after I got there. I couldn't believe it."

She laughed. "That's the place. There's a song about it. Very, very old. Have you heard of Los Amantes?"

"Los Amantes de Teruel? Tonta ella y tonto el?" Yes, I had heard of it, it was a favourite Republican marching song. Los Amantes were a romantic, young, seriously over-pious, Romeo and Juliette-ish couple in the thirteenth century, separated by death but remembered, forever together, in song: "The two lovers of Teruel. Stupid her. And stupid him."

Elena was only briefly surprised. She was getting used to the oddities I had picked up from studying the Civil War. Then she remembered why she'd called. "I've found someone who wants to talk."

The interviewee was Pilar, the rich aunt of a well-off couple Elena had worked for as a cleaner and nanny when she left school at fifteen. A lifelong communist, she mourned the lack of interest in the war of those around her. I must have been a revelation to her, and her attitude turned from doubt that a foreigner would know anything worthwhile about that time, to delight that I did. As Elena sat slightly apart Pilar began to talk, gabble really, too fast for me to understand everything, waving her hands the whole time.

Journalist-style, I let her get started before casually bringing out a pad and asking if she minded if I took notes. She grabbed it from me, slammed it onto the table and insisted that I did.

"I was as old as the decade when the war began. Six in '36. At first my parents tried to keep from me what was happening, but they couldn't. All around was chaos. Almost overnight people changed the way they dressed, and the streets were suddenly full of men and women in overalls or clattering up and down the roads packed into lorries and cars, waving these long rifles and shouting slogans. One day there'd be no food then the next they'd have taken over a shop and would be handing out bread to the crowd. I don't think the shop ever reopened mind you. Later I learned that for many the greatest fear was of being taken for a paseo. You don't know that means, I suppose."

"Yes, in English a stroll. But in this sense what the Americans call being taken for a ride. Driven away and shot."

"That's right. But I knew nothing of that. My parents needn't have bothered to try and shield me from everything. To a child it was a carnival. The air raids hadn't begun yet."

It was the first time she paused. I thought she was searching for a memory, but she might as easily have been repressing one.

"Those Italian sons of whores. Their bombers came over, these little black shapes, like flies, so far away they seemed to take forever to cross the sky. I shit on their mothers; I don't know why they flew so high, no one had anything to shoot back at them with. Of course, Comrade Stalin gave us guns and fighters, but we never saw them here. I am sure he sent them where they were most needed. All the other countries were too cowardly to sell us weapons. Make sure you write that down."

I'd heard the same thing so many times before that I responded without thinking. "I think, to be fair, other countries did sell arms at first. Czechoslovakia. Mexico. Even France planned to until the British persuaded them to stop. And Stalin didn't really *give* the weapons. He took all the gold reserves of the Spanish Republic to Russia at the beginning of the war 'for safekeeping', and he didn't exactly send any back..."

I should have known better. Her eyes burned at me, and she spoke with genuine anger.

"Well even if that is true, better *he* had it than that son of a whore Franco." Then she composed herself and began again.

"Later the Germans came, flying lower, but the day I remember it was planes way up in the sky. The street was full of women and children, queuing for food. Someone pointed and shouted 'Aviones!' and everyone ran for the nearest public shelter, which was nothing more than a well-built shop – all stone – with the front sandbagged. I lost my mother in the rush but someone else pushed me inside. In my memory there was the noise of explosions but I'm not sure I really heard any after the first one went off and deafened us all.

Instead, there was a feeling like great hammers beating the earth and a huge cloud of dust rolled across the road towards the entrance. Like a wave at the beach, almost that fast. Then everything went dark. There was no door. A woman hesitated for a second at the entrance. Young, no more than twenty, holding shopping in a string bag. She was the last one in and perhaps she couldn't see where to step next, because the lights inside had gone out as soon as the first bombs fell. Then she was gone. Her top half was cut away as if by a giant blade, and there were just her legs left, still standing, in darned stockings and a woollen skirt. The bombing stopped and the legs stayed there, leaning against the wall. I was next to them, and I began to cry and scream, but no one wanted to touch them. Instead, they turned me away so I couldn't see. My mother found me soon after and led me out. I don't know if they were still there when I left, covered in her blood and fragments of her flesh and bones...."

She began to cry, deeply and uncontrollably. Elena put her arms around her and comforted her. I sat, uselessly, waiting for the right moment to apologise for bringing up the memories. But when I did, she became instantly animated.

"No, no, I want to tell more. There was one moment I pray I will never forget. Listen. This is something you will want to know...after that, after the bombings, after the fascists took town after town and there seemed to be nothing anyone could do stop them...the foreign troops came. The world went round that an army had come to fight for us, and we all ran to see them. Dios mío, my God, what men. All blond and fair-skinned, and all so tall. Like giants. English (she used the Spanish catch-all term for anyone British). Americans. French. Thousands of them, all singing the Internationale at the tops of their voices. The road trembled with the crash of their boots. They held their heads so high while we children ran alongside them and the crowd pelted them with anything they had to give them, flowers and cigarettes, oranges and nuts.

I had read about that day, how a group of International Brigaders marched up the avenue then doubled back through the backstreets and joined the rear of the column, so that hundreds seemed like a thousand. I knew that they couldn't all have been huge and blond and booted, except to a child or to citizens desperate for hope. But there would have been enough First World War veterans and Territorial Army members among them to ensure they marched roughly in step and to a British Army pace that was well suited to the Internationale's rhythm. Ill-equipped, but exuding to the crowds a patina of foreign military professionalism. It must have looked as though Spain's problems were over.

"In that moment we believed that we could not be beaten. More than believed. *Knew.*"

She stared at me intently, making sure that I held her gaze, tears once again in her eyes, her voice trailing away a little as she travelled back almost sixty years, willing me to see it the way she did.

"They were magnificent."

Somehow, perhaps in the way that I treated Pilar, I had passed a test in Elena's eyes. As we descended the stairs to the street, she put her hand out for a second to pat mine, then quickly withdrew it, the move unfinished. I knew that she'd be expected at home but as we walked back to the metro she dawdled slightly, as though she needed time to decide.

"Back in my village it will soon be the Festival of the Virgin."

She paused, and I mentally waved a sad goodbye to the double entendres that had suddenly flared to life in my mind, only for me to smother them, unspoken, at birth.

"Everyone who was born there tries to get back for those days. Maybe you might want to come. I can explain that you are a foreign friend," (She left unsaid the fact that I would need to rigorously abide by this partial truth). "It's your birthday next week, isn't it? You could spend it there. It might be, I think, interesting for you."

"Oh, you think I'm ready, do you?" I asked, even though I suspected that behaving myself, rather than readiness, was the test that I had passed.

"Ready? Oh no. I told you once before, you cannot imagine how it is until you get there. You're not from La Mancha and you're not from a village. You'll just have to go and hope for the best. Until you do, you'll never be ready."

Chapter Twenty-Three

I put my luggage together and booked out, glad to save for a week the cost of the hotel which, though cheap, was eating greedily into my funds. The last thing I did before leaving town was to pick up the photos of Elena and me at the beach, that uncomfortable day when she'd been so wary of my intentions. I was shocked to find that the pictures of us, tanned, gleaming and near naked in our swimming costumes, seemed to show an underlying sexuality that had in no way been evident at the time.

I thought about that pretty obsessively right up till I arrived at Valencia Station, where I put it out of my mind, since I would be spending half a day travelling alone with her. She had told me that Paco, tired of the demands of two families, had cried off attending the festival, claiming that he couldn't get time off work. She, in turn, had a few days off from her cleaning and bar jobs.

Coming towards me across the concourse she looked stern, and more conservatively dressed than normal. If I'd worried about what we would talk about on the journey I needn't have, given that she had a lifetime's memories of the village that she was keen to air. And I had some questions too. "What I don't understand is this idea of a local virgin."

She explained patiently: "Every town or village has its own festival. There's always one going on somewhere. For teenagers it's an excuse to party, but there'll be special church services as well, and chosen groups of people will take the statue of the virgin, and maybe Christ and the saints as well, from the church and carry them around the streets. The heavier the statues the greater the honour. You know the kind of thing. A big procession."

"Yes, I've seen a few. Some of them look pretty sinister. You know, the scarily mediaeval ones you see in the airline magazines, where the effigies are carried by penitents dressed up in those scarlet, pointed-hooded robes the Inquisition wore. But I thought that kind of thing was just for Easter or religious holidays."

"Oh, every day is a holiday somewhere in Spain. The virgins have different days you see."

109

"But that's what I don't understand. Isn't there just the one virgin? Mary. Isn't she your village's virgin?"

"No. ours is the Virgen de La Encarnación. Where I live in Valencia it's the Virgen de La Victoria. I don't know how many more there are, there's a virgin for unemployed people, there's the Virgin of Guadeloupe, the Virgin of Fatima."

"That's what I mean. How many virgins can there be? I was brought up in the Church of England. There's only one virgin and you don't even really believe in her. Are they saints?"

Her patience was running thin. "No, virgins. Some may be saints, but they don't have to be. They just have to be virgins. Well, one or two have children."

No wonder all the Roman Catholics I'd known had complained of the endless religious instruction they'd endured as children. How else could they keep track of it all? "I give up. Maybe if I'd been brought up a Catholic, I'd understand."

"If you'd been brought up a Catholic, you'd know not to ask questions," she told me.

The train journey was long, but grandiosely scenic in a way I hadn't expected a European one could still be. We passed from the city into a landscape of rice fields and miles and miles of orange groves, which turn the air almost into an intoxicant when they blossom, then fields of lemons and vines for as far as the land is irrigated enough to support them. Among the crops were dotted occasional towns and remote, often-deserted farmhouses. And, always alone, haciendas – sometimes dilapidated but invariably exquisitely decorated, the once grand mansions of the latifundia system, still high-walled and heavily-gated to protect them against past royalist wars, eighteenth century brigands and, no doubt, the workers who laboured for their owners in near feudal conditions almost until modern times.

Later even those occasional buildings began to thin out as we entered the foothills and the land dried and turned rocky and orange. Except where the occasional stunning river plunged deep into its own precipitous valley made agriculture possible, all signs of habitation, apart from an ancient shepherd's or quarry worker's hut, disappeared for miles at a time. Then we were in the mountains, with a sheer precipice on one side and the track clinging to the rock on the other, hugging the mountainside so closely that at times the diesel loco would appear almost alongside the carriages it was struggling to pull, but on the next hairpin bend, separated from us by a yawning drop into the tree-sprinkled valley below. Occasionally we would stop but pick up no one at a station whose existence was a mystery, since it seemed to serve only a cluster of houses half a mile away and a hundred feet below. Then, further along the line we'd pass its sister structures, abandoned but non-vandalised, gracious nineteenth century railway buildings that in Britain we'd fight to convert to habitations.

From there we disappeared into a tunnel and emerged onto a bridge spanning a deep, easily defensible defile, and I imagined the Republican troops with their obsolescent, overlong Russian rifles and rope-soled sandals panting as they pushed and dragged the weighty Soviet-supplied, Tsarist-era Maxim machine guns on their back-breakingly heavy iron wheels up the near vertical slope, maybe thrashing some poor mule nearly to death to make it carry the ammunition, while on the other side the insurgent troops, better shod, their tight woollen tunics buttoned, by order, to the neck despite the killing heat, struggled to approach them, blinded by sweat and desperate to stay out of the way of the flailing sticks and riding crops of their bullying NCOs and high-booted officers, furious at having to leave their superb cavalry horses behind and scramble up the burning rock like the rest.

From the station we took the little minibus that scrapes its living by travelling the old roads between the isolated villages that punctuate the plain of La Mancha. The main road, such as it was, was almost deserted, used, since the building of the new motorways to Madrid, only by the most local traffic. The bars and restaurants that dotted it were either long closed (their once brightly painted exteriors and enamel signs surviving as faded reminders of the 1940s) or just clinging to life as venues for the wedding and christening parties that still brought families back to the villages they had left decades before in the mass migrations to the cities that left the countryside populated mainly by the old.

Every few miles we would bump off the highway into an anonymous, unmetalled, single lane road that apparently went nowhere. At least until, just as it would have for someone on foot or donkey five hundred years before, a church, always the highest building, showed over the horizon, revealing the otherwise hidden village it overshadowed.

This was Don Quixote country. The windmills had gone, but the people, or at least the eldest ones, remained. As the little bus clattered to a stop to offload one or two villagers, parcels or livestock, it would be met by squat, thick-accented old men and women, with brown-baked, deeply lined faces, and few teeth. Recessed, squinting-against-the-sun eyes watched everything. The men were collarless, their shirts buttoned to the top, all dressed in flat caps and cardigans despite the heat, the women in shapeless dresses and aprons, often in mourning black. The males looked like Sancho Panza (Elena told me that a big gut is still called a "Panza" there), so uniformly sized that I found myself looking at a line of them and thinking that you could run planks along their heads to make shelves.

Ineffectual curtains tried to block the sun from the vehicle's cramped interior as we carried on through a landscape of flatness that was varied only by occasional ridges of stone or, here and there, a small enclosure of almond or olive trees, or a goat feeding on a patch of spiny grass.

Mostly, though it was just sky and desert-like earth too stony and dry for anyone to work, crossed only by an occasional dirt track that might lead to a field, a hamlet, a farm or perhaps to nothing. Then the driver dropped nosily down through the gears, and we jolted onto another unsignposted lane that had the vehicle rocking on its springs.

"Look," Elena told me, "The Angel's Wings." She pointed to a lunar landscape of whiteness dotted with jagged sandstone that flanked us as far as the horizon, where it gave way to the piercing aquamarine of the sky. "Salt flats. Every, perhaps, ten years, when it rains in summer, it floods here and makes a lake, and then the road is closed." There was a slight incline and then a rise fringed with stunted olive trees whose parched branches clawed at the sky like arthritic fingers. Then behind them, raising itself into view as we approached, came the tower of a squat church that seemed to have been carved out of the hillock of rock that surrounded it and on which, like children clinging to their mother's skirts for protection, fifty or sixty whitewashed houses clustered.

"We're here."

Chapter Twenty-Four

After spending an hour with my legs squeezed in between the tiny seats I nearly stumbled as I climbed out of the minibus but, thankfully, recovered and stepped as manfully as possible into the blinding light of the village's centre.

I looked at the square, the square looked back. It was clearly the main public area: a sandy arena bordered by small, picturesque houses, with a dry fountain; benches; a single, elegantly antique streetlamp fixed to a wall that also held torn posters for long-past elections; and, here and there in the shade of their doorways, an aged grandmother sitting, knitting or warming her rheumatic bones, or a flat-capped older man standing, unmoving, studiously watching everything except the stranger. It was timeless. What a place.

Elena's bag bumped into my back as she tried to step down from the bus. "Come on dreamer," she told me, then uttered the six words that sooner or later you're going to have to hear in any serious relationship, "It's time to meet my family".

Their home was nearby in a steep, flinty lane that gave off the square (come to think of it, that description would be true of almost any of the houses there). Too close for me to linger over the surroundings which, goggle-eyed, I was trying to take in all-in-one go. I just had time to notice how small the windows were, then Elena opened an unlocked and deeply recessed front door and, ducking my head, I entered the darkness inside.

The hugely thick, heat-defying walls created a reverse Tardis effect, making the house even smaller inside than it looked from out, and we quickly went from the unlit, narrow entrance passage into a little, boxlike kitchen, whose only light came from the open back door. Her mother was inside cooking, with her back to us, unaware of our arrival till Elena called out "Mama!". She jumped, shrilled in pleased surprise, quickly wiped her hands on her apron, then, with much cooing, embraced her daughter. She was a small, older woman, hard of hearing, bent from a lifetime of hard work, and dressed in mourning black.

"Mama," Elena introduced us, "This is Tomás – Tom – from England. Tom, this is my mother, Señora Amparo." She said hello, calling me "Ton", missed my proffered hand, moved fussing around Elena, asking her about the journey, saying she was too thin, picked up then put down her luggage, then shrieked as the fat in the frying pan she'd been heating caught fire. She quickly extinguished it with a combination of more shrieks and her apron, then continued the same way while she cooked the meal, which she'd delayed until our bus arrived.

"And Papa?" Elena asked.

Her tone became momentarily frosty. "He is next door. You'd better say hello."

We went into the front room, where he was sitting on the sofa that also served as his chair for the dining table pulled up against it and watching a dubbed cowboy film. The room was dark, tiny, tatty and filled by his presence. He greeted Elena warmly without turning down the sound or rising, then acknowledged me, as I leaned over the table to shake his hand.

"Tomás, my father, Señor Augusto Vilar. Father, this is Tom, a friend I knew in England who has come to Spain to visit our village."

He was small, made smaller by sitting in the age-sunken sofa with the table up to his chest. Nearly bald, sun-darkened and leathery, with gimlet eyes, a huge jaw and, I suspected, a hair-trigger temper. The patriarch in his autumn, one-time absolute ruler of his family. An otherwise undistinguished man who had always made the gift of his fists freely available to them. Only now he was becoming too aged to inspire the fear to which he had been accustomed, and the society he inhabited was moving on from its acceptance of the man as the caudillo of the home. Elena had told me that, much though she had feared him before and impossible though she found it to forgive him for his treatment of her mother, she found herself feeling sorry for the shrunken, almost friendless old man he was becoming.

He waved us to the table, and we sat as his wife brought in the lunch, with me waiting for her to join us before I began to eat. Suddenly he moved his face near mine, hit the tabletop and shouted something. His accent was too thick for me to understand. What the hell had I done wrong? He did it again. When I failed to reply he smacked the wood and barked something more. Elena finally translated it into understandable Spanish for me. "Come on! Eat!" So, I did. He boomed something else that I guessed was a question about the food, so I quickly praised it, and he sat back, briefly satisfied, his attention momentarily diverted by the booming TV.

The mother still hadn't joined us, and I was out of practice meeting girlfriend's fathers. All I had to go on was teenage memories of trying to make a good impression on middle-aged men who spent their spare time fixing things around the house, using screws that they kept, sorted by size, in old tobacco tins.

Here though I had more reason to make a good impression. I decided to take my cue from Elena's remark that I had come to study the village, by acting as though it were indeed the centre of the world, all its products paragons and its people giants among men. I continued to do this in the subsequent days with everyone. No one found it odd.

When enough time had gone by without me complimenting something he asked me about the food. Everything, he told me with pride, was "del pueblo", from the village. With him watching me closely, and with Elena's mother now sitting with us – though silently in the presence of her husband – I began.

Me: "Mmm, this meat is very tasty."

Him, pleased: "Es del pueblo."

Me: "The tomatoes are very good, aren't they."

Him: "Sí, cómo no? Son del pueblo."

Me: "How refreshing the water is."

Him, nodding vigorously: "Es del pueblo."

And so on. Maybe it would have been a good time to say that I'd been sleeping with his daughter. He might have been delighted. She was from the village too.

With the meal finished and his attention diverted by an attack on the cowboys' wagon train, we were able to escape the table, which, despite his aggressive protestations that this was women's work, I helped clear, then washed the dishes. He angrily made it known that this was madness, but I carried on anyway, bent over the way-too-low sink, my back killing me, my head knocking against the ceiling.

I was left alone for a while after that. Elena had visits to make and suggested that I unpack. She showed me to the spare bedroom, where, like the rest of the house, no right met no angle, and told me to enjoy it while I could: this was where her young nephews slept on visits and when they arrived, I was likely to lose the fight for the top bunk. I had no great desire to go and sit downstairs with her old man so, deciding to do something that would look like work if anyone came for me, I began to write:

The house seems to be typical of the village. Squat and low-ceilinged (from the street, standing on tiptoe I think I could just about reach the glassless, shuttered window of the first-floor front bedroom). Blindingly white outside, cave-like inside. The sun is the main enemy, so walls are thick and windows few and tiny. It's more important to keep the heat out than to let light in. Removed from their past as rural hovels only by modern additions like unreliable electricity and paved rather than dirt floors, these houses must be miserable in the harsh winters, cold, draughty and damp.

But they have their charm. The yard of this one houses an ancient stone trough that is still used for washing clothes, along with several winters' worth of neatly stacked wood for the potbellied stove that will be the only heating. A flush toilet and truncated bath were put in an unheated outhouse twenty years ago to replace the earth closet.

To enter the house is to step from light into darkness. A stubby, windowless corridor leads into the kitchen and the small main room, again without window, shabbily furnished and ornamented with flyblown religious paintings and charmless plastic souvenirs of bullrings from the sixties and seventies. From there a step-up leads into the main bedroom, another to the narrow stairs, built from rock and so shadowed and hemmed in by the walls and lack of light that you feel you're underground. A narrow window, almost like a medieval archer's slit and one of only two on the ground floor, gives onto this space. Some light comes from the votive candle that burns day and night on the steps for the soul of some dead family member.

The stairs lead to the first floor, which is given over to two bedrooms, one facing front, mine facing back towards the yard and the fields beyond, and just above the pitched tile roof that covers the kitchen. Which houses a butane cylinder stove, a low sink and some cabinets of depressing cheapness and age teetering on the heavily sloping floor. The kitchen can take two people at a time, and I can't stand up in it. The back door is usually left open and gives onto the toilet facilities outside in the yard, which they still call the "corral", even though the division of property among each generation means that it is now too small to house animals. It slopes down to the back gates and is hemmed in with high stone walls. Rather charmingly it is overgrown with a roof of vines heavy with purple grapes.

I didn't mention that I had been slightly shocked to see a gleaming – all stainless steel and blond wood – pump action shotgun standing on the stairs next to the candle. But I was less used to the village then and to the long history of putting food on the table by poaching. After I had seen the casual way firearms were left around within reach of visiting children, I was less surprised to open a cabinet in "my" room and find it full of boxes of shells and .22 bullets. At the bottom of the single cupboard was an old up and over shotgun similar to the kind I'd occasionally shot back home (I'd never yet fired a pump-action). A gun case in there I left alone, though it appeared to contain a hunting rifle considerably larger than a .22. I don't know where its ammunition was kept. Probably down the village crèche.

Little though I wanted to I guessed that I couldn't put off going downstairs any longer. I prayed the cowboys were still doing their stuff so I wouldn't have to try and converse with the dad, but as I descended the sound of the film ending came from the front room.

Then the front door opened, and Elena came in. She studied my face. I must have looked desperate to get out and explore.

"Come on", she said, "I'll show you the village."

As we went out, I clapped my hands together once. "Well, that's meeting your family over."

She looked sideways at me and gave a short little laugh. "You're joking, aren't you? You've hardly begun."

Chapter Twenty-Five

Out of tradition and common sense no one went outside under the afternoon sun by choice, so we had a chance to explore without attracting too much attention. Village telepathy meant that almost everyone knew by now of the arrival of their first ever foreign tourist. Elena took me to the village's one sight for visitors, a chapel in miniature, built years back by a local farmer's pious son. As we crossed his yard to look inside it, he came out, now an old man, and challenged us. Not by asking what we wanted or who we were but by soliciting the more important information: "¿De quién son?" Whose are you?

"I am of Augusto and Amparo," Elena replied, and, having established that at least one of us was of the village, he showed us his creation, let us scramble inside and then solemnly sent us on our way under God's protection.

Elena was in her element. Here, it was the reverse of how things had been in London, with her taking care to ensure that I was enjoying myself (she need hardly have bothered, I was already fascinated by the place) and was included in what was going on. We ambled among the extraordinarily silent streets, which were made narrow by the housefronts that hemmed them on both sides.

The buildings were uniformly low, topped by roofs of thick, rounded terracotta tiles and so whitewashed that even through sunglasses the reflected light hurt your eyes. Elena explained that unless they were owned by someone well off enough to bring in modern building materials, they demanded a top to bottom limewash each year. Uncared for, they'd quickly collapse. With their castle-thick walls it seemed unbelievable till I saw how many of the streets had the missing tooth of just such a picturesque and seemingly ancient ruin: barn toppled, skeletal walls crumbling, an iron-grilled window or a crude door that may have outlived several houses the only things standing. A wall-supporting door lintel would be revealed as a branch no thicker than a finger. In this wood-starved near desert, without real mortar, a house could turn into a ruin after only five years' neglect. Resistance to heat was the key to their design. That and the dearth of local materials apart from stone, the one crop in which the fields would always be rich. Each house, though based on a common style, was unique, each surrendering its family tree to inspection. Here the first, humble, basic structure, one room above, one below. There the later additions, as stone or space became available. Here the divisions, the reduction of the unit into smaller ones to keep jealous brothers happy. There the repairs, the telltale use of different-sized rocks. Generations, even centuries, could be traced by eye. All around was evidence of ancient beams, doors or window surrounds recycled from other structures and used out of place in larger apertures; the resulting gaps being filled with clay, stone or mortared tiles, or patched with the remains of a long-lost wagon.

Everywhere there were details and images: visible historical progressions, local eccentricities, contrasts of absolute light and darkness, flowers cascading, lichens making patterns, the shadows of fig trees and vines painting themselves as blackly as silhouettes across the overpowering white of the walls.

I tried to store them up until I could come out with my camera alone. In the meantime, I wandered in a state of childlike wonder at the difference between this village, a survivor in time, and what I had thought I knew of modern Spain.

It was all on a human scale. Even the houses of the returned (relatively) rich, which could climb higher due to the use of bricks and cement, were constrained by the narrow frontage available to them, and the feeling that nothing should challenge the modest height of the church. Just as the distances between villages and market town were determined by the distance a person carrying a load could walk in a day, so the width of the lanes had been fixed centuries before at that necessary for a single wagon to pass. Where they were too steep for a cart to climb it shrunk to that needed by two people walking or a donkey with panniers.

Poverty made it unthinkable that two wagons would need to pass anywhere within the village, so the only wider road was that approaching and leaving it via the square. On this we continued our stroll, Elena happily pointing out the locations of her childhood memories, as we entered the fields that bordered the village.

The surprise was that, unlike the south and eastern approaches, here there was enough water to bring forth a crop of triffid-sized, gloriously bright, giant-headed sunflowers. Miles of them, all blazing away against the cloudless blue of the sky. Like a British wood, they made me wish I could paint; only here you'd need something more vivid than the watercolours that suit the countryside at home so well. The beige of the stacked hay was the only shade that wasn't a primary colour. Despite the cliché the sky really was azure, and the flowers rose massively to meet it in a carpet of orange and yellow that was punctured here and there by the burning white of a wellhead or an antique beehive-shaped rock shelter, where in times past someone would have slept to protect the crops from thieves. The tallest thing in sight, which could have been placed there by an artist who wanted to make sure that no element was missing, was a lone tree that advertised the existence of a spring in the very middle of the flowers.

"They're beautiful," I told her.

"They're the last chance," she replied. "Sunflowers and hay are the only things that are economic to grow here now. When I was little, it was wheat and grapes. But the heat killed the crops and the farmers who didn't try something else went out of business. For a while there was money in cultivating tomatoes, but they needed too much water. I think this is the fifth year of the sunflowers. My father would know. One year it was too hot, and they failed. They looked terrible, all sparse and stunted and drooping. If a crop can't pay for itself in three years, then that'll be the end of it. Or of the farmer. Mind you, in the old days it would have meant the end of the village. But yes," she added, "they are beautiful, aren't they."

We detoured around a heat-exhausted but dangerous-looking dog guarding a farmyard that was littered with the obsolete equipment that it seems no farmer anywhere can bear to get rid of. Chickens ran around it and onto the road, allowing Elena and I to return to our well-rehearsed disagreement over what noise cockerels make. I stuck with "cock a doodle do", even though I remembered from the last time we'd discussed it that it isn't particularly accurate when you actually listen to one. But even knowing that she had grown up surrounded by them it still seemed more acceptable than the Spanish alternative, "Quiquiriquí," (Key-ricky-ricky-ree), which would always sound a bit effeminate to me.

We looped our way round to the north of the village, where the earth was thinner, supporting only the huertas, the subsistence smallholdings guarded for centuries by those families lucky enough to own one, and whose produce might be all that had stood between them and starvation in the past. Their crops could only be brought forth at the expense of laboriously dragging buckets of water to them daily, yet each small patch of land was regarded like treasure by its owners. Some held tomatoes, others beans or lettuces, and a few boasted olive trees whose twisted branches formed tortured patterns that looked like they had been sculpted by a particularly demented bonsai expert.

Out there, alone, five hundred yards from the village, was its cemetery, an incongruous, otherworldly, tall-walled enclosure about half the size of a small English country churchyard. It cried out for Arnold Böcklin to paint its high windowless walls, which were broken only by a heavily barred arched gate. It was a strange white oasis, far better built than any of the houses, overgrown and shaded by tall dark green cypresses, all in the middle of acres of red, dusty soil.

I tried the gate. "Locked."

"Yes, I think it's opened for a few hours on Sundays so people can visit the graves, and there are religious days when families go to visit their dead relatives. You could ask the priest to unlock it for you. I'm sure he wouldn't mind..."

"Oh, no, no, don't worry about it."

"...but I don't think people would like it if you took photos. I remember how surprised I was when I first saw children playing in churchyards in England and climbing on the tombs. Even that the graveyards were always part of the villages in your country, not kept outside. Then I decided that those were healthy things. Death is different here."

I peered through the bars at the unaccustomed green of the interior, which was kept in shadow by the trees and high walls. The available space was taken up by the marble sepulchres of the departed local rich, while everyone else was buried in niches in two of the walls. I couldn't help sneaking a look at the other walls to see if there was the chest-high gouge that would show if the cemetery, like so many others, had been used for firing squad killings in the Civil War, but they were unblemished and sparkling, innocent of blood. Or maybe just repaired and repainted.

I could have spent the whole day just walking around looking at everything, but the afternoon was lengthening, the cicadas were starting up and it was time to go home. Here and there we'd see a lizard, apparently as immobile as the rock on which it lay. But if I approached it would fly off with a speed and movement like the crack of a whip. As we left the fields we passed Elena's old school where, she told me, the children – the first generation to all receive an education up to age fifteen – had shared a single classroom with a terrifying collection of tortured wooden saints, carved in the throes of agonising martyrdom, which the church could no longer accommodate but was unwilling to throw away. Now it was a social centre for the "third age", the senior citizens who made up the majority of the village's inhabitants. Opposite it was a brand new but empty nursery and playground, both built with outside funds in an attempt to bring young families back to the place.

We wandered back, a little reluctantly. Past the church and the single bar, shop and bakery – each essential in a place that was almost totally without cars. As the afternoon lengthened more old people had come out to sit on stools in front of their houses, and our return was slow, as Elena stopped to talk with them and catch up on the little she had missed since her last visit.

Apart from illnesses the only news was of grandchildren and her one-time classmates: who had finished their military service, who was doing well in Madrid. I would be politely introduced but there was no suspicion about our relationship. Their accents were too strong for me to understand at first and I was quickly relegated to the status of foreign simpleton. It would seem unnatural to them that a local girl would look further than the village for a partner, so it was inconceivable that she had chosen me for anything more than the act of kindness of showing me around her nation – though one of them thought that England was actually a part of Spain, with just a particularly distinctive regional dialect. After we'd said our goodbyes to each of them, I'd ask Elena who they were again, and be told that they were the mothers or grandmothers or great grandmothers of sisters- or brothers-in-law, or first or second cousins.

"Surely not everyone we've met can be a relative of yours."

"No?" She seemed puzzled. "Why not?"

Chapter Twenty-Six

"Dinner! To the table!"

At the call everyone went to the toilet or found something to do they'd been putting off all day. I once again marvelled that no matter how hungry they are, if you want to galvanise the Spanish into action all you have to do is tell them there's a hot meal ready for them. Only later, when it's going cold, will they approach the food.

Elena and her mother brought in loaves of fresh bread which were put straight onto the old and cigarette-burned plastic tablecloth, to be cut and eaten without butter, along with a bowl of salty salad that I'd been told we'd each eat directly from, rather than transferring it onto our plates. Then fried beef offcuts, fried salted aubergines in batter, cut thin enough to go around four, and a fried potato tortilla so good I had to discreetly mentally relegate Elena's to second best position.

Elena's father was quieter than at lunch, and ate using only a heavy pocketknife that, in true countryside style, he would produce and open one-handed when needed. It was humble food, but good. The only thing more I could have asked for would have been wine with it, but I realised that to buy some would be seen as being a bit too flash.

Afterwards there was fruit, and the father produced almonds that he had picked that afternoon in the distant huerta he visited daily on a decrepit moped. He opened them with his knife, and we ate them fresh, fried, warm and salted. In fact, apart from the salad, the only things that weren't fried and salted were the bread and water – presumably because the bread wouldn't mop up all the juices if it were, and the water because they haven't worked out how to. Yet.

I thought of how we are told that the longevity of the Spanish, which was in full view in the village, was due to a supposed Mediterranean diet of lightly grilled fresh fish and abundant salads sparingly tossed in extra virgin olive oil. Then wondered how, on the contrary, they all lived so long on a regimen of salty fry-ups. A clue came when everyone got up for the after-dinner paseo, and we walked out to the old main road. Along its length, strung out at intervals, most of the population of the village, no matter how old, was enjoying their post-prandial constitutional, a daily two-mile stroll with their families.

When we returned to the house Elena asked me if I wanted a coffee and, when I said yes, went next door to her Aunt Esperanza's to borrow some and one of those little single cup espresso pots. I was embarrassed to have asked for something that was obviously such a luxury that the basic machinery for its consumption had never been brought into the household. Her mother suggested that if we both wanted a cup it might be easier to have it in the bar, and I enthusiastically agreed. I asked them if they wanted to come but the father, thankfully, went to bed early and she was in mourning for a brother who had died less than a year before, so she could not drink alcohol or go to a place where it was consumed.

The bar was just down the road, quiet from outside but raucous and smoke-choked within. There were no more than fifteen or twenty people inside, mostly old men, but they were all conversing gruffly at maximum volume. I'd wondered if it would all go quiet when I entered, but nothing would have stopped them talking. The only women were a mother with husband and children drinking after-dinner coffees and hot chocolates, Elena, and the owner, who greeted her warmly.

They talked at the bar, which you approached by crunching over the salted sunflower seed shells and bottle tops dropped by those drinking at it, while others waited their turn to talk or be served. After ten minutes we were able to disengage and sit at a table with our carajillos, the burning brandy and espresso mix that can be drunk after dinner for the energy to go out half the night. By then of course they were cold.

I wanted to relax with a cigarette and Elena's company, but I was conscious of being on view. There was no hostility, just poorly masked curiosity, at least till one of the few younger men came over. He was thin (if you wanted to be really uncharitable, you'd say he was slightly rat-faced) and had a city haircut and clothes, which were cut just a bit too tight. He helped himself to a chair and I noticed that Elena, though outwardly friendly, failed to give him the usual two kisses. She introduced him as Ramón, an ex-classmate of Paco's, and asked him the usual: how he was getting on in

Madrid, how his family were, if he was just back for the fiestas. He talked freely with her but said nothing to me and I marked him down as someone with a grudge, who, if he had any suspicions about the two of us, would not be slow to air them. It might, I decided, be necessary to try and avoid him.

After a while one of his oversized friends got up, came over and crashed into a chair. Unlike everyone else there he was drunk. He put his head too close to mine and, after Elena had introduced him as Bernardo, went into a rambling diatribe about how the English ran the European Union and had bankrupted Spanish agriculture, leaving no job for him. Occasionally, slack-mouthed, he would look at me from below his disordered eyebrows and mussed up hair, and beerily assure me that, despite this, he had nothing against me personally, while Ramón looked on, amused.

This complaint was, at least, a new one to me. I had no illusions about how the British are regarded in Spain. As individuals we can be welcomed, and being polite and speaking just a little of the language goes a long way. There is still a residual, affectionate memory of us as the well-mannered Holmesian gentlemen of fiction, and a love of our bands, but we may as well admit that too many Brits, especially the English, have pissed on our own chips. In the resort areas where we've been seen the most, the stereotype of us is likely to be of an over-proud race given to constantly complaining – if you're lucky. If not it's of the "gambas" – the prawns – the sunburned, vomiting, abusive, street-pissing, thuggish packs of tourists who can't hold their drink, their temper, their cocks in their Union Jack shorts or their tits in their over-tight tops.

Bernardo only stopped when a young woman came in and tried to take him home to his hours-old dinner. He blustered to her that he was with his friends, and how often did they come back to visit, and what was a missed meal compared to them? When she saw Elena, she tried to put on a brave face, but was clearly embarrassed. She left Bernardo for a moment to eagerly ask her how she and Paco were doing in Valencia, and how England had been.

"I'd love to go there for a holiday. Or to any other country, really", she said wistfully, sounding like she knew she never would, then in answer to Elena's questions, told her that her baby was doing fine "It's at home with Mama, I should get back, she doesn't like to...you know...it isn't always easy living with her, and...I should get back." She left quickly without the husband she'd come to collect, and shortly afterwards Elena and I did the same.

"Not sure I thought much of Ramón," I told her.

"Pah, he's harmless, just one of those people who are always looking to make trouble. He has the vice, which makes it worse."

I did my poor impression of someone who can raise an eyebrow in order to ask a question.

"Cocaine," she explained. "They went to school together, but Paco doesn't like him much, no matter what Ramón thinks. I'm sorry about Bernardo going on at you; he's becoming the local drunk, even though he's still in his twenties and one of the only young people here. He's never worked. He lives off his mum's pension and what he can screw out of his mother-in-law. Ignore him."

"I planned to." I wouldn't tell her it but like most men, I suspect, I was constantly sizing up the other bloke in any situation like that and deciding if I could take them if it came to a fight. I had quickly decided that in Bernardo or Ramón's case I could. "So, he's not a relative of yours?"

"No."

"Probably just as well."

"His wife is. A second cousin. We grew up together. She's lovely, but she never managed to leave the village. Now she's married to him she never will. She wears sunglasses out a lot these days", she told me, then added, in case I hadn't understood, "Including at night. You know what I mean?"

"Yes. Poor her."

"Yes," she agreed. "Poor her."

It had made her think of something. "I've told you about my father and his tempers, but there's something that is usually forgotten," she told me. "Whatever else he was and is, there are things that he never did. He never chased other women. He never drank away his money. Many did. What little he had he always put on the table. That is not often spoken of in our family. But maybe it should be."

Spanish bars are usually pretty good places – as this one should have been – and I felt slightly cheated of the peaceful drink and talk I'd hoped for. Maybe Elena did too.

"Do you want to go straight home?" She asked, "Only my younger sister, Paulina, well she's a bit hippy and when I told her I was bringing a visitor here she said I should take you out to see the night sky."

What else was I going to say?

"Sí, cómo no?"

We deliberately didn't look up till we'd left the houses behind, along with the dog guarding a few sheep (whose milk is used for the local cheese) which did its best to alert the whole area to our passing. Half a mile out from it, the dimly lit village and its four struggling public streetlamps disappeared behind a low ridge and then all artificial light was gone. We didn't need a torch; we could follow the dusty road by the moonlight reflected off it as we walked out into the darkness and the hugeness of La Mancha. When we were completely alone, and feeling like the only people in a world that was utterly silent apart from our breathing, we looked up. And our breathing stopped.

Above us the sky spanned the earth in an immensity I'd never witnessed before, like a vast dome that dwarfed even the great empty distances of land that surrounded us. I felt an urge to reach up and touch it, as though its immeasurable depth would yield like velvet. Everywhere thousands of stars shone, literally shone, through air that was so pure and thin and clear that there was nothing to dim their light. The Milky Way, far more perfect than any book illustration, hung over us like a vast blanket of incandescence and as we turned, we saw other great swathes of star clusters painted across the sky like giant brushstrokes of phosphorescence in a tropical night sea. And between and around them meteors flaring across the night for a second then dying away, constellations, a satellite blinking, and stars. Everywhere stars, glowing white hot, bright enough for us to see each other's faces and the wonder they showed.

I'd never seen anything quite like it.

I didn't want to call it a day, but it was late, and we had to walk back. Reluctantly we did, freed from the constraints of the village, protected by the darkness, holding hands.

Chapter Twenty-Seven

The next day began with a breakfast of cakes from the bakery, with hot chocolates for the others and tea – which I slightly embarrassedly had brought with me from England – for me. As usual it felt decadent to start the day with icing sugar-dusted madeleines rather than Dour 'n' Puritan bran cereal, but I was learning that it was part of the pattern of food and rest that allows the Spanish to make it through their long, early starting days and still have the energy to go out afterwards.

(A typical day might be breakfast at six or seven, to work by eight, a snack at mid-morning, then a midday break for a large lunch and siesta, and afterwards back to work till eight or nine at night. Dinner could be as late as 10 or 11 o'clock, often followed by the whole family, including children, going for a paseo and a coffee in a bar, then to bed or out on the town. You can't really begrudge them a bit of sugary assistance the following morning.)

Afterwards, before the sun could get going, Elena's father took us for a walk to a patch of land he owned outside the village. It was no bigger than a large allotment, a barren outcrop of solid rock from which in his youth he had gouged stone for building with home-made explosives. Among the rubble were the remains of a crumbling adobe and stone outhouse and for a second, I thought of a future in which we brought it back to life as a modest house sitting in the tiny quarry which, with decent earth and irrigation, could be made to flower.

But it was pointless. Too far from electricity and piped water, and, as Elena explained later, he wouldn't part with it anyway, despite the fact that it was virtually valueless. Houses in the village could be bought for less than twenty thousand quid anyway, so why bother? As proud as he was of the place, which he saw as his birthright, it quickly became obvious that he was even prouder of his skill at blowing things up.

I think that with every girlfriend's father there is a topic that, if you can only find it, you can use to make contact. This was all too clearly his. He darted around surprisingly nimbly, pointing out where to place a charge to split a vein of rock and declaiming on the different mixes of dynamite he had created in his shed – including one made from locally available materials that, being "del pueblo" was, naturally, ten times more destructive than anything that could be bought anywhere else. With glee he told of how one time he had set out to blast a boulder apart and after the explosion there was nothing there. Only on his return to the village did he find it, buried in the square. It had nearly landed on two women, he told us, wiping away tears of laughter, and "Ay! What a scandal there was" when they found out who had done it. With a faraway look of unaccustomed good humour, he reluctantly let the memory slip away and began a rambling exposition on making his own ammunition; but blowing things to hell was obviously his first love.

He was, as they say, a bit of a character.

To make conversation I asked him if we could see his almond trees, but he turned cagey. Possibly they were too far to visit on foot, more likely they were his more by tradition and occupation than by legal right. Instead, we went back to the narrow lanes, stopping here and there for him to present me to someone, all the while keeping up a stream of proud and often fantastic anecdotes.

There were more women than men setting up their seats outside their doors, and Elena had to stop to greet a succession of biblically named ancients. As well as innumerable saints, Eves and Marys I met Lourdes, remedies (Remedios), two rosaries (Rosario), a mercies (Mercedes), two pains (neither Dolores used the much racier short form "Lola"), one incarnation (Encarnación) and an immaculate conception (Inmaculada Concepción). I also got to hear what Jesus (Jesús) was up to. His mother, the blind near-centenarian Great Aunt Catalina, told me that he was away doing his military service. Quite an achievement, given that he must have been seventy years old (unless he was *that* Jesus in which case make that roughly 2,090 years old).

Gripping my hand, she asked me if I was old enough to have to do mine soon. I tried to explain that I was a foreigner and Spain was getting rid of national service anyway, but it was pointless. I might as well have asked her if she was named after history's most attractive flying boat, or indeed, if it was named after her. She was happy enough just to have someone to talk to. Snapping her fan shut and tapping me on the arm with it for emphasis she bade me goodbye with the advice that if I just did what the sergeant said and kept my boots and buttons shiny, it would all be over soon.

I wanted to talk to Elena alone. I was hoping that the father would tire of accruing status by showing off a foreigner to his few remaining male friends and noted that he had little patience for the conversation of women. Finally, he began to look fidgety, and I politely asked if we might take just one stroll around the outside of the village. Brusquely he told us that he had things to do and left us to it. We stood for a moment in the middle of the one-time main road to Madrid, watching his retreating back and standing innocently apart. I didn't know what to say to Elena that wouldn't risk ruining the fragile gains in friendship made since my unwanted arrival on her doorstep.

While I waited for her dad to get out of earshot I saw a cloud of dust half a mile away. As it approached it resolved itself into two cars. We stepped aside to let them pass and I blessed them for the extra minute they'd given me to screw up my courage. Then the first one hooted long and hard at us and braked in a flurry of grit and sand. Packed into it was luggage, a man, woman and three unseatbelted boys, all pushing to look out of the same window and crying out Elena's name. As the second car stopped, the passengers, one a younger version of Elena and the other an older one, called out "Hola sister!"

Delightedly she clapped her hands, "My family is arriving!"

The house was soon riotous with them. Sister Paz and her husband Felipe, along with their three lively and likeable sons. Sisters Carmen and Paulina had come in the second car with brother Alicio, who was dropping them off on his way to Madrid where he would be bullfighting. Elena's other siblings couldn't make it this year and were back in Valencia, where the whole family now lived either next door to each other or within about ten minutes' walk.

Only the father was excluded, spending half the year with them and half in the village for the good its unpolluted air did his lungs, which he'd damaged by smoking the now extinct brands of ruinous, rough black tobacco that cost pennies and had been the consolation of the Spanish male working class in decades past. They were cigarettes so cheap and vile that they made smokers of Capstan Extra Strength seem like jessies, and buyers of Gitanes look like effete pseudo-intellectuals (Actually, scratch "look like" from that sentence). The mother, meanwhile, used any excuse to stay in Valencia, surrounded by her offspring.

After an hour of them catching up and reminiscing we left the heaving house so Elena could introduce me to Alicio, who had gone straight to see his Aunt Marisol, the father's older sister whose temper, almost a match for his own, had condemned her to lifelong spinsterhood.

We arrived as he was finishing paying his respects to her. Unusually, Elena presented me to him and then left us to it. He appeared to be avoiding his father and, instead of going to the parental home, with his aunt's permission he showed me around her house, which had survived the centuries virtually unchanged. Denied an education after the age of eight, he had developed a keen interest in Spanish history, and he quietly but enthusiastically explained its features.

It was living history. Unusually, it had been willed to Aunt Marisol and not her brothers, in the failed hope that it would act as a dowry and ensure her a husband. Childless, she had made almost no changes in fifty years. It was like one of those twisted, eccentric old farmhouses you might rent for a week in the countryside back home with a bunch of mates then suddenly find yourself wondering when your life went wrong and why you don't live in a place like that. All trapdoors and short, tiny corridors leading to little stairways and windowless rooms. The ground floor was similar to Elena's parents, with the same narrow, dark entrance leading into the undersized main room, off which were the stairs, kitchen and bedroom.

I asked about the Alice in Wonderland door set low into one wall and he opened it to reveal a closet-sized space sunk into the rock below. I hadn't seen one in any of the other houses and even as I asked if there were more realised what the filled-in space next to the stairs at the other home had been. "It is a larder. All the houses had them built into the ground, I think," he told me "but it's true, you don't see many now. The rock would keep the food chilled. Perhaps they were all filled in when people first got refrigerators. Now here's something you must see. It's totally original."

He showed me into the heavily sloping, windowless, smoke-blackened, coffin-wide space that was the ex-kitchen. It still had a dirt floor, and its only feature was a medieval-looking open fireplace into which had been driven ancient hooks for hanging pots above the flames. He told me that it had only fallen out of use about five years before with the installation of a modern kitchen and bathroom by Alberto the builder, the amiable dreamer who was Elena's oldest brother. In true village style, with room to spare indoors, it had been inexplicably situated outside in the one-time stable. As always there seemed to be some resistance to the idea that on a freezing cold winter's night it might be alright to go for a crap inside.

If the plan of the ground floor could be easily understood, upstairs it became a labyrinth in miniature. Halfway up the stairs another child-sized door opened into a kind of closed mezzanine floor that ran long and low out over the outhouses, and still held the collection of precious wooden beams, half empty sacks of grain and basic farming hand tools that had lain unused since the death of her father half a century before. Returning to the stairs we ascended to the unused attic floor proper, which was far higher-roofed than the low rooms downstairs.

It was like an English watermill, although much smaller, heavily beamed in honey-coloured wood and lit by piercing sunbeams that entered through chinks in the rafters and little unexplained windows that were all too high- or low-placed for logical use but which created a circus of movement as each ray of sunlight picked up the airborne arabesques of the chaff and grain dust that our entry had disturbed for the first time in decades.

Outside was similarly intriguing. In the cobble-floored former stable that housed the kitchen and bathroom the whitewashed walls still held feeders for the long-gone four-legged occupants. A gravity-defying staircase of unbelievable picturesqueness wound unsupported up to another un-entered attic crammed with old lamps, harnesses, an ox yoke and one of those straw hats for donkeys that I'd thought were an invention for tourists.

By the back door, sunk into the ground, were two of the huge clay cistern-like amphora for holding oil and water whose design could be traced back to the Moorish occupation of Spain and beyond that even to the Romans. A tiny clump of herbs and vegetables fought with a fig tree and grapevine for occupation of the only flinty patch of soil in the otherwise unforgivingly stony ground of the corral, among which a collection of chickens picked their way lethargically before returning to their home in a straw-filled antique ox wagon that any museum would fight to call its own.

"It's perfect," I told Alicio, as we sat down in the shade of the tree.

"Well, not perfect, but very interesting. If you were to live here there is a lot that you would want to modernise, perhaps."

"If I lived here, I wouldn't want to change a thing."

He looked at his watch then across the yard. "In an hour or so I will be leaving for Madrid. I'll be back in a few days to pick up my sisters."

"Are you going to your parents' house now? I'll walk back with you."

"No, I'll go there only to say goodbye to everyone."

There was a pause. Sooner or later there was something difficult we were going to have to talk about and it wasn't the Spanish Civil War. Or even the fact that back in London I had been having a thing with his sister.

And was beginning to wonder if I might not be doing so again quite soon.

Chapter Twenty-Eight

Time passed differently in the village. Everything was slower. The days were longer. So were the pauses.

I looked at the quiet, thoughtful man opposite me and wished we didn't have to have the argument about bullfighting that was inevitable between us.

You would not immediately guess whose son he was, nor his peasant origins. Middle aged, he carried himself with a lithe dignity that went with his work, and you could almost imagine his bearded, serious face in one of those dark old Spanish portraits, wearing a ruff at the neck and a metal breastplate, one hand on a sword's hilt or holding a rolled parchment.

Oh well, Tom, say something: "So you're not staying in the village for the fiestas?"

"No, I rarely stay in my father's house. Anyway, I'm working tonight."

"Tonight?"

"Yes. Evening is when the corrida de toros mostly takes place. You have never been?"

"No. I'm sorry, I know it's your livelihood, but I find it indefensible."

"If you have never been, are you sure that you can judge that? Your objection is the killing of the bull, I imagine," When I agreed he continued. "Do you know that they are an ancient breed that the Romans fought, and the Cretans worshipped, and which would be extinct without the corrida? That each is loved and cherished by its owner, respected as an equal by its opponent, and goes to the ring only after a life that is better than that of many of the world's poor?"

"Yes, but they are unable to give their consent to that trade off, and no one can convince me that a beast dying for reasons he doesn't understand, surrounded by tens of thousands of roaring people, is consoled by human concepts of love and respect."

I had had violent arguments in the past with aficionados of the bullring, the last with a deeply conservative, highly educated Spanish woman (who at least had the excuse of having been brought up in its tradition. Those foreigners who embrace and mythologise it are worse). She had raged at me and the argument ended up being fuelled by mutual contempt: hers for someone who could not recognise it as an art rather than a bloodsport, and mine for someone who could revel in the staged persecution of an animal. With Alicio it was different. Not only was he more thoughtful – more interested in discussing the topic than in converting me – but he actually got his hands dirty. I couldn't help but wonder what it does to a man to suppress his fears and go daily to face his own possible death.

Tentatively, I asked him about the reports we'd heard in the UK of dirty tricks being played, like drugging the bull or shaving its horns just before the bout.

He thought for a moment. "I haven't seen it. They blunt the horns at a fiesta where ordinary people get in the ring, but not professionally. I can't say that it doesn't happen sometimes, but it would be very difficult to hide it from the audience. They are expert and utterly unforgiving. The career of a young torero who fights badly can be broken by the crowd's reaction. They would know straight away if we were trying to deceive them, and the blood on the sand would not just be the bull's. More importantly, cheating would be …" he looked for the right word, "…dishonourable. Few toreros make much money. The glamour and fame are for a tiny minority only. The season only lasts six months, the rest of the time you must find other work, or scrabble for a place fighting in Mexico or Colombia for a few weeks."

For the first time his face darkened, and he showed emotion. "Or France. They treat us Spanish with contempt there. I hate it. You come out of the ring desperate for a shower and they put you up in a room with a sink that they expect you to both wash and piss in. And they think there's nothing wrong with that! At the end of a lifetime of work toreros often end up poor, and if they're injured, penniless. A bull lives better than some of the older bullfighters. If an organiser was secretly fixing the contest, then they would be robbing us of the most important things we have. It would take the honour and the skill from us and then what would we be left with?"

He wouldn't know it, but I had learned from Elena that years before he had been thrown, trampled and gored by a bull that had torn the length of his spine open and broken his back. (Their mother had become an instant royalist when King Juan Carlos had phoned to ask how he was, after hearing he had been given the last rites in the arena.) I could only imagine what it would take to re-enter the ring after that. After six months strapped to a board it had cost another year and a half of intense, painful exercise and therapy before he could once again walk, then run, then return to his profession. In all that time the only money coming in was from his family and colleagues.

"If you wish I can arrange for you to visit a plaza de toros and see behind the scenes: the chapel, the infirmary, where the bulls are kept. Then you can watch and decide for yourself. Have you tried to see it as a contest," he asked, "an animal of immense power against a small team of men and, at the end, just one?"

"Yes, but ultimately isn't it still outnumbered, out weaponed and confused? And isn't it true that even if it should beat the matador, it won't be allowed to escape. Another torero will come to fight it, and even if it won that bout, there'd be another waiting to take it on. Thank you for the offer, Alicio, but no, it wouldn't be right for me to go."

He paid me the compliment of not making the easy and valid retort of bringing up fox hunting. Instead, he reflected for a while then said "Most bullfighters I know are soft-hearted. Many of us are involved with animal charities. I would like you to know that we do not do what we do out of cruelty. Anyone who did would be rejected by the rest of those who go into the ring. We do it with pride. For a living, or because it is in our blood, or because of who we are as a nation. Or maybe for all those reasons. And before Spain became richer, we did it to escape from poverty – to have a job when there were few others available to those who were not rich and educated."

We got up and began walking back to the parents' house. On the way we made a little conversation about what we each did to keep fit, and he told me that he ran six kilometres barefoot on sand every day.

"Every day?" I asked, "even when you're touring?"

"Well, if I'm not near the beach then I will try and find grass to run on, but yes, every day. I had…an accident some time ago. There was an injury to my back that stopped me being able to walk for a while. The day I stop exercising is the day that it will begin to return."

Strolling with Alicio I became invisible. Villagers came out to say hello to him or clasp his hand and slap him on the back. He was the village's most famous son.

"You're a celebrity," I told him, relishing my sudden non-existence.

He remained modest. "There is a saying: 'pueblo chico, grande infierno', small village, big hell. How can I explain it? Let's say a village is like a pond. Cast a pebble into the sea and it will be lost unnoticed in its immensity. But throw it into the pond and everyone hears the splash and feels the ripples. It doesn't take much to get noticed."

"In English we call that a storm in a teacup. No, there's a better saying. That someone is a big fish in a small pond."

He thought about it. "Yes, that's good. But this one has a warning to it too. In a place as small as this it can be easier than you think to make waves." He put a friendly hand on my arm for a moment. "It might be good for you to remember that while you're here."

He went in to make his farewells. Despite whatever fame and modest material success he had there was, I felt, an air of sadness about him. I thought about how he'd been robbed of schooling as a child and sent to work in the fields. Of how he must have returned exhausted, only to face hours of the gruelling practice that bullfighting demanded of its applicants. Then of the lifetime spent training, fighting first to succeed, and then against the loss of vital reflexes that hit around the age of 28 or 30. Of the dedication needed to succeed and to carry on. Of the long, marriage-endangering absences and the annual search for half a year's work. I could be wrong, but I suspected that the tinge of melancholy he carried about him came from looking at his life and wondering what he could have achieved if he could only have paired that abundant willpower with a few breaks and a half decent education.

As he made his goodbyes I stood aside, replaying our conversation in my mind, finishing with his piece of advice.

"Small village, big hell". Maybe he did know I'd been sleeping with Elena, after all.

Her sisters certainly seemed to.

They bustled around the house, gossiping, cleaning and throwing amused, knowing glances at me and Elena, who must have confided in them what had happened in London. Paz, the eldest, was the responsible one, and facially close to Elena, despite the age difference. Carmen was the wild one, and dreadlocked Paulina the youngest, whom they all cosseted.

Carmen, fresh from making a whispered double entendre that earned her outraged giggles and a smacked bum from Elena, asked me what I thought of Alicio. I told her that I liked him a lot and that however much I might dislike what he did for a living, it didn't lessen my respect for him as a man. "I'd like to talk to him more. He asked me to the plaza de toros but I said no."

She stopped what she was doing. "He asked you to the bullring? You're honoured then. It's an offer he only makes rarely. I know why you don't want to go but it's a shame you couldn't. Afterwards he would have taken you to a Gypsy place where they do flamenco. Real flamenco, right through the night. The kind where they only choose the location at the last minute and tell no one that isn't known to them. You know, the type of place you wouldn't want to stumble into if you didn't want to stumble out later without your money. They respect Alicio and his job and his love of the music, so you'd be alright with him. Alone it could be risky."

Paulina chipped in, "My God, though, you'd have seen something special. The dancers and singers he knows really have duende."

They all agreed, and not for the first time I asked what it meant. Elena handed me a collection of mismatched knives and forks and pointed me outside, where the table had been placed beneath the vines. When I'd laid them out, I went back to stand in the doorway, and she told me.

"A duende is like a bad fairy. An ugly, malicious spirit that delights in doing bad things. You told me once about similar superstitions in your home. Evil sprites with funny names."

I switched to English, "Goblins? Brownies? Changelings?"

Paz joined in. "That's true, sister, but that's only part of it. There's another meaning that maybe grew from that first one of something, maybe bad, maybe too strong to bear, that can possess a person. It may be an evil spirit, or it may allow them to transcend what they are and do something extraordinary. A poet or an artist, or especially a dancer or singer, will seek duende and surrender themselves to it in order to achieve something that is almost beyond their human ability. Extraordinary but maybe dangerous too. Like making a pact with the devil."

"And you may also hear it used approvingly, to say that someone has a special gift for something or is unusually lucky," Elena added, "Or as a warning that they have the evil eye."

Paz turned to her other sister. "Carmen, you're the one with the most education of us all. You explain it."

"I don't know if I can. We all know what it is but ask us and we will all explain it differently. Are my old books still in the chest upstairs? Wait here while I look."

When I came back from putting tumblers and a jug of water on the table she had returned and was flicking through a dog-eared and broken-spined old textbook. She held it up to show me. "Lorca. Our most famous poet. He wrote about it. Wait...here it is, *The Theory and Function of Duende*. Listen. "...people speak constantly of duende and discover it wherever it appears with an instinctive ease...all that has dark sound has duende. These black sounds are the mystery, the roots that thrust into the fertile earth that we all know, that we all ignore but from which comes all that is fundamental in art."

Then the mother came in and interrupted her, flapping her apron at them and jokingly chivvying them over how come they hadn't got the table ready yet. When they told her that they'd been explaining duende to me she rolled her eyes and reflexively touched the small crucifix she wore. "¡Dios mío! As if we haven't got enough bad luck already without you inviting *that* into the house!" Then, clucking, she drove them out of the kitchen and shortly afterwards declared "Dinner! To the table, little ones!"

The food smelled delicious. I went to help serve it, but she waved away the offer, so I hurried to take my place at the table while it was still hot, expecting the others to do the same. Five minutes later I was still waiting, alone. I don't suppose I'll ever learn.

Chapter Twenty-Nine

At least the delay gave me a little time to think – a precious commodity amongst a family that size. I wondered about duende, and how something that implies not just a flirtation with elemental forces but also despair, sensuality and passion, can be reconciled with Spain's formal Catholicism.

I'd heard of it before, of how a flamenco dancer will yield to it in order to temporarily achieve superhuman abilities, but had not realised to what extent something that comes from inside was portrayed as an external force, rising from the earth, or a personal demon. I began matching the idea to the people I'd met. Everyone believed in it, so who had it and who didn't? In Elena's family was it the fear I saw in them that the temper, or maybe madness, that infected their father was carried in their blood too? Did the village possess it? The nation? Was Spain's duende in its people's pride, or in the pessimism they displayed even when everything was going right? And was it that spirit of madness that had been loosed by both sides in the Civil War, so that, even when it was over, the genie of fratricidal persecution could not be put back in the bottle for so many years?

Sitting under the grape-heavy vines and wittering on to myself like this I felt a very long way from London. Almost a different person. For the first time there I thought about my job, and it seemed inconceivable that I could go back to it. Instead, I toyed with ideas of how to stay longer, and daydreamed of writing a book about the village and its characters that would pay for my escape. It was an impossible idea.

Even if I could afford it would I want to stay there without Elena? And if I was somehow with her could our relationship and hers with the village survive a public airing of its private affairs? In her, her brothers and sisters you could see a mixture of emotions about the place: affection for it, memories of happy times in childhood, but also pride at having escaped it to make a fuller and more fulfilling life elsewhere in other jobs and another city that, if they lived there for ten times as long as they had here, would never quite seem like home.

To write with honesty about the place would be to banish myself and maybe Elena too from it for ever. Still, it was fun searching fruitlessly for a title and imagining recording on paper all that I'd seen of it in just the little time that I'd been there.

Finally, they began to turn up. Señora Amparo first (the father had eaten earlier and wouldn't be joining us). Then Paz and Felipe – their children were having dinner at an aunt's, they said, though actually I suspected they were still gleefully enjoying the opportunities to safely make riot that the village afforded them. I had seen them shortly before, waving to me from their bicycles while picnicking on crisps and taking turns to illegally ride an aged moped through fields and over heaps of rocks.

Then Carmen came to the table with Elena and Paulina, joining Paz in a gaggle of giggling sisterhood. As we made ready to eat beneath the grapes and the dusky sky, Felipe, middle aged and moustached, part-Spanish and part-Moroccan, produced a bottle of wine, whose provenance and vintage he proudly explained to me.

It was one of those evenings you want to put in your memory to taste at other, more mundane times. We ate and talked and drank, free from the pall that the father's presence might have cast over the table, while the first stars began to come out above our heads and a slight breeze eased the day's heat from our bodies. The sorority gossiped and joked and coaxed old sayings and a song from the mother, who was so delighted to have her family around her that she even let herself be persuaded into dancing a copla, on condition that I put my camera away. Paulina, the youngest, offered to show me the miniature chapel the next day, and when I told her that I'd already visited it said "Paf! Our first ever tourist and already he's seen everything there is to see. What are we to do?"

In reply Carmen suggested I should try and infiltrate the secret mass she swore was held for the village inhabitants who were too inbred to be seen in the usual service. Half scandalised, the mother tried to reassure me that there was no such thing. Carmen kept a straight face while she insisted, "Mama! How can you say that? You know it's true! The attics are full of them. Haven't you heard about the girl without a forehead who is hidden in one of the houses and is so hairy that they have to shave her face every day? They start at the eyebrows and work their way down. You must know her, she's a cousin of ours."

When we'd eaten all the food the mother went contentedly to bed, after being kissed by all her daughters, and we finished the wine, the sisters all refusing another drink but then agreeing on condition that it was just half a glass topped up with gaseosa lemonade.

Apart from Felipe, who was a regular, most of us were now only occasional smokers, who kept cigarettes for special occasions. I passed around my English packet, which met with particular approval from him, and he told me that when he was young and in the Spanish Foreign Legion, he had spent all his money on flashy, imported brands like Senior Service and Dunhill.

"A Ronson lighter and a box of Craven A and there was not a more sophisticated man anywhere in North Africa."

One of his sons poked a head around the gate to ask if they could stay out playing in the dark, received a "yes" then got called back to run an errand to the bar first. Five minutes later one of the staff arrived with a tray of coffees. They turned out to have been laced with whisky, on Felipe's instructions, and the women, now slightly pink-faced, waved imaginary fans in front of their faces in response to their involvement in this unaccustomed alcoholic excess.

They reminisced, including stories of their father publicly losing control, like the time, dressed only in underpants and waving a shotgun, he had threatened revellers from the balcony of the family's flat in Valencia, infuriated by the noise they were making as part of the huge, cacophonic and unstoppable annual Fallas festival.

Then it was Felipe's turn. "I remember when I was walking out with Paz, and I wanted to make a good impression on him. I thought it was time to take him somewhere, even though I was in terror of his temper. Do you remember?" he turned to Paz, "you said it was safest if we went somewhere where there wouldn't be many people. So, I asked him if he wanted to go fishing."

He broke off while the others ribbed him over his angling exploits, his expensive equipment and lack of success at actually catching anything with it, then resumed.

"We went up into the foothills to a place I knew in the woods. A lovely pool, very secluded and peaceful, with a waterfall tumbling into it from a smaller pond in this cliff maybe three or four metres above. I laid out my gear and offered your father a rod, but he said I could start without him. He had made a firecracker, he told me, and he was going to throw it into the top pool "to scare the fish down to me". Well, he scrambled off up the rock with just his pack and I started fishing. Just standing there, you know. Then, my God, there was a great flash of white and I was knocked off my feet. I looked up and above me was this huge mass of water, just hanging, suspended in the air. Then, whoosh, it fell and broke over everything and nearly washed me into the pond. I was flat on my back, stunned by the blast and the deluge. As I started to recover my senses your father's face appeared over me, grinning like a madman. The waterfall had stopped. The top pool was empty. All around me, and hanging from the trees were fish, dead or knocked senseless by the explosion. 'Well that scared them,' he told me."

We carried on like that, laughing and smoking and sending for more coffees till the moon was high and even the boys were too tired to play anymore, and everyone went reluctantly to their beds. We were all still chuckling at Felipe's story, and I thought: *Fishing with Augusto.*

If ever I did write a book about this place, I had the title.

Chapter Thirty

I've got a few minutes; I must write a bit about this place.

Last night when everyone else went to bed I decided to go for a walk out into the fields. I crept out by the light of the candle on the stairs, careful not to knock over the shotgun leaning next to it, which shimmered silver in its flickering light. Once again, the stars were of an intensity and number I've never witnessed before, even in the mountains of South or Central America. Maybe twice as many as I've ever seen in a single sky, with spirals and clusters visible unaided, piercingly bright in the pure transparency of this air so near to heaven.

This is La Mancha. Literally "the stain", where the earth is as close to the colour of blood as you can get. The sun's anvil. An arid plateau, broken only by ridges of rock; miles of flat, baked space, raised to the sky, too close to the sun's merciless power, but possessed of the same celestial light and purity of air Velasquez captured four centuries and 130 kilometres away in Madrid, Europe's highest capital.

It's extraordinary really. I am being given access to a place and culture I did not know still existed. It's like the first time I went abroad as an adult all over again: every detail is fascinating, every object different from our own, every custom and artefact new or redolent of what I've read of but thought lost. It is as though Elena has taken my hand and led me back centuries to a Spain that I believed – we all believed – was gone forever. A place that is so familiar from old books that it feels almost like I have come back to somewhere I've been before.

An example: I remember something that stuck with me when I first read Homage to Catalonia, *aged eleven. George Orwell wrote of his shock when he saw what he thought was a torture instrument, a door-like rectangle of wood, with hundreds of sharpened flints sunk into it in grooved rows. To his horror he realised it was a harrow, and that all over Spain in the twentieth century peasants were still so poor they were using Stone Age implements. At the same time, I knew, the aristocracy would have been driving in Hispano Suiza limousines to parties where fascist sympathiser Juan de la*

Cierva might land on the lawn in one of his new autogyros to amuse them as they arrived fresh from kissing the jewelled fingers of the bishops who preached hard work and acceptance to the near-starving poor, while the hated Guardia Civil stood ready to deal with any who disagreed. Now all this history is being laid before me. Suddenly I am seeing those harrows too. They are a common sight here, obviously only abandoned in the last few decades, left lying in huertas and gardens or serving, now flintless, as doors – each painstakingly pitted with row upon row of short vertical notches agonisingly carved to grip the now-absent stones.

This is what as an outsider I would normally never see. A village that has barely moved on during centuries, an unexpected survivor of feudal Spain. Yet I am seeing it. I'm finding a different Spain to the one I thought I knew, one that I believed had passed away. It's fantastic really. Absolutely bloody fantastic.

From Tom Drummond's notes, found with the rest of his luggage abandoned in the house of Augusto Vilar and his wife, Amparo.

Chapter Thirty-One

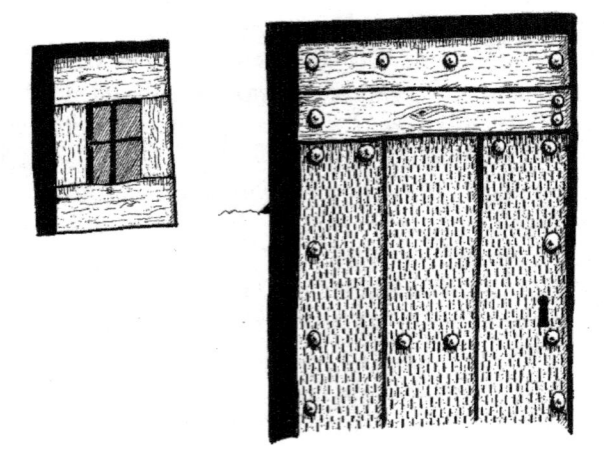

In the town square was a stone pool where women beat clothes clean in water that was good enough for washing and for animals, but not for drinking. It was in this, Señora Amparo told me, that "forasteros" – outsiders from the neighbouring settlements – would be thrown in the old days if they tried to marry a local girl without first buying all the village's young men a drink. For potable water, right up until the 1980s, the women had had to make a daily mile-long journey to the fuente vieja, the old fountain.

It was to this spring that we set off walking the following morning: the four sisters, the mother, Aunt Marisol and her brother, Elena's father, who followed behind on his moped, too wheezy to match the pace set by the septuagenarian women. Even the daughters found it difficult to keep up with their mother and aunt, who effortlessly strode out on what, for almost a lifetime, had been part of their daily duties.

The water was clear, cold and sparkling. It flowed into an aged stone cistern, across which diamonds of reflected sunlight played, and alongside which the dynamic young local mayor had had a concrete barbeque and picnic table built, as part of his campaign to make this once again a place for younger families to live. In one direction the distant houses began to shimmer as the sun's intensity grew. In the others sunflowers commenced their slow, head-turning day. And beyond them, past the little stone shelters and ridges of rock, miles of the thin, reddened, unforgiving soil stretched to the horizon.

It was nothing like the rich, dark, soft, friable English loam and it seemed inconceivable that families could be split for generations over who had inherited some, and that people would fight, die or kill for a piece of it. Yet just sixty-odd years ago they had, and the blood spilled would have soaked into the thirsty red earth leaving almost no trace. And still, no one talks about it.

Including me, if I knew what was good for me. Instead, I marvelled at the landscape, took photos and, like the rest, drank the icy water which, the elders assured me as they bottled some to take home, was good for the kidneys. Its temperature showed that it had travelled far underground, which was more than I had done. I had failed to find the hidden subterranean side of the village, which common sense and a look at the local rock formations told me must exist. Yet I could discover no crypt, no caves, no legends of tunnels, no smugglers' niches, not even any cellars, beyond the now filled-in sunken larders. I would have to ask Elena's mother, who was revealing herself as a repository of local folklore and archaic sayings, what I was missing.

It was she who signalled to us that the sun was getting high in the sky, and we should begin the return walk. Elena and her sisters rose reluctantly to their feet, kicking the dust from their shoes, talking among themselves or having a last drink, while their father cycled his moped into sputtering life and wobbled off to his hidden almond trees, then we set off.

I knew that I would be out again later. I used noontime a lot during those days to explore and take photos in peace. And maybe also to prove something. In singlet and shorts, desert-booted (seven months on, they'd dried out) and capped (because I quite enjoy the excuse to wear one, rather than because of the local belief that you'd be instantly struck dead if you went out without covering your head) I'd walk serious distances under the sun's continuous hammering. Mostly I chose that time, considered too dangerously hot to be outside without very good reason, for the freedom it afforded from the constant surveillance. But if I was honest, I'd admit that I also didn't mind showing that it was possible to wash dishes and avoid killing animals for sport and still be a man.

That was the idea, anyway. More likely they thought I was loco.

The research on Nathan was on hold. This place was too fascinating, too all-consuming, to allow it. I had carefully mapped all the known locations where the British Battalion fought, trained or billeted, and none were really close. It wasn't a surprise. I'd already been told I was the first foreign visitor – then later felt piqued to hear of a resident called el Alemán, the German. It had to be explained to me that he was no forastero, he was village-born and -bred. His name came because he was good at fixing clocks, a talent considered Teutonically technically minded.

It didn't stop me trying to see things through Nathan's eyes, though. The past was so tantalisingly close here that it almost breathed. If walking the village brought me a little closer to the reality of those years, it also brought me in contact with memories of my own father. Mindful of the fact that everything I did on my walks was reported around the village – despite the apparent lack of any witnesses – I chose one particularly empty stretch of landscape to give him a spoken report of what I had been up to. And what my plans were. I knew my dad couldn't hear. Death is death, after all. There will be no reunion. But it felt good. A bit embarrassing, a little illogical. But right, somehow. He too deserved to be remembered.

On one of these walks, I slipped into a garden sandwiched between two houses that had been tempting me since I first saw it – especially after learning that one of the nephews had once found a Civil War steel helmet nearby. The wall around it was mostly intact and within were the ruins of a collapsed house. The building was mainly rubble, with all signs of habitation gone, bar a rusted tin bowl and some shards of unglazed pottery. But the sun-dappled garden was a delight, just big enough to hold me, a gone-wild fig tree and one of the very few wells I'd seen in the village.

There are places that cry out to be explored. I wanted to poke around but was sure that even though the spot wasn't directly overlooked, and there was certainly no one on the streets, someone, somehow, was bound to be watching me.

So, I sat on a heap of stones surrounded by wild grass, cicadas and history, and plucked, peeled and ate figs fresh from the tree that was breaking the sunlight into brushstrokes of light and shade. It was a happy moment that cried out for – and got – the sacrifice of a cigarette to make it complete.

The wellhead was low but bulky. Made of rings of cut stone blocks, maybe centuries old, now thickly covered and capped over with porous cement in which when wet someone had inscribed 1939. A well and someone literate enough to write a date; this must have been the house of someone comparatively well off. Frost and heat had cracked the cement across in several places. Trying to look casual, I nosed a chunk free with my foot, hoping to make a fissure just big enough to allow me to slip my pen torch in and be the first person to peek inside since what for us had been the beginning of the Second World War. Grating, the crack grew. I made ready to pantomime surprise and dismay if the whole thing broke free, and tried not to think that if it did the biggest chunk would crash onto my toes.

When I first learned first aid at the age of fourteen, they still used to make you study the structure of the circulatory and nervous systems and the human skeleton. Sadly, I'd forgotten most of that theoretical knowledge. But I still knew what a human ribcage looked like when I saw one in front of me.

I am neither an actor nor a convincing liar. I jerked my foot back and stood up when I should have done neither. If anyone was watching, I had just signalled my discovery of something that would have been better not found. Because even if there were some tiny possibilities that a dried-up well might have been used as a legal resting place in the emergency that was Spain in the 30s, I still fence. So, I have some knowledge of swords. Which means that I recognised what was pinning the bones into the earth which filled the well shaft as a rusty estoca, the weapon used in the corrida to kill the bull.

I quickly decided to mention it to nobody. This was a historical death, I told myself. No different to the centuries-old human bones I had sometimes found but not reported by the Thames. It was the same there as here: any crime committed was beyond investigation now.

The year of the killing gave the reason for it. One more political execution. I wondered what had happened to the rest of the family. Someone had covered that well and recorded the date. Then they might have continued living there until maybe twenty or thirty years ago, probably too frightened to remove the remains during the Franco years, when those who had chosen the losing side in the war lived for decades in justified fear of reprisals. Poor sods. Including the Topos, the half-blind "moles" who, after the Generalissimo's death in 1975, emerged from the holes and wall cavities they'd been hiding in since 1939.

The occupants of this house wouldn't have been alone, either. During Elena's endless rounds of visits to relatives the one sure topic of conversation was always the past. Old photos were scarce, limited perhaps to one family portrait per generation, probably taken when a travelling fair passed. But always there was someone who was not mentioned, whose story had stopped. If I or Elena innocently asked about them the reply was that they had died before their time, poor thing, may they rest in peace, or had "gone away". It was in complete contrast to the minutiae that you heard about everyone else, and it suggested a deliberate loss of memory among the old people.

Why not, after all? It wasn't just that the Civil War was "tabu" and not to be spoken of. I thought of when someone is killed in a road accident. If the family has to pass the spot every day, do they always stop and look? Or do they learn to lessen the pain by passing by? And perhaps there comes a point when they decide not to burden their children with the facts. Especially in Spain, where for decades any association with the Republic could be a death sentence and had to be kept as a secret, ruthlessly suppressed.

I remembered when, even in liberal Barcelona in 1988, my attempts to buy an International Brigade or Republican Army memento had been treated with suspicion, disbelief and denial that such a thing existed. Finally, a militaria seller had taken me into a back room and sold me a leftist cap badge under strict secrecy and the promise that I'd never tell where I'd got it.

I resolved to return as casually as possible to the parents' house and say nothing. Inevitably, on my way I passed the occasional old man or woman warming their arthritic bones in the shade of a doorway.

They knew me by now, and wished me Adios as I passed, all saying it the same way, broken into two words. A dios. With that little thrill of pleasure you get from making a linguistic breakthrough I realised that they must be using an archaic root of the modern word, both as a greeting and a farewell.

They were sending me A Dios.

To God.

I didn't know that within a few days they wouldn't just be doing it verbally.

Chapter Thirty-Two

Then the fiestas began.

They started with the procession of the Virgin, a boringly pious-looking, gilded effigy carried on a heavy wooden litter by struggling, red-faced, elderly acolytes. "The more difficult it is for them the greater the penance," Elena, standing at my side, explained. "In Easter it is worse, they all wear penitents' robes and pointed hoods, and if someone wants to really prove how devout they are they'll do it barefoot."

I looked at the little collection of aged churchgoers taking turns to shoulder the burden in the already oppressive heat. Already they were, to use the Spanish phrase, sweating like chickens. At least one looked ready to faint. "What do they do if one of them drops down dead?"

"Congratulate him probably."

"Eh?"

"Well, he'd be straight off to heaven, wouldn't he?" She jerked a thumb skywards. "Express ticket."

It was probably as well that they weren't in robes. Those were part of Spain's history that went further back than I wanted to explore, to the victims of the Inquisition. "Heretics" were made to wear them in processions not too dissimilar to this one, as they were marched to the auto da fe, the "act of faith", in which they'd be burned alive for their sins. Right up to the early 19th century. There'd be someone there with bellows to blow the smoke away from those who refused to recant, in order to spare them the too-easy death of asphyxiation.

Luckily, this watching crowd was small, old and harmless. It was early and the younger visitors, raised in the cities, where huger festivals and vast carnival floats were common, were still in bed. The youngsters' arrival, when it came, was announced by the fireworks they threw in the streets and desperation on their part to get things going and have some fun.

Which was provided by the annual Moors versus Christians battle. In this, adolescents in intricate homemade armour liberated the village from "Moors" – other, turbaned, scimitar-wielding youngsters blacked up in a way that would be impossible in Britain. Afterwards, in a local twist, the participants were replaced by another group, dressed like devil-worshipping Morris dancers. Their clothes were scarlet, and they were hung with metal plates that, despite the cushions they wore tied across their torsos, clearly bashed bruisingly against them as they leaped among the spectators to briefly pursue a shrieking girl or compliantly screaming child. From each one's neck a heavy cowbell hung.

"They are the strongest and fittest young men," Elena told me, "They need to be to wear all that metal," It was true, you wouldn't want to carry that amount of hardware in that heat, let alone run in it. "They have to keep moving to make the clanking noise that scares off Los Diablos. That's what this bit is called, The Devils"

"But what does it all mean? They look like *they're* the demons."

"I don't know. Does it have to mean anything?" Then, pedantically, she added "Anyway it's devils, not demons. There is a difference you know."

"Well pardon me. I may be an atheist now, but I was brought up in the Church of England. It's a bit more relaxed about these things; you're not expected to actually believe in much. They long ago decided that there's no such place as hell."

She was slightly taken aback. "Next you'll tell me that they don't believe in heaven either."

"I'll need to check on that and get back to you. I wouldn't get your hopes too high, though."

I asked what further celebrations we could expect, but in answer was reminded that Elena, her parents and sisters were travelling the next day to visit family in Madrid; in particular the romantically-named Soledad (solitude), one of her favourite cousins, who was nearing the end of a difficult, health-endangering pregnancy.

"Alicio will come for us, and we'll travel in his and Felipe's cars. It's family. You should stay here. We'll be back the next day in time for your birthday. You can enjoy yourself till then."

"Of course. I'll explore a bit more," I assured her, remembering what I'd already found by doing that. I wondered again about mentioning the bones, thought better of it, but was unable to back away from the subject altogether.

"Elena, do you know anything about what happened here in the Civil War?"

"Very little. Family stuff. I only ever heard one thing. My grandparents were peasants, they couldn't have been poorer. But they cut a little window in the front of the house so they could sell eggs from the chickens they kept, and they put every spare céntimo they had earned slaving in the fields to buy packets of rice and a handful of tins of food to sell. When the communists came, they stole what little there was and dragged my grandfather into the square, saying it proved he was a bourgeois. They beat him in public and every day he expected to be killed. In the end he survived. Just. Others didn't, I think. But no one talks about it. I don't know what happened before or after that. This is a small place. Maybe the war just passed it by."

The war passed no place by. I told her some of what I already knew from the history books. That this area was under anarchist control and its towns were used to publicise what their philosophy could achieve: self-determination by debate, the abolition of money and the feeding of all through the pooling of resources and by everyone working for the common good.

At least in theory. In reality the system frequently broke down amid food shortages, greed, political terror, favouritism and incompetence. Human nature in other words. Whether the anarchists were in charge or not it would all have begun the same way anyway, with the shooting or worse of any cleric or landowner not fast enough to escape. (I told her how in one Andalusian village they had been made to run in a human corrida, and killed with banderillas, the spears used to madden and weaken the bull.)

Anyone educated who was not seen to be on the side of the people would be in danger, even teachers and doctors. The church would have been sacked. If there was a garrison of the insurgent falangist army near enough to attack, the young men and women would have formed militias and jammed into the slogan-daubed cars they had confiscated from the rich. Then clattered off to rout the enemy, clinging to the running boards, with scraps of red or red and black cloth around their necks or tied to one arm, waving their guns, joyous, certain of the righteousness of their cause. That after centuries of injustice and oppression the people had finally risen and nothing on earth could stop them defending what was rightfully theirs.

Untrained. Armed with homemade dynamite and shotguns with a killing range of 100 yards. Against conscript soldiers carrying Mauser rifles accurate to twenty times that distance. Most of them would never even see the enemy who killed them.

Later in the war the Communist Party, empowered by their role as vendors of arms to the Republic, took over the whole area, having broken the power of their political rivals.

Suddenly the rules changed. Anyone who wasn't a party member was suspect. The anarchist leaders were doomed. Those who had gained influence under them, or even just cooperated with their system, were in danger. The time was now up for those landowners and priests who had been spared before because they were known to have treated the poor well. The executions – the enduring disgrace of the great experiment that was the Spanish Republic, and which had barely stopped – began again.

And what came after, when Franco's falangist troops arrived? That I couldn't tell Elena. When defeat came it marched in hand in hand with horror. Atrocity followed atrocity. Is it any wonder that people don't want to talk about it?

Today was another time, and another world, thank God. The village sustained an aged but universally pensioned population, with a small senior citizen clinic and the services of a visiting district nurse. And for now, even the music was for them. Later it would surrender to the demands of the youngsters who had come to visit, and become a stream of unchanging techno that continued, boomingly, till three in the morning (broken unexpectedly only twice, by Dexy's Midnight Runners and Led Zeppelin). But for now, it was a mix of old hits designed to get grannies dancing with their grandchildren, and the classic coplas. Voices from the thirties, forties and fifties sang plangent laments from other times. Songs of emigration, of eyes as green as wheat, of a pony running in a bewitched Seville night.

And among them, suddenly, was a familiar song exhorting us to accentuate the positive, eliminate the negative, and not mess with Mr In-Between. If we didn't, we were told, then pandemonium was liable to walk upon the scene.

I smiled to myself and was glad that Elena didn't notice and ask me to explain. Years back I had a girlfriend, Caitlín, who shared my affection for those singing, Bing Crosby and the Andrews Sisters. "Mr In-Between" had been her nickname for a part of my anatomy.

Well, I'd done my best. As they suggested, I had tried to accentuate and eliminate, have faith, spread joy and bring down gloom. But Mr In-Between and I had been putting ourselves about with a local girl. I should have listened to Bing, Patty, Maxene and LaVerne. They were right. Sooner or later pandemonium *was* going to walk upon the scene.

But first everyone went to lunch.

Chapter Thirty-Three

The entertainment stopped at one, when people broke to eat and get out of the sun. Food was being served from trestle tables in the shadow of the church but, like many others, we went for a family meal instead, in the large backyard of another of Elena's mother's sisters, Aunt María Jesús. There we squeezed into refectory tables and ate paellas cooked in huge shallow pans, outside over a woodfire.

Unfortunately, when I failed to understand the first thing the thickly accented and almost instantly irritating aunt said to me, she immediately told the whole table that, poor thing, I didn't speak Spanish. I was sat apart from Elena, her sisters and mother and any time I began to converse with anyone María Jesús would butt in and say, very loudly, "It's no use. He doesn't understand a word you're saying". I actually began to feel that I'd rather be back with the father, whose response on being invited had been: "Spend lunch with that stuck-up witch? I'd rather die."

The meal felt endless. I was drifting away, trying to look like somebody who welcomed conversation, while actually hoping that nobody wanted to try, when someone asked if the seat next to me was free. I looked up. He was dark, in his late twenties, and I didn't need to notice that he was too well dressed and groomed to be from here. His Madrid accent gave it away. He asked me if I had a moment, shook my hand and introduced himself as the mayor.

He began with the usual generalities, welcoming me and asking me what I thought of the village. I could sincerely say how fascinating I found it, and praise the advances – benches, playground and public telephone – he had secured for it.

"That's nothing," he told me. "Next year or the year after we will pave the square, and later surface all the streets."

I said that I hoped the changes wouldn't endanger the character of the place, but he waved away the thought.

"We have to remake this village to attract young families. We must create jobs here, and for those we can't, make this a place where they will want their children to live while they commute to work elsewhere."

"Are there children here then? I thought all the youngsters had come especially for the festival."

"Just three at the moment, from two families. In both cases their parents live and work in Madrid so during the week the children stay here with their grandparents. They are bussed to school in another town. But we are close to achieving the funds for a new school."

He went on to ask me my opinion of European Union politics. I noted that he shared the national amnesia for the fact that it is that institution that has supplied the massive funds that have transformed the country. I marvelled at the idea of getting a grant to build a school for a village that could only boast three children, but had to hand it to them. Spain, along with Portugal, had milked its original poor southern European status to wheelbarrow out vast sums of EU loot.

At least they had used it imaginatively, on soaring architecture, inspired improvements and future-embracing projects like high-speed train links, but coming from the rundown, underfunded Britain that had supplied a good bit of that money, I couldn't help thinking that some recognition of the fact might be nice.

That aside, he was stimulating company, the only person so far apart from the shopkeeper (another "forastero") whose conversation roamed outside the village. I imagined that he could also talk as easily about purely parochial affairs to someone whose gaze had never lifted above a horizon dominated by its church. It was possible to see how, even though he was an outsider, he had been accepted.

As he continued, I began to suspect that he was leading up to something. I tried to second guess him, hoping it wasn't going to be some embarrassingly impossible request. Like securing more funds for improvements or trumpeting the modernisation in the newspaper that he perhaps erroneously believed I worked for.

Then the moment came. He stopped, glanced down at his hands, loosely clenched into fists on the table, and his gaze fixed on them, unfocused. For a minute he almost looked like he was going to ask me if I wanted to hear the story of good hand and bad hand. He didn't, but they were telling a story nevertheless. They were thin-fingered, clean. The hands of a person from the city. Not the short, cracked, spade-like ones of someone who had only ever lived in the village.

He lowered his voice. "I believe you are interested in a particular moment in history here." He was no longer looking at me as he spoke. "I will tell you something about this that you may not know and then I think it would be best if you did not raise the matter any further."

There was just enough delay in my translating what he'd said to make him think I knew what he was talking about. If I'd have been quicker to understand I'd have answered with a denial, or a platitude and he would probably have gone no further. Instead, he looked around him, then at me and even more quietly began: "Perhaps you already know more about it than I do. I have only heard fragments of what happened. Hints. The pained ramblings of someone on her deathbed. A few clues told in the strictest confidence. You should understand that what was done was done under duress.

"This village was unlucky. Advancing soldiers from Franco's army were quartered near here for three days. They were looking for victims and those here, who were almost blameless, were the closest. When they arrived the anarchists and communists were dead or fled.

"Those who were left were people who had nowhere else to go. The ordinary villagers. But they were still to be punished. 'Cleansed', the victors called it. You have guessed, I suppose, that almost every family had to give up one member to be killed?"

I nodded, even though I hadn't. The gaps in photos and histories and family conversations had begun to point in that direction, but I had never suspected that it was that harsh. That ordered.

My mind rushed to catch up with why he was telling me this. What he thought I knew, and why. Had he somehow heard about my discovery at the well? Or was it because of my noonday expeditions and innocent questions about local history and folklore?

"That was the sentence on this village, the price it had to pay," he continued. "I don't know how they were killed or where they were buried, and I don't want to. You shouldn't either. But before you decide that they all acted like cowards, or sheep, or stupid, helpless peasants, there is something else you should know. Most of those who were killed sacrificed themselves. Grandparents and parents went voluntarily in order to protect their children. There was no choice. There were hundreds of Moroccans among the falangist troops. The officers told the villagers that if they didn't surrender their own for execution, they would let them loose. Do you know what that would have meant?"

I did. The fifteenth century reconquest of Spain from the occupying Moors is still as essential in understanding Spain as World War Two is in Britain. As we'd just seen, it is played out annually across the country. Spain's patron saint is Santiago Matamoros – St James Moor-Slayer, Son of Thunder – often shown surrounded by the severed heads of Moroccan invaders. Yet Franco loosed those same Moors to loot, castrate and mutilate. And above all to rape, to an extreme that would only be surpassed by the Japanese Army in Nanking, and the Stakhanovite efforts of the Red Army in the following decade. They were his duende, his darkest and most terrible force, the mere whisper of which filled his enemies with disabling terror.

The mayor saw that what he had said had sunk home. "Oh, and there's one more thing you should know. You were wrong. This was a poor village. But honest. The church was never plundered."

So that was it. Someone had been eavesdropping on my conversation with Elena in the street earlier and told him that I knew what had happened at the Civil War's end. Yet I had been speaking generally. Had they misunderstood, maybe overheard a detail that they thought was specific to this village, not realising, because of the national blanket of silence, that similar things had happened elsewhere?

I realised too that he thought that I was going to talk or write about it all. Maybe he even believed that I had come here especially for that purpose. I was trying to put into words something that would reassure him, that would prove that I understood they were a private people and would respect that, when we both noticed a shadow loom over us.

She spoke very slowly, as though by mere contact with me he too had also been turned into a dribbling idiot. "It's no good. You're wasting your time. He doesn't understand a thing you're saying".

He stood up politely, then answered María Jesús more graciously than I would have managed. I couldn't decide if what he said contained a compliment or a complaint.

"Our guest here? Oh no, I think you'll find that he misses nothing."

Chapter Thirty-Four

I was becoming burdened with secrets, and I had only myself to blame. I didn't want to hide something from Elena, yet at the same time I didn't dare mention it. Despite my affection for the place, I had unwittingly come dangerously close to insulting the village. And an offence against the village would be an offence against her family. And an offence against her family...

History should be a lesson, a reminder and, if we choose it, a fascination for us. It shouldn't intrude dangerously into the present.

Someone should tell it.

I wondered if I should just discount it all. How true was it anyway? Exaggeration is part of the fabric of Spanish life, woven into almost every conversation. What I had been told could easily be nine-tenths myth. A mix of Chinese whispers and the national obsession with moaning about things being worse than they actually are. (In Spanish to complain is theoretically a reflexive verb, so they don't complain, they complain to themselves. If only.) There must have been at least sixty families back then. So up to sixty people to be killed, supposedly. Where would they have been able to hide so many bodies in such a tiny place? Impossible, surely. Except...

You get an eye for it. Something that interests you teaches you to see things differently from other people. Like that every house was built from local stone, yet nowhere was there a quarry large enough to have supplied it all. People must have gone to a lot of trouble to fill it in and cover it over. For the same reason that someone had concreted over a well in a nearby garden?

The meal finally ground down to a point where I could escape. Elena stayed, chatting, and I decided that it would not hurt for us to be seen apart a little more. I headed back to the house, where I found her mother glued to a dire Latin American telenovela. When it finished, she moved to the kitchen to begin preparing food for dinner and I went to help, just as the father putt-putted into the backyard on his moped, in time for the start of that day's cowboy film.

Señora Amparo had become fond of teaching me lines from old songs and archaic sayings. The day before I had asked her about the area's legends, expecting an equivalent to a British village's tales of wind-swayed gibbets, grey ladies, crashing coaches and highwaymen who didn't yet know they were dead.

Instead, she had launched into what I think was a story involving men in olden times being dressed in cloaks and posted on stilts or platforms to guard against crop thieves. The punchline may have involved one of these scaring returning citizens half to death and into the fountain by speaking to them out of the night sky through the primitive trumpet with which he was equipped to rouse the village. But I wouldn't like to swear to it.

As the tale neared its climax, so her accent deepened and her voice quickened, and by the end I was nodding like a madman and understanding nothing. Even Elena's speech was changing the more time she spent there. She had taken to adding "What times those were" to all conversations about family and past times (which is to say more or less all the conversations in the place). She'd also adopted, or maybe re-adopted, the other local verbal tic of punctuating every statement with the confirmation-requesting "A que sí?", which I took to be a contraction of "Verdad que sí?", Isn't it so?

But today we compared truisms. I would translate an English language saying and the mother would pause, think, and then match it with the Spanish equivalent. If I told her that a bird in the hand is worth two in the bush, a man is known by the company he keeps, and that you shouldn't throw the baby out with the bathwater, she'd reply that a bird in the hand is worth a hundred flying, that if you tell me with whom you walk I'll tell you who you are, and that you shouldn't throw the house out of the window. And, she'd remind me, God helps an early riser, and if you've been given a horse, you shouldn't check its milk teeth. The only one I couldn't find a British equivalent for was a darkly sinister phrase that had lodged in my imagination since I'd heard Elena use it back in London: "Cría cuervos y te sacarán los ojos." Raise crows and they'll take out your eyes.

I didn't realise that we had passed an hour talking until someone came in unannounced through the front door, which was never locked before bedtime. I was, after all, too busy feeling pleased at the universality of folk knowledge and the breakthrough in my understanding of the local dialect.

"Sister," a now-familiar voice came from behind me, "I've told everyone before. It's no good. He doesn't speak Spanish."

Elena looked surprised when she came home and found me talking warmly with her father. At least she did until she discovered that Aunt María Jesús was in the kitchen.

That night her, the sisters and I went for a paseo to the square, where racks of lamb were being roasted over flaming barbeque pits. Meanwhile, in that Spanish manner where a job put off for months will suddenly and miraculously be done, rows of benches and barriers were all being swiftly assembled.

Ramón was there. He called out to Elena, pointing to the gates that were being installed at the plaza's exits.

"Ah, it's the Englishman. Will he be running with us tomorrow when they loose the bulls?" He made it sound like he was sure my answer would be no.

"What's this," I asked Elena, "a bull run through the streets, like they do in Pamplona?"

"Yes, an encierro," she raised her voice so Ramón could hear. "Except here it will only be two or three bullocks chasing the young and those who don't realise they are no longer young. It is not something you need to do, Tomás. You are not one who has anything to prove."

If people who take exercise seem to divide into either natural swimmers or natural runners, then I'm the former. I've never run for fun, only wearily for exercise and because you never know when your life may depend on it. But sprinting from bulls wouldn't bother me. I'd survive and so would they. Hell, I'd enjoy the thrill. I was careful not to give Ramón the satisfaction of an answer, but I had already decided I was more than ready to give it a try. I hoped he'd have a great evening and drink, smoke and party the night away. Because tomorrow I was going to do my damnedest to beat the bastard.

Then the sisters were pulling at my arm. "Come on, this is something you should see. El pelele. It's very traditional."

The term was vaguely familiar, but I couldn't remember why. A circle of people was holding a large sheet, in the middle of which the pelele lay, a life-sized manikin, which would be sent flying when they all gave the cloth a tug.

I experienced a thrill of recognition. I'd seen the same thing in a centuries-old Goya painting of pastoral pastimes, in which a similar scarecrowish figure was flung into the air, smiling across its painted face, its body lolling. But, typically for Goya, even in the superficially sunny picture there was a sense of a menacing blackness, ready to move in from the edges. The apparent innocence and the painted smile hinted at a darker side, that it might just as easily be a living person being hurled, broken-limbed, into the air for the crowd's enjoyment.

With the flames of the barbeque pit painting tiger stripes across the half-shadowed watchers there was that same feeling of the circus of the night about the scene in the plaza. It looked as though if you gave the villagers flaming torches, they'd be straight off to attack Baron Frankenstein's castle. I greedily marked it all down in my memory as another sight that I had never expected to see played out in this century.

Away from the fire's circle of light stood three figures, instantly recognisable, even in silhouette: Ramón; Bernardo, drunk and weaving slightly; and Francisco, a semi-employed young local of limited intelligence, but one of the new generation of Spaniards, who, finally fed a decent diet, have grown into absolute giants. They were clustered together in a conspiratorial group, the night providing cover for whatever petty act of vandalism or drug-taking they were planning. The shadows covered their faces in hoods of darkness, making them look black-robed and hunched.

Like the crows were gathering.

Chapter Thirty-Five

We were a conspiracy of two. The mother and father would already be asleep. Felipe, Paz and the children had relocated that day to Aunt Marisol's house, and Carmen and Paulina were awaiting a lift to a party in the neighbouring village, Islaverano, which they confidently expected to last all night. There was nothing to keep us in the square.

"Do you want to stay here or go for a walk in the fields?" I asked, remembering the holding of hands last time, and wondering where we could go from there.

"No. I want us to spend the night together. The house is as good as empty. We're not going to get another chance like this."

It was so unexpected that I wasted a minute wondering if she meant what I thought she meant. "You're sure?"

"Very sure. What's the matter? Don't you want an early birthday present?"

Locking the doors behind us we crept to her bedroom, leaving the parents sleeping soundly below. Outside, music boomed from the square, but we were still scrupulously careful to stay silent throughout the night. When she came Elena would bite down painfully on my arm or stuff her mouth with blanket, so as not to let a scream escape. We could not have been more cautious.

At five, an hour before her mother would wake, we had to stop. I pulled my trousers on and moved quietly back to the bedroom where I was expected to be sleeping, stopping first to squint out through the shutter to the deserted street below. Bathed in that metallic early light that promises a burningly hot day, the whole place was sleeping. I felt confident that what had happened was our secret.

Chapter Thirty-Six

There are no secrets in the village.

Ever fallen in love with someone you shouldn't have fallen in love with?

Chapter Thirty-Seven

Where am I?

In the village.

Elena brings me out of the confusion of sleep by stroking my shoulder. I'm not sure how I know this, but I realise she has been standing, dressed, watching me for a few minutes before waking me.

"Good morning, sleepyhead," she says, her head tilted affectionately to see me better. I raise myself to kiss her, but she puts a finger to her lips and gives a little shake of her head.

"Sorry, there's no time. It's late. We're late. We're leaving for Madrid. I didn't want to go without saying goodbye."

I scramble into clothes and rush downstairs. The cars are waiting outside for the mother, who is fussing and waving her hands while the father curses in response. She sees me and panics over whether I am capable of making my own breakfast, then, when assured that I can, worries whether I will manage if left alone all day.

"Oh well, there'll be plenty to keep you busy. And there's a free meal after the corrida. They cook the bullocks, though the meat can be quite tough,"

The smile on my face suddenly feels fixed and false, and my answer sounds as foolish to me as it must to her. "Corrida? What corrida? It's an encierro today. I was planning to take part."

"Oh yes," the Señora tells me reassuringly. "The encierro is to drive the bulls to the plaza, where they have the bullfight. It's quite exciting for the young men. Any of them who fancies himself as a torero can jump in the ring and have a go. The bulls aren't the real breed of course, but they'll do for amateurs. And when they're all killed, they roast them for the audience. Yes, yes! I'm coming! Well, adios. Until tomorrow." And she bustles out, closing the door behind her.

"Fuck."

Well, I can't go then. Not if the bull run is a prelude to their killing. Even if it does mean I'll be considered a coward.

Instead, I kick around the house, looking for something to do, ears unwittingly tuned to the sounds from outside.

Conversations, celebrations, then the brassy fanfare that announces a bullfight.

There's nothing to read apart from a few old textbooks in a trunk which are the house's only books.

The antiquated television yields only one channel, showing the inevitable telenovela. Others flicker in and out but require too much adjusting of the old rabbit's ears aerial sellotaped to the wall in order to maintain the picture.

Outside there are cheers from the square.

I wander around the house studying the age-spotted religious pictures of children running to angels.

In my room I aimlessly count the ammunition in the cabinet. Four boxes of shotgun shells, plus many more loose ones. Eight boxes of .22 bullets. A collection of old military rifle rounds and one from each of the common pistol calibres, probably dating back to someone's military service.

Lack of knowledge of firearms is a feature of many of my generation's leftwingers. In our teenage years we tended to reject martial arts and the cadet corps in favour of protest and nuclear disarmament. The 1980s had rubbed some of those edges off me. Anti-fascist work had reduced the former gap, and South America the latter. That decade taught me that if there are things worth fighting for – and there are – then it's worth knowing how. I now have a passing knowledge of common weapons that my sixteen-year-old pacifist self would have found distasteful. So it is with some regret that I leave the guns well alone, certain that someone would somehow know if I touched one.

The sound of cheering dies down and the coplas begin again, occasionally interspersed with other oldies for the oldies – mambos, cha-cha-chas and Nat King Cole singing Quizas, Quizas, Quizas.

With one of my teabags, I make a cup of tea – it'll have to be the only one till I go out and buy some more milk – and sit in the yard. For an hour I look for patterns in the stacked wood or study the old homemade tools. In the streets, fireworks are thrown and echo boomingly against the housefronts.

Back inside, with nothing else to read, I take out my pad and flick through my notes on Nathan and the Civil War. When those too are exhausted, I turn to a blank page, even though I know that I will never use what I am about to write.

"*Most families had to give up one member*". That means dozens, maybe scores, murdered. Where? The cemetery is too small. There was no bullring or football stadium, those favourite sites for executions. No, here it would have to have been the village square. Everyone would have been driven from their homes and made to watch. That was the way it usually worked. To show reciprocity and punish the many for what had been done to the priests and landowners at the beginning of the war. Proving that the eye of God had been watching all along and the hand of God waiting for this moment.

And, of course, to show how the future was going to be. "Cleansing", they called it.

And afterwards? The bodies would have been left for the villagers to dispose of. They would have wanted to make ready their dead for burial, but how could they? What had the mayor said? That the troops had been camped nearby for three days. No one, especially no women, who traditionally wash and prepare corpses, could dare to leave home to fetch water until they had gone. So, in the height of summer, they would have hidden, hot, hungry and thirsty, terrified, their ears pressed to the shutters and bolted doors, hoping to hear the soldiers leaving, while beside them the bloody and broken body of a loved one lay putrefying. How would they have coped if they didn't have an outhouse or a dried up well they could temporarily move the corpse to?

Christ. It's been staring me in the face.

Of course. The little underground larders. The only cool place in the house. That was why so many were filled in. Even afterwards, when the beloved dead might have been transferred at night to whatever quarry or pit was chosen as their secret communal resting place, who would ever want to use them again to store food?

Even as I write there is something nagging at me, demanding attention. Something related to my immediate surroundings. I begin to look a slow circle around the room, trying to nudge my subconscious into surrendering what it is. It takes three or four circuits before my gaze stops at the notebook I've just been using. I had taken it out from among the clean clothes in my luggage, when it should have been on top of them. In this house, where the doors are never locked till nightfall, someone has entered sometime in the last week and gone through my things. What is gone or has been moved? Not clothes, penknife or camera. Not the rolls of film I've taken here. Something similar though.

I open the card folder of those sexually-charged photos of Elena and me at the beach – intimate and half-naked, swimsuited and tanned. Has someone looked at them? At first, I can't be sure. I'm careful to hold the prints by the edges. But someone else hasn't been. Tilting them to the light, I can see fingerprints on the emulsion. From hands that are just that bit too large and agricultural to be mine.

Which cuts the list of suspects down to the male half of the village's population. I tell myself it's no good worrying about it. The worst thing is going to be letting Elena know. Then I'll have to leave this place before my presence here makes life difficult for her. If I do, things will probably blow over.

It's evening. From outside comes the smell of smoke, blood and meat, and I realise I haven't eaten since breakfast. A look in the fridge shows only water chilling, marge, a few vegetables and a large plate of chicken scraps that I know Señora Amparo will somehow turn into something tasty. The cupboard yields a pack of madeleines and some chorizo, neither of which I would feel right about taking. The bread bag surrenders a dry loaf, and despite what the mother has told me, that to real hunger there is no such thing as hard bread, I decide that I am going to have to risk going out to buy something. Out of boredom as much as anything else.

It might be just as well to wait till darkness, though. The village store stays open till ten.

Later I quietly push the door open onto the night-dark street.

They're sitting in the shadows down the road, passing a bottle among themselves. "There he is! Hey, Englishman! You missed the bull run. But don't worry, we don't mind having another one just for you."

Chapter Thirty-Eight

Ramón, Bernardo, Francisco.

What can I do except go with them? It would be dishonourable not to. And I don't believe that they are a serious threat. At least not if they're handled properly.

It's the fag end of the festival. The celebrations have finished, and rather than face the inevitable comedown, they're trying to keep the excitement going, from the mouth of a bottle on a deserted street. And failing. No doubt my arrival offers them the possibility of a little forastero-in-the-fountain fun.

Yeah, well, we'll see.

Inevitably it's the square were headed for. Dark and abandoned, littered with the day's detritus, bottles and half-eaten portions of meat in paper napkins. The streamer-strewn barriers and benches for the corrida are all still in place, but the blood has been hosed away.

I accept a drink from the proffered bottle of brandy, and in return offer my cigarettes. Only Bernardo takes one, and I'm glad to see that my hands aren't shaking as I light it for him. He is swaying and for a second, he holds my wrists to keep match and cigarette from parting – and for a second, I think about breaking loose and kicking off here and now. But his move is innocent, and I'm glad that I won't have to take on three blokes at the same time. Especially when one of them is the enormous Francisco.

Ramón is the first to speak, his voice dripping with heavy irony and pretend concern. "I'm sorry my friend Paco can't be here. Have you met him? He's the boyfriend of your friend Elena. He missed out on today's encierro and corrida. So did you. What happened? We were expecting you."

I shrug, prepared to voice the old arguments. "I'd have liked to have run, but not when it's part of the corrida. I don't believe in killing animals for fun."

He ignores me, unable to wait to say what he's prepared. "I know!" (as though he's suddenly had a great idea) "We could have one now. That way you won't miss out, and we can tell Paco what his girlfriend's new friend made of our little customs."

"No. I told you. I don't treat animals that way."

"Well," things are clearly getting better and better for him. "If you don't want any bulls to get hurt, we won't use any. In fact, *you* can be the bull."

Bernardo is sniggering, while Francisco remains mute and stony-faced. So, this is what they're leading up to. A rougher version of the kind of mock bullfight that Spanish children play.

"Hombre. La capa," Ramón tells Bernardo, who in place of a cape hands him a jacket. Then, leaving me with the other two, he disappears into a nearby house. A minute later he is back, carrying a pair of short, spear-like banderillas and an estoca, the bullfighter's sword.

I'm trying to keep an eye on the weapons, hoping they're the blunted, souvenir kind. At the same time, I'm sizing up my chances of breaking away. Meanwhile, with no sense of timing, my subconscious is once again nagging at me that it's got something it wants to reveal.

Is it better to carry on with their stupid game and hope that a little humiliation is all it involves, or risk fighting them? Three of them. One a brick-built shithouse.

How far I can let this go? Risk assessment: the weapons look like souvenirs, so if things get out of hand and I'm accidentally stuck with one of them it's likely to be painful, rather than deadly.

I try to put aside the little mental itch that is inappropriately clamouring for attention...

...but it suddenly clicks into place. Something about all this. Something about a rusted sword lodged in a buried ribcage. Something about the banderillas, and how by mentioning them in the street the mayor thought I knew about what happened here in 1939. Something about the ease with which the bullfight suggests itself to these people when they decide someone has to be punished...

I realise that without meaning to I've dug up what was buried here: both in the ground and in the village's memory. Like those nineteenth century sewer hunters looking for lost gold I've become a tosher. Only I've got it the wrong way around. Surrounded by treasure, I've discovered the shit.

I blurt it out. "My God, that's what they did here, isn't it. They held a corrida using the prisoners instead of bulls. Every family would have had to watch one of their own getting slaughtered. What did they do? Tie their hands and make them run? Let them think that if they could knock down their tormentors they'd get away? Or just tell them that if they didn't make a good show of it, it'd be their wives and children next?"

They're staring at me with total incomprehension, but I can't stop the sudden realisations from spilling out. "The Civil War. What happened at the end. What your grandparents covered up and your parents preferred not to know. What Franco's soldiers did when they occupied this place. How they rounded up their sacrifices and butchered them right here."

The same way these three will do with me now if I don't shut up. Because the more I think about it the more I wonder if it could have been even worse. Was it only the soldiers who carried out the executions? Or did someone decide that the lesson would be more effective if they picked out some of the prisoners or the spectators and forced them to do the killing. Especially if there was a point to it, in their eyes. Why? Because maybe, like the town in Andalusia I'd been overheard talking about, the war here began with the village's young headcases murdering the local rich the same way.

These three didn't know. Any of it. I can see it in their expressions. Ramón puts his face – tight and furious – into mine and hisses: "You foreigners haven't a whore's idea what happened in the war. Now shut up and do what you're told. You'll run with the bulls, or you'll run for us."

Bernardo joins in. "What's the matter? Don't you know how to be a bull?" He bends over, putting his hands to his head, fingers extended, weaving his thick neck and skull from side to side, pawing the ground and snorting. The stupid drunk doesn't know where this is going. "Come on! Be a bull! Dance for us!"

Part of me says this is my own fault. I've pushed the boundaries of this place with my questions and my relationship with Elena. A lifetime of trying to see things from the other person's point of view tells me that if three people think I deserve to be punished for it, then maybe they have a point. But just because I dug below the surface it doesn't mean I'm...I'm what? An image from home comes to me. The mice you see from the platforms on the London Underground, with tourists pointing at them in disbelief. Dirty, outnumbered and running around for the amusement of foreigners. No. I'm a human being. OK, I'm not my father. My job proves that. But I never disgraced him when it came to honesty and acting honourably. I'm told he was proud of me.

I'm not the man he was. But maybe I'm getting there.

I look at them. These three are everything that's bad about Spain. Pride, ignorance, machismo and dependency. Do they deserve to do this to me?

No. Fuck them. I shit on their mothers.

Ramón straightens his arm, prodding the point of the sword into my chest. "Run!" he commands.

So, I hit him.

Chapter Thirty-Nine

A straight left, only it glances off his jaw, hurting my fist more than it does him. But I've been practising this for years. Even as it impacts, I've let go with a much stronger right. It's searching for a stopping place inches behind his head, but his face is in the way. I feel his nose crack as it lands. He staggers backwards, losing balance, shocked into inaction, and falls on his arse…

…catching me by surprise as I move in ready to give him an uppercut or elbow strike and knee to the balls. Two punches. Is that it? Call that a fight?

I'm burning with adrenaline. My training says that I should continue the attack, but I want to try and end this here and now.

Bernardo stops his stupid jig. I don't want to hit him if I don't have to. Instead, I stab two rigid fingers painfully into the soft flesh of the suprasternal notch at the base of his neck and, arm straight, stride forward, making him stumble backwards, the submissive partner in a stiff-legged two-step. He asked if I could dance, didn't he? Here's his answer then.

Yes sir, I *can* boogie.

He's off balance, retreating. Without it (hopefully) looking like I mean to, I'm keeping him between me and Francisco. I don't want to have to take him on.

"I don't have a fight with you, Bernardo." I release him with a contemptuous push that sends him tumbling back, fighting for his balance, nod to the big man, and walk away.

I know I should run. It's what I've been taught to do. Maybe I don't because it would send a dangerous signal. More likely it's pride. "I run when I choose to." I wanted to tell them that but couldn't think of the words.

I hear their footsteps and look back, apparently casually. Ramón disappearing into his house, Bernardo struggling to his feet, Francisco waiting for an order from his leader.

Once I get round the corner ahead, I'm safe. Out of their view I'll sprint for the house. Anyone who tries to enter before the family comes back will get the first limb they put through any window or door broken for them.

There go the birthday celebrations, I tell myself inconsequentially. I'll definitely have to be on that little minibus out of here tomorrow.

I'm forgetting two things:

1. Spanish pride
2. Shotguns

I feel the pellets pass before I hear the shot. Blood runs from where one has pierced my ear and soaks my shoulder, which is suddenly striped with a row of shallow, scorched cuts.

Bloody hell. They want to kill me.

So, I run, after all.

Chapter Forty

As fast as I've ever run, sprinting down the narrow, sloping road. A lumbering figure appears out of the darkness at the bottom. Francisco. Must've used a gap between the houses to cut me off.

There's a shout from behind me. "Where are you going, you son of a whore?" I risk a look back. But don't need to see his shadowed, hateful face to know it's Ramón. A bottle in one hand, a gun in the other. Bernardo puffing behind him, unarmed. The bastards have got both ends of the street blocked.

I could bang on doors, but no one would answer in time. I'm almost at Elena's family's house, but if I stop to unlock the door, they'll have me, so at full speed I vault the high wall of the corral...

... and at full speed hit it with my knee as I go over.

There's just time to collapse through the back door into the kitchen before I am disabled by the pain. It's like a kick to the balls: delay, then nausea, shock, the sensation of blood draining from my face. I fight the need to vomit.

The house is empty, cave-like, pitch black except for the votive candle on the stairs.

I can't yet move to save my life.

So now might be a good time to review my options.

If I hide here, they'll find me. If they find me, I believe they'll probably kill me.

No one is going to help. The villagers will look the other way. I'm the forastero who shouldn't have poked his nose in. They won't like it, and they won't approve, but they're too old, too insular. I'm not one of theirs. An outsider will die, and the village will close up behind its wayward sons. They'll cover it up.

They've got history.

I can try for the fields, but I'll be unarmed and limping. Easy meat for a shotgun. "We thought he was a burglar stealing the crops. An outsider. We shot only to scare him off. Ay, Que pena, what pain it gives us!"

What can I do against three of them, all probably arriving out front now, deciding what to do next, detailing one to go round the back, one to the front? And one to peer through the narrow window into the darkness which hides me for now, despite the giveaway glow of the candle on the stairs.

Which paints the faintest sheen of silver on the shotgun leaning near it. Another option then. Get the gun. Go right through whoever's guarding the back and get away across country. Give him the gunbutt in the face if he's unarmed. And if he's not? Shoot him. In the legs if possible. It could be done.

In danger our minds work at astonishing speed, building mental cathedrals of facts and probabilities, constructing an instant wall of possibility, undermining it with doubt then throwing up a flying buttress of hypothesis to support it. Plans are sifted, the good kept, the bad discarded. All in a fraction of a second.

My brain even allows me the unwanted luxury of considering that if I do get away it's all over. If I live to see tomorrow, I'll just be a dusty, hobbling 34-year-old hitching a lift away from here. The village will close in again, Spain will continue to make its own accommodations with what happened sixty years ago. No one outside will believe that anything happened tonight. The locals will swear that it was nothing more than a bit of drunken high spirits.

And whatever I do I've almost certainly lost Elena. I've crossed the one boundary that she won't forgive by bringing shame to her family.

I'm so focused I don't even jump when the church clock begins to strike its warning that my time is running out. Eleven o'clock. At any moment they're likely to come crashing in, one at the front, one at the back. Then whichever way I turn I'm a target to whoever is surely on his way to the little window overlooking the stairs.

But from where I'm crouching down there are handfuls of bowls and plates within reach. If I fix the scene in my mind so I can run it in darkness and then throw one at the candle I could be at the shotgun in maybe three paces. If the window-watcher shoots I'm dead, but any minute now he'll see me, and I'll be dead anyway.

Will my leg hold me? Will the gun on the stairs be loaded? Assume not. Grab it and get upstairs as fast as this knee will let me. Take a blast in the back or make it to the bedroom.

Swing the bunk across the door and grab the shells from the cupboard there. Work out how to load and ready it. Squeeze out the window onto the kitchen roof; if there's someone with a weapon watching the back, surprise them. Shoot if necessary – let the village invent a drunken accident for the police. Use the darkness and confusion to get away. Hitch to Madrid, leave, fly out. Keep quiet for six months then do whatever it takes to get Elena back.

The clock strikes for just the second time.
    My, we are thinking fast, Tom.
    I pick up a bowl, try and fix the distance to the candle. Shut my eyes to give them a few seconds to get ready for the loss of its light.
    The bell sounds for the third time.
    Ring out the old year, ring in the new.
    From outside the window comes the sound of a footstep on gravel.
    They're here.
    Time to go.
    Got to run.

Appendix

From *London Unlimited* magazine, January 1988:

Hidden Depths

In the latest of his explorations into hidden London, Tom Drummond discovers that still waters really do run deep
London is a valley built on clay. A huge basin, like two cupped hands, with water struggling to pass through from the porous chalk below. Where the clay is thinnest it rises, taking advantage of any opening or weakness to bubble up to the surface. Once there it is ruled by gravity and must search for any slope, gutter or fissure to make its way downhill to river valley and sea.

In London you're never far from water. Not just the Thames, not just water pipes, but streams, canals, sewers, storm drains, water mains, even central heating and air conditioning networks.

Then there are the forgotten watercourses, sometimes still or dry now, sometimes not. Buried brooks and ponds. Paved-over lidos and swimming pools, public baths and laundries. Hundreds of thousands of cesspits, banned and covered in 1847 and into which occasional wagons and horses were still disappearing for a horrible death years later. Water supplies for underground steam trains. Tannery pits (in 1927 a woman nearly drowned when she fell through her Bermondsey back garden into one). Accumulator towers and aquifers. Below-ground interchanges where goods could be transferred from canal barge to train and wagon. Blitz-era emergency water tanks. Underground reservoirs. Thousands of wells, the Roman ones often with sacrificial dogs buried in them. The hundreds of advanced Victorian below-street toilets closed without replacement in the last 20 years. Ancient culverts, buried aqueducts and wooden pipes. Roman bathhouses. Ice factories. The 186-mile-long venous network of the London Hydraulic Power Company, down which water was once pumped at high pressure to power the cranes of the London Docks, theatre safety curtains, hotel, department store and private lifts, lock gates, swing bridges and the lifting needs of London's industry. Watergates, like the one in Victoria Embankment Gardens built in 1626 and now marooned 100 yards from the river. Plus, other gone dry mementos of former pleasure seeking and philanthropy: spas, pleasure gardens, drinking fountains and horse troughs.

And then there are London's lost rivers.

The Return of the Seven

Seven sisters: seven north and, like twins, seven south. They were once clear springs and tumbling streams, growing as they picked up tributaries along their way to the Thames floodplain. Old engravings show them as the centrepiece of idyllic rural scenes or the site of tiny sylvan hamlets like Highgate and Banyard's Watering Place (Bayswater).

But London was growing too. Waterways joining the Thames made natural harbours and docks. Medieval London's burgeoning industries were ruthless in their need for water and power. The rivers were channelled for watermills and thirsty, polluting industries such as cloth dyeing and leather tanning. Upstream of them the water might still be clear and drinkable, but downstream it was quickly clogged with by-products and human excrement. And the unpopulated upstream was shrinking all the time.

Little by little, as the city grew, each of the rivers was pushed down and covered over. Forced into tunnels and forgotten. But they could never be stopped and they're still there now, running in the darkness below us.

If only one hidden river is remembered it is likely to be the Fleet, once London's second waterway and a dark allegory for the capital's development. Thanks to its integral role in the city's history and topography it has survived better than any other in street names: Fleet Street, Turnmill Street (site of a watermill), Cowcross Street (a crossing for cattle), Angler's Lane, Old Fleet Lane and Seacoal Lane (which shows how far seagoing colliers once sailed up it).

We would now be traveling on London Underground's Fleet Line if, in a piece of monarchist flattery, it hadn't been redesignated the Jubilee in 1977.

Rising from springs, the Fleet fills the Hampstead and Highgate Ponds, dug as early reservoirs, before disappearing underground – though it's just audible through the grille in the road at the junction of Ray Street and Farringdon Road – for its five-mile journey to the Thames.

After flowing below Camden, Kentish Town and Kings Cross it continues to Clerkenwell, where it was roofed in and the Metropolitan Line built on top of it, with Farringdon Road on top of that. (In 1862 it broke triumphantly free and swept away the hundred foot deep, massively buttressed trenches being readied for the revolutionary new underground railway). After that it burrows beneath Holborn Viaduct, built to span its still-visible valley, and down New Bridge Road to its subsummation in the greater Thames.

If it seems strange that it is remembered despite its centuries of enforced concealment, then the explanation is in its history of despoliation, delinquency and despair. Its lower stretch was the site of some of the worst horrors of old London. Miles of prisons, gallows, slums, "rookeries" and nests of vice and crime – sink estates of a more ancient type.

The mouth of the Fleet was once three hundred feet wide, a desirable Thameside location that attracted the Dominican Black Friars and Carmelite Whitefriars. But as early as 1290 the monks were complaining about the blood and offal being dumped into the river at Smithfield Market. It could only get worse. Even the neighbouring palace only lasted as a royal residence for decades before becoming a house of correction, setting the pattern for the land around the foetid Fleet: slums of unimaginable deprivation and overcrowding, and gin palaces that were the hunting grounds of muggers, whores and murderers. And between them local jails, places of execution and prisons: the Bridewell, the Fleet, Ludgate, Coldbath Fields and the most feared of all, Newgate Gaol.

And if the hangings and the punishments didn't send the prisoners to an early grave, then the filth of the Fleet would help them on their way. Over the centuries the buildings along its way would provide rich human harvests for plague, gaol fever (typhus, which laid waste to Newgate), White Plague (TB), typhoid and cholera.

The filthy Fleet
By the 1650s it was almost impossible for boats to push through the floating carrion and human excrement. Even a noble attempt by Sir Christopher Wren to canalise the estuary into an elegant dockside basin failed in the face of the intestine-choked, red-running waters. It is likely that the four graceful bridges he built between Holborn and Bridewell are still there, underneath the modern streets.

In 1728 Alexander Pope wrote of the Fleet rolling its "tribute of dogs to the Thames". Jonathan Swift described how a shower would rapidly swell it with "puppies, stinking sprats, all drenched in mud, dead cats and turnip-tops". (The phrase "raining cats and dogs" survives from when a rainstorm would fill London's gutters and rivers with street animals drowned in their quickly flooded refuges.) The Fleet soon became a journalistic cliché, a lazy metaphor for London's ability to turn purity into filth that still turns up today.

And so bit by bit the effluent Fleet was turned into a sewer and bricked over. But not without protests, such as occasional floods and the massive methane explosion of 1846 that sent a tsunami of shit sweeping through Clerkenwell and battered a Thames steamer against Blackfriars Bridge. Now it is a storm sewer that emerges into the Thames at the point where it changes from a salt to a freshwater river. If you lean out from the steps on the northwest side of Blackfriars Bridge at low water and look down you will see the slightly mysterious looking, massively gated arch of its outfall below. For 300 yards downriver the Thames foreshore is incredibly rich with reminders of the past: shells of the oysters that were a staple food of London's poor, fragments of seventeenth century bottles and pottery.

Put on gloves and take the wooden river steps near Stew Lane down to the north bank, crunch over two millennia of history and human remains and you should find an easily dated clay pipe within minutes. At Queenhithe – where Londoners haggled desperately with the watermen during the Great Fire, begging them to take them and their possessions to safety on the South Bank – you'll find traces of the goods jettisoned in the face of the boatmen's extortionate demands or when overloaded craft capsized. The plague pipes smoked as the crowd waited to board will be all around you.

And among these mementoes of those who lived and died along, and sometimes in, the Fleet – prisoner, pauper, warder and monk – are the centuries-old, age-blackened bones and teeth of thousands of slaughtered animals washed down from the river they helped to choke the life out of.

Silent running
What happened to the Fleet happened even earlier to the Walbrook, which marked the eastern boundary of mediaeval London in the same way its sister river did the western. The Romans used it as a natural harbour and source of clean water, and built a Temple to Mithras by its banks, but as early as the thirteenth century it was being covered over to suppress the stink of the sewage filling it.

Long lost, the Walbrook made a sudden reappearance in 1732, when it flooded the excavations for the new Bank of England. It was found again the following century during other building work, 19 feet down, even though in Roman times it had been at street level. Now pressed into use as a storm drain, it emerges into the Thames through an ingloriously small metal hatch and concrete channel next to Walbrook Dock, between Southwark and Cannon Street Bridges, where barges used to leave carrying London's rubbish.

All the river exits have been gated, hatched or barred since the 1840s to keep out toshermen, scavengers who entered illegally to search the indescribable filth for recyclables and coins dropped down the privies above. It was a ghastly job. Unknown numbers were swept away when the tunnels filled with rainwater. If disease or other toshers didn't get them, they could also be eaten by swarming rats, killed by gas, drowned falling into holes in the slime, or crushed by the collapsing roofs of the faeces-filled mediaeval tunnels through which they crawled.

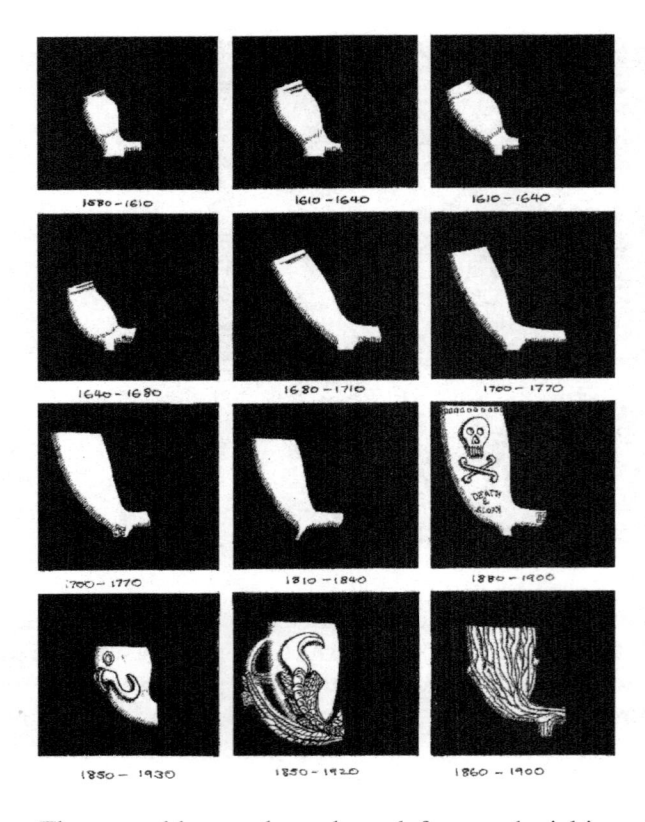

1580-1610	1610-1640	1610-1640
1640-1680	1680-1710	1700-1770
1700-1770	1810-1840	1880-1900
1850-1930	1850-1920	1860-1900

They would once have hoped for good pickings in the Westbourne, another river that rises in Hampstead. What's known of its route to the Thames at Chelsea is noticeably posh – Maida Vale, Westbourne Grove, underneath the Grand Union Canal and on to Hyde Park and Kensington Gardens, where George II's wife, Queen Caroline, had it dammed to create the Long Water (the brick arches incongruously submerged in the grass were its outfall) and the Serpentine. It crosses the Circle and District Lines at Sloane Square Station, where it flows through a large iron pipe just below the platform ceilings, and on to the Thames.

The Tyburn is another Hampstead-sourced river fated to become a royal plaything. Once it used to flood the swamp that would later become St James's Park, where it would be used to create the lake. Its original riverbed is said to be still visible when the lake is drained. Apart from this the Tyburn has been hidden for years – except in 1941, when it was reportedly seen running through the bottom of a bomb crater. This is the river/sewer that passes under Buckingham Palace before flowing on to empty into the Thames at Pimlico. Its outfall is through another impressive riverside arch, off Grosvenor Road, that can be seen from across Vauxhall Bridge. Inside, a tunnel runs underground for 60 feet before it is blocked by an old sluice gate. Tides and dangerously deep, stinking mud make getting this close a risky, reeking journey. Go just for a look from the opposite bank though, and you can also see the Effra, South London's longest hidden river, trickling from its nearby outlet.

Completely hidden throughout its course, the Effra rises near Crystal Palace and runs below Norwood, Dulwich, Brixton, Kennington and Vauxhall, passing the Oval cricket ground, whose raised banks were built with the earth excavated when the river was buried in the nineteenth century. Once navigable by boat, it was 12 foot wide and six deep where it flowed down the east side of Brixton Road (the houses needed bridges to reach their front doors), but its lower reaches were already a sewer by 1636. The not quite emasculated Effra has also reappeared at the bottom of a bomb crater, in occasional floods, and with enough volume of water 35 feet below the earth to force the cancellation of a planned World War Two air raid shelter for over 9,000 people at Oval.

The South London river with the darkest past is the Neckinger. Its name may have come from its looping course's resemblance to the "devil's neckerchief", a slang term for a gallows noose, like the one nearby where pirates were hanged. The river was used for watermills as early as the eleventh century, then for the tanneries that would become Bermondsey's main but disfiguring industry. By the nineteenth century it was an unmappable collection of half buried, lost, polluted, unused millraces, bottlenecks, pirated diversions, creeks and ditches, that at their end held in their stagnant embrace Jacob's Island, "the Venice of Drains".

In *Oliver Twist*, Charles Dickens made this the lair and deathplace of Bill Sikes, "the filthiest, the strangest, the most extraordinary of the many localities that are hidden in London, wholly unknown, even by name, to the great mass of its inhabitants". He wasn't exaggerating when he wrote how "a stranger, looking from one of the wooden bridges thrown across it at Mill Lane, will see the inhabitants of the houses on either side lowering from their back doors and windows, buckets, pails, domestic utensils of all kinds, in which to haul the water up; and when his eye is turned from these operations to the houses themselves, his utmost astonishment will be excited by the scene before him.

Crazy wooden galleries...with holes from which to look upon the slime beneath; windows, broken and patched...wooden chambers thrusting themselves out above the mud, and threatening to fall into it – as some have done; dirt-besmeared walls and decaying foundations; every repulsive lineament of poverty, every loathsome indication of filth, rot, and garbage."

Right by the former site of Jacob's Island and among the streets named after it and its watermills, the Neckinger can be seen from the junction of Shad Thames and Jamaica Road, trickling from pipes into St Saviour's Dock, its estuary and the last part of it that survives open to the air.

Stand at the dock's other, Thames end on a grey, deserted day, squint past the Conranised frontages, and this surviving remnant can still look eerily Dickensian.

A plague on all their houses

The misery Dickens described was about to be shared. A disease was coming that would give Jacob's Island a new name "The Capital of Cholera".

It reached Britain in the 1830s, 1840s (when 130,000 died in a single year) and 1850s. Real efforts were made to battle it, but they were undermined by the belief that infection came from mephitic vapours, a killing stink, an invisible miasma emanating from unhealthy places. The connection between disease, poverty and squalor had been made but, without an understanding of cholera as a waterborne organism, the clean-ups that followed only made things worse.

London's countless cesspits, which filled cellars, choked ditches, putrefied in every scrap of waste ground, polluted wells and rose through the floors of the poor, were ordered covered over. Meaning that, with nowhere else to go, the refuse of three million people entered the lost rivers and ancient sewers – just as they were being vigorously flushed into the Thames as a disease prevention measure.

Soon the river stank. London stank. Drinking water was routinely piped up from the Thames just yards from where tons of diseased sewage disgorged daily. This was no longer nuisance and smells, an inconvenience to rich friars or a killer of toshers hidden in their excremental underworld. Old Father Thames, London's parent and reason for being, had democratised disease and was killing off its offspring. The world's greatest city was poisoning itself. It took cholera and The Great Stink of 1858, when Parliament made ready to abandon Westminster and boats had to creep along, so they didn't stir up the river's putrefying breath, to force action.

And what action. Over the next few decades miles of embankment were constructed, providing road above, sewers, access tunnels and underground railway below, and narrowing and speeding the river so that it would wash away the faecal ooze at its bottom. The hidden rivers were incorporated into a new metropolitan sewer system. It was a near perfect solution for its times. The warnings are there of what will happen if it isn't maintained and updated to grow with London.

So, the lost rivers stay hidden. They no longer explode into the streets above, but they continue to surface as floods after heavy storms, fill cellars and submerge building sites foolish enough not to pump their foundations dry. They're still there, river phoenixes, always moving. They run deep under our feet, renamed, humbled, diverted, ditched, their waters drawn off into forgotten culverts, millraces and drains – but never stopped.

George Nathan

Tom Drummond's research notes, largely written at his desk at Montressor Publishing.

There's plenty of written information on Nathan. Most history books tend to agree that he was the only Jewish Guards officer in the First World War and was born in the East End (though one says Manchester). The minor disagreements should be easy to settle. A good start might be to establish his place and date of birth. Find out how the area was back then, and then go and see how it is now.

Only it isn't so easy. I can't find a register of birth for a George Montague Nathan anywhere in London or Manchester, so start looking nationwide. Nothing. There's a George born in Kings Norton in 1894 and two Londoners with George as a middle name, in 1895 and 1897. The only photo I've seen of him in the Spanish Civil War shows a man of forty or more. Any of them would be about the right age.

Still, it should at least be easy to trace his service history, then work back from there.

Should be. I began at the Imperial War Museum, in the wonderful tower reading room that was the chapel when the building was Bedlam, the Royal Bethlem Hospital. And where the Army Lists quickly proved that there was no officer named Nathan in any Guards regiment. Which went against everything I'd ever read about him. Thankfully there were other possible candidates in other units. All lieutenants: one in the Durham Light Infantry, another in The London Regiment, a third with the Royal Warwickshire Regiment.

I'm going to have to plough through every contemporary record I can find, especially those written by combatants in the Spanish conflict. One, by fellow brigader Joe Monks, has already proved helpful. He describes Nathan as a man at first humbled by poverty who, in command, was transformed into a natural leader, suddenly adopting once again the immaculate dress, professionalism and clipped upper class accent he had learned when he joined the officer class twenty years before. Most importantly, Monks gives a date for Nathan's birth. 1895. I go enthusiastically back to my notes. Only there was no listing in the records for a George born that year, just one in 1894. I think I'll send a cheque off for that birth certificate and see if it leads somewhere.

I try the *Honour Book of British Jewry*, a 1922 record of some of the estimated 50,000 Jewish men and women who served in the forces in 1914-1918. Yesterday I spent two hurried hours – squeezed in between a health and safety press conference and a product launch – in the Jewish Museum, rushing my way through it.

There was no sign of the GSM Nathan in the Royal Warwicks shown in the Army Lists, but the other two lieutenants were here. Interestingly, the one in the Durham Light Infantry had previously been a sergeant in the

Honourable Artillery Company, one of the Army's oldest regiments. Might it have been considered to have the cachet of the Guards?

I had what looked like a piece of luck. *The Honour Book* had a 1915 or 1916 portrait of four Nathans, including, fourth from the left, "Sergt (Later Lieut. Durham Light Infantry) G. Nathan, Honourable Artillery Company". Only it was nothing like the lean, aristocratic-looking, pipe-smoking major in a 1937 photo from Spain. For a minute I hoped I'd read the caption wrong and that it should have applied to the tall, moustachioed figure standing two to his right, with his hand on a seated, older comrades' shoulder, who actually did look like he might possibly be a younger version of the Nathan in Spain. I checked the name of that soldier. Well, well. "Bombardier G Nathan, Honourable Artillery Company". Was this the man I was looking for? But the rank was wrong.

I kept studying the picture, willing it to somehow reveal that this was a 21- or 22-year-old version of the man we know from Spain. Only, he should have been a sergeant and according to the caption he wasn't and another of the four Nathans in the photo was.

Could there have been a mistake? Neither of the two men in the Honourable Artillery Company had their arms in full view, so no sergeant's chevrons were showing. However, I finally realised, some stripes were visible on another soldier in the group who was listed as a private, while the sleeve of the one who was meant to be a sergeant major was bare. And shouldn't be. It proved that a mix up had occurred when the photo was captioned. I might have just found the earliest picture of the Spanish Civil War hero.

Oh Parker, well done.

I went back through my notes looking for corroboration and found the date Joe Monks gave for Nathan's commission. It tallied with the one I'd found in the Imperial War Museum for the GSM Nathan in the Royal Warwickshire Regiment. For whom there is no record of birth.

Ahead of me I can see a long and slow research task. I'm going to have to somehow fit in more visits to record offices, libraries and military museums. And my trip to Spain is coming up fast.

The thing is, in a funny sort of way I feel I owe it to him to do something. He's been ignored for too long. Someone needs to do what it takes to keep his memory going.

Why? Here's one reason; this is how he died. He was out organising the first proper meal his troops would eat in weeks when he met the American brigader Steve Nelson and offered him "a snifter" in honour of Nelson's recent promotion. A flight of German bombers attacked.

"Better make a hit for cover", Nathan told him, and they ran, leaped a wall and waited for the bombing to end. Nelson was sure that Nathan was unhurt, but found him in agony, unable to raise himself, struggling with the Sam Browne belt that signalled his officer status – maybe trying to pass it on to him.

Later, Nelson wrote: "Nathan, good and wise and capable, cheerful and jaunty. Strolling blithely along under the heaviest fire, swinging his foolish little cane. The rawest recruit couldn't be frightened when he was around. Nathan had taken the most outrageous chances, exposed himself hundreds of times in the grandly arrogant manner. Now death had found him, in the tragic accident of a bomb splinter – a pure, blind, bloody chance."

Yesterday I slipped off early and went to the British Film Institute, where I'd booked a showing of a short 1937 silent film on the International Brigades. I sat in the basement, in a narrow, monitor-packed underground room, where I could watch it on VHS. It was the most dated of the Civil War footage I've viewed recently. All long, static shots that wouldn't have looked out of place in a Great War newsreel, yet punctuated with almost modern product placement (Pravda, the Daily Worker, a Partido Comunista poster) intended to subliminally suggest that the war against Franco was being mostly fought by the Communist Party.

It was evident how ill-equipped the Brigaders – all dressed in mismatched uniforms – were. You couldn't help noticing that the cavalry squadron shown displaying its riding skills was unarmed.

A group was shown learning to use three machine guns: the excellent American Lewis, a Great War Russian Maxim and a French Chauchat, the world's worst ever automatic weapon. No bullets were fired. There was no ammunition. Then a caption "Three Englishmen" and suddenly, there he was. Sitting in the shade of a tree. Smoking his pipe, dressed in a jacket, roll neck pullover, breeches, cavalry boots and Sam Browne belt, his hair oiled, his moustache trimmed. It was true; you could have put him in any Hollywood film of the era as the reliable older British officer who would be like a father to his men. His two comrades appeared uncomfortable, ruffled by the heat, conscious of being filmed. But not him. It was striking how confident he looked. Not playing up for the camera. In command. But very weary too.

I paused the tape and ran the segment back over and over again. And, yes, at the end, I felt like I maybe knew him just a tiny bit better. I also realised that the only two confirmed photos I had ever seen of him had been taken from the film I'd just watched.

The birth certificate I ordered has arrived. George Nathan, born in Edgbaston in 1894. With this I can track him through the census returns. They show that by 1901 they were living in Number 1 South Villas, Camden Square, London. Nothing to prove or disprove that this is the right man.

Back to the Public Records Office.

I'll have to gamble another several quid on buying a birth certificate for the next candidate on my list, Joseph George Nathan. Or should I try Samuel George M Nathan? I try not to remember how time is running out for the work I wanted to have done before I attempt to pick up his trail in Spain.

If there is one thing that blackens Nathan's memory it is the allegation that in the Irish War of Independence, he murdered the Mayor and ex-Mayor of Limerick. The source of this accusation is a single, speculative, 1961 *New Statesman* article by a Richard Bennett. (When I embarked on this research it seemed that I entered a world of niceness. Phoning the magazine they disdain to charge for seeking out, copying and posting it to me, instead asking me to just buy a copy of the current issue "and push our circulation up one".)

I read the article dispassionately, determined to try and judge it on the standard of evidence it provides. It's not high. The accusation, we're told, comes from two anonymous ex-members of the "Dublin Castle Murder Gang" known only to the author. Their identification of Nathan is on the basis of his name and the murderer having been a fearless, "roaring homosexual", "typical Jew-boy" ex-Guardsman. That and a photo from IRA Intelligence, which we're not shown. Possibly it's the one used by them in 1920 to identify what they called the Cairo Gang, a group of British agents, most of whom they murdered. When I find a copy of this photo it's immediately obvious that none of the men in it is Nathan.

It could all be true, but it doesn't feel it. It appears to have convinced neither those who knew Nathan, nor the historians of the Spanish Civil War, who it nevertheless has left duty-bound to at least record the allegation whenever they mention him. The best answer to the charges belonged to the ex-Irish brigader Joe Monks, whose quietly dignified response appeared in the following week's issue: "Perhaps it is fair to say that Nathan, the volunteer for liberty, who gave such magnificent service to the anti-Fascist cause in the last year of his life, did not seem in character with the officer portrayed in Mr. Bennett's article."

Yet if those accusations had been made in 1937, they would have cost Nathan his life. Back then, Irish International Brigaders called a hearing to put him on trial for his possible association, as a British officer, with the Black and Tans, the thuggish and justly detested police auxiliaries recruited during the Irish War of Independence. Nathan made no secret of having served in Ireland but said that it was behind him. "We're all socialists now", he told them and, in the light of his superb record in Spain, this was grudgingly accepted.

I realised I was losing my objectivity when I began to feel defensive of Nathan, and that his accusers might have usefully given thought to other matters, such as why they were so heavily outnumbered by their countrymen fighting for Franco under the command of one of their old IRA colleagues. (Though, admittedly, the Irish rightist volunteers quickly gained a reputation for military uselessness that surpassed even that of the Portuguese division, and the 75,000 Italians, whose hubristic defeats delighted their allies as much as they did the Republicans. Speaking of which, it was here that Hitler learned contempt for his Italian allies-to-be. "The only hard Latins are the Spanish," he noted.)

The relative usefulness of the war-winning help given to Franco was shown in a prescient observation by Air Commodore LEO Charlton, CB, CMG, DSO, who predicted that he could not win unless "the Republican military staff committed egregious folly, Italy sent another ten or twelve well equipped divisions (i.e., around 120,000 to 144,000 men) and the Germans 10,000". Unfortunately, all three proved capable of doing pretty well that.

Yet the Republic had been strong in manpower, in the justice of its cause and in a will to win that was stoked by news of the appalling atrocities that followed each Francoist victory. But, thanks to the British government's policy of "non-intervention" it was starved of the outside help that was pouring into the insurgent side. By blocking its legitimate right to buy arms from, say, France, Poland and Czechoslovakia, Chamberlain and his fellow appeasers pushed it into Stalin's bloody embrace.

It helped cost the Republic the war, depriving it of the modern weaponry that Mussolini and Hitler were supplying to its opponents in the Franco camp. Only in two areas was there parity. The interceptor aircraft sold by Russia were initially at least as good as anything the fascists were sending, but by the end they were outnumbered by Italian machines and outclassed by the evolving German fighters and the skill of their pilots.

The USSR also supplied its copies of what were then arguably the two best tanks in the world, the British Vickers Six-Ton and the American Christie. Both were superior to the under-gunned and thinly armoured Italian and German tankettes. But under Soviet control they were wasted in abortive actions. (In 1937 Stalin's high command took as its lesson from the Spanish Civil War that independent tank warfare had no future. The Germans, in contrast, noted that even the Italians had been able to achieve one major victory by using a fast-moving armoured column supported by motorised infantry and artillery, and backed by ground attack aircraft.)

Why else did the Republic lose? Partly because it refused to trust its own officer class, instead treating them with suspicion and setting Soviet-style commissars to watch and supplant them. And, perhaps, it was defeated because it had forfeited its own sense of rightness. Stalin's megalomaniac control increased in direct proportion to the arrival of Soviet arms. Amid the murder of allies, the coming of the Soviet NKVD torture teams, the annihilation of political opponents and the crushing of dissent, the Republic lost its soul.

However, I digress. I do that sometimes.

The people at the Marx Library were as helpful as those at the Imperial War Museum, letting me dig through old boxes of secret reports sent from Spain by party official Peter Kerrigan to his boss Harry Pollitt, the General Secretary of the Communist Party of Great Britain. They held the first warning signs of the trouble between Nathan and Irish Brigaders: Moloney "a dodger" and Black "a really vicious type", who was leading an antisemitic campaign against Nathan and other Jewish comrades (estimated as making up as many as one in four of all the Internationals). Then dismay when the Irish – led by "bad elements and non-party people" – seceded from their British colleagues, ending the dream of International Brigades freed from all national enmities by the common anti-fascist cause.

Here too were repeated pleas for binoculars, compasses, tobacco. Then Kerrigan's pride when mad, murderous Marty, the International Brigades' chief commissar (who allegedly had hundreds of brigaders executed as "fifth columnists" or just for being insufficiently ideologically sound) announced that the British company was the finest fighting unit, singling out Nathan for particular praise. He was commended too in the confidential dispatches back to Party headquarters in London: a "grand fellow" who also appeared in a brief and intriguing note that he had been told that he would not "at the moment" be allowed to join the Party.

His name appears also in the requests for the CP to send more officers "like Nathan", rather than students, "odds and sods from Bloomsbury" "bad types" and "Trotskyite infection". Any time I was beginning to feel sympathy for Kerrigan in his constant struggle for supplies and men I'd find one of his icy vilifications of combatants who had a Trotskyist family member, or his inhuman, execution-inciting reports for the *Daily Worker* of the show trial against the leaders of the rival POUM party. With just a few name changes they could have been used by the Christ in the Kremlin, Stalin, for his party purges, by the Nazi People's Court, or by the Ministry of Truth.

Meanwhile, the second and third birth certificates have arrived. My best guess has to be that he was one of two Londoners. Maybe Joseph George Nathan, born 29 April 1895 at 27 Planet Street in Saint George in the East (back when people navigated London by parishes rather than tube stations; now we'd call it Shadwell or Stepney). Son of Henry, a fish market porter and Frances Harriet Nathan, who signed her name with an X when she registered his birth.

On the weekend I go and look at the area. Planet Street is now Hainton Close, a short avenue lined with good quality modern social housing, but back then it was right in the middle of Jack the Ripper's killing grounds and part of a virtual Jewish ghetto. There's a description of it, then known as Star Street, in the book *Ragged London* by Victorian reforming journalist John Hollingshead, who used it to illustrate all that was bad about the slums of Whitechapel and "St George in the Dirt".

He records its sixty or so hovels, whose rooms – which all measured nine and a half feet by nine and a half feet – held up to thirteen lodgers. It's no surprise to also find it in the first map I go to, the 1898 plan drawn up by another campaigner, Charles Booth, who sought to quantify the levels of London's poverty and criminality on a street-by-street basis. Planet Street fell into the worst possible category: "Their life is the life of savages, with vicissitudes of extreme hardship and their only luxury is drink". A true slum then. So maybe even the mud and blood and carnage of Flanders might have looked like an escape to a young man suddenly receiving decent rations, a lieutenant's pay, and the respect earned by someone who, by becoming a British officer, also automatically became a gentleman.

Did Spain offer a chance to recapture the life-transforming promise of those days which – like for so many other returning servicemen – was broken post-war? Was it an opportunity to leave behind middle age and failure and relive a youth in which he had been unexpectedly lifted from poverty and prejudice by the Army?

Nathan explained his political belief as a mixture of gut socialism and anger when the British Union of Fascists tried to deny Jews like him the nationality of the country he had fought for. If Planet Street was his birthplace, then he came from the heart of the area that Moseley's blackshirted wideboys sought to dominate, and just a few steps from Cable Street, where they were humiliatingly defeated the same year the Spanish conflict began.

So, Joseph George is the right year and the right area. And if it's not him? Then maybe it's Samuel George M Nathan, son of Maud and Samuel, a butcher. Born 21st December 1896 at 11 White Post Lane, Hackney Wick (the Booth poverty map shows it as edged in by the multiple and heavily polluting tar, dye, varnish and other chemical works for which the area was known, and its inhabitants as ranging from "Poor. 18 to 21 shillings a week" to "Mixed. Some comfortable others poor").

When I visit, the road is still there but bombs and clearance have left almost nothing that he would recognise: a crumbling brick wall topped with broken glass, decaying arched entrances to long-gone factories, a fragment of Victorian masonry, its windows bricked up. And all around, industrial units, building sites, rubble, a junkyard behind collapsing barriers of corrugated iron. The rumble of lorries and forklifts and the smell of diesel and spilt engine oil.

The birth certificate informs me, perhaps crucially, that M stands for Montague. He would have been named Samuel for his father, but maybe he preferred George and changed the order, which could make him the GSM Nathan of the Warwickshire Regiment.

Between the two of them I should have enough to give me some chance of tracing Nathan's service record and the details of his Irish posting at the Public Records Office. Once I get back, that is.

I have a clearer picture now of who he was. An enigma of his own making, delighting in muddying the waters of his past. A showman too, as deliberately idiosyncratic as the great TE Lawrence (another brigader, Hugh Slater, described finding him outside, under a tree, enjoying an after-lunch smoke sitting in an armchair at a table with checkered tablecloth while shells burst all around him. "Somehow it was almost impossible to be frightened when Major George Nathan was around," he said.) And, like Lawrence of Arabia, capable of displaying a theatrically reckless, almost self-destructive bravery that among the half-trained, polyglot, sometimes crumbling units in Spain was an inspiration; the embodiment of the British Army officers' maxim: "Don't duck. The men don't like it."

"Have you seen Nathan today?" His men would ask. "Did he have his gold-tipped cane with him?" If the answer was yes then, they told themselves, none of them would die that day. He was their good luck charm, their legend, their perfect gentleman. A totem of calm, charm, competence and indestructibility. A self-made hero.

From *London Unlimited* magazine, December 1989:

The Second City

A visitor's guide to subterranean London, by Tom Drummond
Beneath our feet is London's shadowy double, a city in negative, with thoroughfares, rivers, stations and shops bathed by darkness instead of light.

It's a second world of vaults, crypts, catacombs and charnel houses. Of 113 miles of working underground railway and 1,300 miles of Victorian sewers. It conceals the arteries without which London could not function, carrying its people, power, communications and water. All passing above, below or alongside other tunnels and spaces whose existence is denied, forgotten or lost.

In fact, they're so tantalisingly close that by making a few connections it would be possible to roam the hidden city alone and unobserved. Passing through the doors that connect vast bomb shelters to the Northern and Central Lines, along miles of unused train tunnels, in and out of the sewers, lingering in cellars, atomic bunkers and ghost stations.

Yet, apart from the passengers on the tube and a few essential workers, it remains empty. Only once have the people of London interacted intimately with this world. That was during World War Two when, faced with danger, like the earliest inhabitants, they returned to caves.

Uncountable subterranean spaces were pressed into use and uncounted ones remain, their entrances blocked, their walls hung with collapsing benches and faded signs pointing to forgotten first aid posts.

In the 1930s the bomber airplane was thought to be unstoppable. The film Things to Come shows the shape the imminent conflict was expected to take. Within minutes of war being declared, thousands of aircraft would blacken the skies, unleashing a rain of explosives and poison gas that would drive society back into its primitive past.

At the time, the government was ignoring calls for the tubes to be used as civilian shelters, in case the population refused to leave them to go to work. They feared that if people were too well accommodated beneath the earth they might "go native" and, like the Time Machine's troglodytic Morlocks, never come up again. However, this didn't stop them casting about for sanctuaries for their, the armed forces and the royal family's use.

Gimme Shelter
The policy on deep level protection for civilians was only reversed with the fall of Chamberlain as Prime Minister, and when Londoners occupied the tubes. It was not a bloodless victory. The precedent, especially in the East End, that a way could be forced into a shelter past officials shouting that it was dangerous to do so would find dark echoes at Bethnal Green, in vandalism and theft, and a refusal to vacate tunnels earmarked for desperately needed arms factories.

Thankfully, in 1938 the *Air Raid Precautions (ARP) Act* had begun the process of setting up networks of air raid wardens, civil defence workers, and other volunteers. Once the Blitz began, any space that was suitable was pressed into service: corpse-filled crypts, basement flats, wine vaults and warehouses. Even railway arches and pedestrian underpasses. Millions of the well-designed Morrison and Anderson shelters were provided free or at cost price. And below London's squares and in virtually every park and playing field, concrete-roofed trench shelters were dug. Tens of thousands of them, maybe more. No one knows how many remain, sealed and forgotten, but many are still visible as a telltale grassed hump or, like on Ealing Common, as cement caps to the entrances.

They provided good blast protection, but if there was a direct hit – as happened to one in Kennington Park – the occupants were likely to be atomised. They were usually uncomfortable places too, damp and with no toilet facilities beyond stinking and overflowing buckets. Meanwhile, on the Underground the ventilation was at first turned down in case of gas attack. Vermin, bedbugs and mosquitoes thrived among the heaving platforms. The smell, the overcrowding and the noise were often enough to drive occupants out into the blacked-out streets and persuade them to look to the kitchen table and understairs cupboard for safety in future.

But organisation and the volunteer spirit would arrive and win through. In time London Underground laid on medical posts and bunks for 22,800 people. Each night refreshment trains supplied 30,000 buns, 21,000 pieces of cake, 13,000 gallons of cocoa and lakes of morale-building tea. All for a penny or two a serving, but you had to bring your own teacup. And through it all Londoners confounded the pessimistic expectations by returning to work after each night's bombing.

Up to 177,500 people took cover on the Underground (just 4 per cent of those in public shelters), but safety was not guaranteed. At Balham an explosion ruptured the water mains, flooding the tunnel faster than those inside it could escape the wave of water and sewage that crashed out of the sudden blackness. Sixty-eight drowned. Even at Bank, inner London's deepest station, a bomb pierced the surface, bored through the station concourse and smashed into a machine room, where it detonated, sending a deadly blast wave down the escalators and leaving a vast crater in the road above.

The worst loss of life, though, wasn't due to enemy action. On the Third of March 1943 shelterers were descending the nineteen-step stairway to the unfinished Bethnal Green Underground station. The stairs were wet, the only light was from a 25-watt bulb, no handrail had yet been fitted, and the local council had baulked at the cost of installing barriers. As the people entering surged forward – probably panicked by the sound of an anti-aircraft rocket battery firing nearby – a woman fell. Someone tripped over her. Almost immediately the stairs became blocked with fallen people. Above them others continued to push forward. Three hundred people crammed into six and a half yards of stairwell. Within seconds those at the bottom were fighting to breathe. Within minutes 173 people, 62 of them children, were dead.

London Transport offered over fifteen miles of tunnel for ARP use, including "ghost" stations, unfinished extensions and obsolete routes like the approaches to King William Street station, abandoned since 1900, which was made into shelter space for thousands of people. Most of it remains, punctured here and there by later building work, the darkness hiding the stalactites and peeling posters warning that Careless Talk Costs Lives.

As well as civilian shelters the tube hosted factories, the Elgin Marbles, and, at Down Street station, the War Cabinet, who were awaiting completion of their dedicated Whitehall HQ. To get there a train would nose its way into a station so that Churchill could be stuffed into the driver's compartment while the rest of the carriages, and their unwitting passengers, lingered unaware in the tunnel. At Down Street it would again make an unexplained stop, alongside the door to the railway headquarters that had been secretly built out of the platforms abandoned in 1930.

Too late for the Blitz came eight twin-tunnel, double-deck, gasproof, deep level "shelter cities", each capable of sleeping 9,600 people. These subterranean towns were finally opened to the public during the V2 bombings. They were designed for post-war conversion to a high speed, ultra-deep, cross-London express tube line, but by the time the war ended Britain was broke. Instead, they temporarily housed national servicemen, visitors to the Festival of Britain and, at Clapham South, job-seeking West Indian arrivals from the Empire Windrush.

The nearest Labour Exchange to the shelter was at Brixton and it was this that would lead to the transformation of the area's racial makeup. Now a few serve as private security and document stores, but most are empty and unused, proof that there is storey upon storey of descending levels beneath us.

As deep as you go in the stations to which they are linked they are still underneath you, huge, dark and deeper still.

Their blockhouse entrances, like art deco pillboxes, can still be seen near the stations at Belsize Park, Camden Town, Goodge Street (walk from the main entrance in North Crescent to the secondary one opposite Habitat and you have covered only a third of the shelter's length), Stockwell, and Clapham North, Common and South.

When the capital's inhabitants went to live underground en masse more of them chose to do so in Chislehurst Caves, Kent, than in any other one place. These eighteenth or early nineteenth century chalk mines had their finest hour when they protected 15,000 Londoners and became a self-governing community, with its own citizens' advice bureau, library, cinema and dance halls.

A baby was born in the underground hospital and christened in the underground chapel with the underground name Cavina. She changed it.

The disused mine had been rediscovered by the Victorians, who invented a fantastic but false history of hauntings, Druidic temples and human sacrifice. In the twentieth century it was put to use for mushroom growing, as a venue for Led Zeppelin and a location for Doctor Who. Lantern-lit full-length tours are still run on Sundays. It's one of the best places where you can get underground without needing specialist equipment or advance permission.

Further out from London are the Hell-Fire Caves at West Wycombe. Dug for local aristocrat Sir Francis Dashwood, they may have hosted a few of the notorious parties of his sacrilegious club, the Knights of St Francis. Dedicated to feasting, fornicating and filthy poetry, the deliberate profanity of their mock religious ceremonies would be exaggerated into Satanism by outsiders, who renamed his "order" the Hell-Fire Club. A 1745 letter to Dashwood from a fellow member identifies his interests as being much more to do with having sex with women dressed as nuns and spending 20 hours a day "upon your own belly, or…laying your cock in every private family that has any place fit to receive it".

Reaching 300 feet below its flint-towered entrance, his mausoleum and unchristian-looking private church, Dashwood's subterranean folly is a product of imagination: damp, steeply descending, crudely made and punctuated with the revellers' macabre carvings of faces and skulls. A great place for children, who will enjoy it even more if you take torches.

The railway that changed London

The world's languages were given the new word "Metro" for a new concept when the Metropolitan, the world's first urban underground railway, opened in 1863. Its history lingers. The Met/Circle Line platforms at Baker Street, Great Portland Street, Paddington, Barbican (formerly Aldersgate) and Farringdon are all relatively unchanged since that time. As on the District, the Met's one-time rival, the trains are still big and boxy, with a seating plan based on their Victorian surface counterparts, and run through shallow, "cut and cover" tunnels dug from the street down (technically neither is a tube line. They also have carriages, while, reflecting their partly American heritage, lines like the Central, Northern and Bakerloo have cars).

The building of the Metropolitan Railway transformed London and the lives of its population, beginning with the inhabitants of the terrible slums clinging to the sides of the Fleet Valley, which were ruthlessly swept away. The poor were ejected without compensation. The rich received more consideration. The early trains were pulled by steam locomotives, whose fumes were a choking inconvenience to passengers and a suffocating misery to drivers and guards. Airholes were vital. One was needed near Bayswater Station, but it would be among the grand houses of Leinster Gardens, W2. From the front numbers 23 and 24 are virtually indistinguishable from their neighbours, but walk around the back to Porchester Terrace, peer over the wall and you can see how the problem was solved. The two stately "houses" are nothing more than elegant five-storey facades hiding a ventilation shaft.

They are typical of the quirky and interesting things that can be found on the Underground. Many stations are worth a look, like little, maroon-tiled Maida Vale, in 1915 the first to be staffed entirely by women. In 1919, as men returned from World War One, they were all sacked. Unloved little Holloway Road, with its unused lift shaft and foot tunnel by the emergency stairs, is another authentic reminder of the old lift-serviced stations.

Other stations such as Sudbury Town, Arnos Grove and Cockfosters, designed by architect Charles Holden, were standard bearers of the new architecture of the interwar years. This design heritage was fostered by London Transport's visionary chief executive Frank Pick and chairman Lord Ashfield. They ensured that every last fitting, from seat covers to lights, matched the style of the next, to form a seamless procession of detail that was not just supremely functional, but also elegant.

Artists were commissioned to design posters, and Harry Beck's brilliantly simple route map – which looked beyond the need for geographical accuracy, and plotted lines and stations using the rules of an electrical diagram – was adopted in 1933. Every underground network in the world now uses a variant of it. London Transport even commissioned its own lettering, the Johnson typeface. It's a timeless piece of typographic perfection that is still in use today, despite an unnecessary 1979 makeover which has dated more than the lean and classical original.

The 1930s were the glory days, when delegations flocked to London from around the world to study its model of a transport system that meshed trains, buses and trams to move millions daily. Just look at a map of the Moscow Metro to see what the visitors learned. Anybody who wants to understand what integrated transport is need only study a contemporary photo of Southgate's combined rail and bus station, built with drop-off and pick-up points, passenger shelters and refreshment outlets, and an indicator to warn bus drivers not to leave when a train was coming.

Stations like Piccadilly Circus, with its 360-degree concourse, marble, bronze and murals, were the modern wonders of the world. Others, like the Odeonesque Park Royal and East Finchley, with its streamlined waiting rooms and statue of a crouching bowman, were temples to modernity and mass transport. In old photos they are like medieval churches, standing proud and alone above the undeveloped land their presence will turn into suburbs.

Riding the ghost train

Before ending a tour of the Underground at the London Transport Museum look out for some of the network's ghost stations, the offspring of change and the wasteful competition of the private enterprise years. There is quaint little 1883 Osterley and Spring Grove, now a bookshop, that was replaced by the modernistic current station in 1934. Between Baker Street and Finchley Road, you can see the once grand but now graffitied and roofless remains of Lords, Marlborough Road and Swiss Cottage stations.

The westbound platform of Wood Lane, a fly in amber that closed in 1947, is visible on the left (when facing the front) of trains leaving White City for Shepherd's Bush. It still has its huge enamel signs and posters for Danny Kaye films intact. There's also grimy little 1890 Stockwell, visible from the Northern Line, a short, dirty run of tiles just north of the current station, which replaced it in 1924. Like many abandoned stations, City Road, built midway between Old Street and Angel in 1901 and closed in 1922, was brought back to life as an air raid shelter. Its dirty and platformless remains can be caught by looking right when going northbound.

On the left just before Tower Hill, when taking a westbound train from Monument, is a platform from its 1884 predecessor, the second of three Underground stations to serve the Tower. It is eerily atmospheric, with sooty columns, shadowed recesses and a cave-like tobacconist's. Above ground the station building survives as a bar in Byward Street, while in the pedestrian subway next to number 16 the noise of trains crashing past the former station escapes through louvre doors that block old stairways down.

There are others too, mostly with their platforms removed to make more room for shelterers during WWII, and now visible only as glimpses of blackened tiles, a ghostly side tunnel, or a single door to the surface maintained so that a train can be evacuated via the driver's compartment.

And then there's British Museum, made superfluous by its bigger and better neighbour, Holborn. It lingers in the collective memory thanks to its use as a wartime shelter and because of some *Daily Mail*-encouraged silliness about it being walked by the ghost of an Egyptian mummy. This inspired Bulldog Jack, a creakingly endearing 1934 comedy set in a fictional "Bloomsbury" station. The genuine sub-surface remains can be seen in both directions on the Central Line, but for the best view look out the right-hand side on a train from Tottenham Court Road and 50 seconds before it arrives at Holborn it's there – an eerie little, white-tiled station, its nameplates gone, its shadowy exits bricked up, its stairs going nowhere.

Many former stations, like St Mary's and Tower of London, are lost and gone forever, while others that seem to have disappeared have just been renamed. Like Post Office (now St Paul's), Great Central (Marylebone), Gillespie Road (Arsenal) and Addison Road (Olympia).

Deathline

It would be nicely appropriate if one particular ghost station were, like its passengers, underground. But sadly, it's not. Waterloo Necropolis Station can still be seen at 121 Westminster Bridge Road. Traces of the platforms and sidings remain behind it, survivors of a 1941 air raid that signalled the end for the London Necropolis & National Mausoleum Company, which once ran sombre funeral trains to the City of the Dead, Brookwood Cemetery in Woking. Even in death coffins and mourners travelled in first, second or third class and to different stations, depending on whether they were C of E or nonconformist. At Waterloo the entire frontage survives, though unfortunately with the company and platform signs removed. I'd like to have been passing the skip the day that happened.

The Underground system is full of anachronisms and displacements, the new alongside the old. Like the pocket-sized art deco Boston Manor station, whose modernist neon finger points boldly skywards, but whose quaintly roofed platforms date from 1883. Or the St Paul's escalator that is rusting away below Wiltshire in a World War Two ammunition depot. At Acton Town there is a curious little bay once used for the Pony, a single carriage that made the 1,232 yards journey to long-gone South Acton station. The drivers called it "the tea run", since you could put the kettle on and get there and back by the time it boiled.

The London Underground is like a tidal shoreline, washed by waves of passengers and modernisation that expose earlier remains. Intriguing little survivors turn up and are covered over. A full-size 1930s Ovaltine poster at Waterloo. No one quite knows what to do with it, so it is panelled over again for a future generation to find. At Clapham Common an enamel nameplate is removed, and underneath is a sign for Nightingale Lane, the station's intended but never-used name.

Old signs stored in the onetime pedestrian tunnel part way along the westbound Central Line platform at Notting Hill Gate are moved and behind them is a poster for the Children's Society (Do you know it costs 25 shillings a minute to keep and clothe our family of 5,000?). Like many others, this disused passage has been incorporated into the underground's ventilation system. Stand in front of its grilled gate when a train comes in if you want to understand how the movement of the tube's flat-fronted trains is used to push fresh air from above around the system.

Mail Rail

London Underground has a rival in the Post Office's own metro, a 23-mile system of driverless narrow-gauge trains that carries mail 22 hours a day, 70 feet below the ground. It entered service in 1927, after spending the First World War protecting art treasures from Zeppelin raids. It was not the first of its kind. In 1859 the Pneumatic Despatch Company built an "atmospheric railway" carrying mail sacks to Euston Station. The venture failed, despite the success of the technology on a smaller scale in systems that carried cash and documents around government buildings and department stores. Six of its carriages were later unexpectedly found when builders stumbled over the forgotten tunnel in which they had been abandoned.

Pneumatic railways were one of the dead-end technologies that excited the Victorians. One was built at Crystal Palace and another, the London Croydon, stretched seven miles. It quickly suffered problems, not least with maintaining a seal between train and tunnel wall. Leather flaps were tried and worked, until the leather dried. It was found that adding animal fat kept it supple. At least it did until rats began eating holes in it. The same short sightedness that saw steam engines as static power sources that would suck and blow trains around a tunnel network was evident in another contemporary favourite, the cable-pulled railway. This outdated coalfield technology was to have been used to power the City & South London Subway, which ran between the Square Mile and Stockwell. Its abandonment before opening day turned it into the world's first true electric tube railway, and now recognisably the core of the Northern Line.

Even more of a Victorian dream was its close cousin, The Tower Subway, which not only used cable power but tapped into another nineteenth century speculative mania, for tunnels under the Thames. Built in 1870, it ran a windowless shuttle in a narrow iron tube from Tower Hill to Tooley Street. It was a failure within months and was later bought by the London Hydraulic Power Company, whose aged water-as-power-source pipes still crisscross the capital. Now it houses fibre optic cables. One of its entrances, a modest little brick roundhouse, can be seen by the Tower of London ticket office at the corner of Lower Thames Street and Petty Wales.

The Beautiful Road to Hades
But the classic tunnel under the Thames is the first one. Begun in 1825 by Sir Marc Brunel, The Thames Tunnel at Wapping was finally completed in 1843 by his son Isambard. Its construction pushed the father into an early grave, ruined the health of his son, killed several workers and injured many others.

It wasn't the first attempt to sink a crossing beneath the water, at a time when to build a bridge would have involved an unacceptable interruption to the Port of London's constant river traffic. But previous attempts had collapsed as fast as the sides of the shafts when the Thames burst into the excavations.

The project began with the building of a huge brick tube 50 feet across, which sank into the earth under its own weight. Then the work started behind a cutting shield, with workmen digging out a few inches of clay, gravel or quicksand, then struggling to jack the shield forward a hand's width, before starting all over again. It was agonisingly slow. In the best months the tunnel moved forward seven feet, during the worst ones just one. As each few inches were gained bricklayers rushed to line the walls before they collapsed. And all the time stinking, polluted Thames water ran over everything. Amidst the poison gases, the oozing excremental mud, the filth and cold, everyone fell ill, some with "tunnel fever" that would blind them for life.

This grinding labour would carry on for almost a quarter of a century, stopping when the money ran out or the river came bursting in, sweeping up Brunel and the workers desperately running for the exit shaft. Seven drowned. The newspapers alternately applauded and vilified the project, praising it as the Beautiful Road to Hades then mocking it as The Great Bore.

Finally, it opened, and its fame went round the world. It was celebrated in verse, song and souvenirs. Within 27 hours of its opening 50,000 people had walked through it. At a time when the population of London was only two and a quarter million people, two million visited it in its first year. In August 1851 it had twice as many visitors as the Great Exhibition.

But *The Times* was right when it noted at the splendid opening that "the very walls were in a cold sweat". Despite the sacrifices, despite the worldwide fame, the tunnel would be a failure. There was no money to build the ramps that would have attracted toll-paying carriages and waggons. At first people paid a penny to descend the stairs and cross on foot or visit the occasional funfairs held there. But the 63 clammy arches, lit by flickering gas lamps, soon filled with muggers, homeless people and prostitutes. In 1865 it was finally sold at a loss for use as a railway tunnel, later becoming part of the Metropolitan Railway (now East London Line) between Wapping and Rotherhithe. Making it the oldest part of the world's oldest underground railway.

At Wapping Station, in the shaft to the platforms, something of the original conception's grandeur can be seen (take the stairs, not the lift). This is where the carriage roadways would have spiralled elegantly down. It is huge, lined with thousands of bricks made from the clay excavated from beneath the Thames. At the other, Rotherhithe end, a small museum, the Marc Brunel Engine House, and the stump of the great shaft can be visited.

Before leaving Rotherhithe station stand awhile at the end of the platform looking into the blackness towards Wapping. You can get a far longer view of the tunnel and its dripping, soot-grimed sides than is normal on the Underground. Especially on a wet day the moss-furred walls are alive with condensation, the air heavy with damp. From far off comes the distant pounding of pumps and rush of water coursing noisily through drainage culverts. As a train sets off from the other side of the river the tracks light up with a sickly reflection of its headlamps and, among the noise and the gloom, it is easy to see how terrible it must have been to work on what even as it opened as a heroic success of sub-aquatic tunnelling was at the same time such a hugely costly failure.

It has its rivals, like the Greenwich Foot Tunnel. But this was the original, and pioneered the tunnelling technology that has been used not just to bore beneath the Thames again and again but to punch almost countless passages through the clay beneath London.

But not always quite so publicly.

Shadowlands

Because beneath the city streets is the hidden obverse of the democratic society. The central nervous system of the endangered nation, or the warrens of the secret state, depending on your point of view.

Since the First World War, governments have recognised that in times of war and civil unrest London's unique strategic importance may need to be defended from underground. The capital had to hold out – and be seen to hold out – for as long as possible.

The secret underworld of the metropolis is made up of acres of bunkers, miles of protected telephone cables and exchanges, broadcasting studios, transport and emergency control rooms, and a number of citadels (sadly for conspiracy theorists the term "citadel" just means a bombproof structure rather than a vast Orwellian state underworld). The best known is the disappointingly shallow Cabinet War Rooms, the heart of government during the Second World War. Below its public level is a still-closed sub-basement, where workers less exalted than the Prime Minister ducked their heads under the four-foot-high ceilings and found their way by torchlight through the rat-scurrying darkness to their army cots.

And somewhere alongside it is the mile-long Whitehall Tunnel, stretching out from Trafalgar Square and linking surface offices, Downing Street and the wartime citadels. The most visible of these is HMS St Vincent, aka "Lenin's tomb", the 1941 Admiralty Citadel, whose ivy clad, pillbox-cornered, above-ground part sits massively on Horse Guards Avenue. Cursed when it was built for its ugliness, it is actually not unattractive given its purpose – to hold out to the last in the desperate street fighting that would have followed the expected Nazi invasion. If central London fell or was destroyed by aerial bombardment, then Black Move would come into effect, and command would have been dispersed to bunkers in Neasden, Harrow and Cricklewood, and finally to Corsham in Wiltshire.

Still in use below the Cabinet Office in Downing Street is the crisis management suite whose acronym is said to have lent its name – Cabinet Office Briefing Room A – to Cobra, the joint committee that meets in times of national emergency.

At the other end of the Whitehall Tunnel(s) are the Rotundas and Horseferry Road Citadel, built on the site of a former gasworks, into whose gasometer wells an estimated three miles of circular corridors and 1,000 rooms were sunk. Gasproof, bombproof, with an artesian well and diesel generators, they could be "buttoned down" for three weeks.

Similarly self-sufficient were the Curzon Street citadel and the Faraday secret telephone exchange, linked to the hundreds of miles of survivable emergency communications cables that the Post Office had far-sightedly begun installing in the tube, the mail railway and its own secret tunnels during the 1920s. Other bunkers included a stronghold below Broadcasting House that was just one of several scattered underground radio broadcasting studios, and a national network of railway control centres.

In the late 1940s plans were drawn up for the minimal upgrades needed to make the tubes, shelters and existing bunkers atomic-bombproof. But the development of the hydrogen bomb brought those plans crashing down almost as fast as the shelter walls would have done in a thermonuclear attack, and ushered in a Cold War building boom of dispersed, H-bomb-protected control, command and communications centres. Whose customers no longer included the civilian population.

By the 1980s it was clear that when the brass bands played, and feet began to pound Margaret Thatcher and friends were going underground. Leaving the rest of us to cower inside the mattress and door "inner refuges" recommended by the government's *Protect and Survive* handbook. There was no equivalent of the Anderson shelter, no helmets and free gasmasks, and no public shelters. Just instructions to be good and stay put, while our betters carried on our behalf, occasionally sending some soldiers to shoot any radiation-scarred survivors foolish enough to try and raid a food depot. Hindsight says that many of those heading below were actually civic-minded volunteers making the agonising decision to leave their families topside while they tried to retrieve some kind of post-bomb civic structure. But even so, it still looks like the senior politicians were ready to write off much of the urban population, and that more thought was to be given to protecting art treasures and the royal family than to the people who pay for them.

And what of those thousands of bunkers now? The government is, bit by bit, taking some of these massively expensive structures off the secret list, while improving the fewer facilities now deemed necessary for its members' use. You are unlikely to be receiving an invitation to join them.

The underworld's underworld

Older, secret spaces have been dug for as long as London has been London. Cubbyholes and smugglers' passages once laced sections of the Thames foreshore. Others surrounded the thiefdom that was the London Docks. Demolition in the nineteenth century thieves' kitchen of Clerkenwell revealed more sinister networks. The area was then a byword for crime (Dickens knew what he was doing when he placed Fagin and his gang in Saffron Hill). False doors, rooftop routes, buried corridors and cesspit cellars allowed crooks to stash goods and evade arrest by escaping to the swarming warrens of Black Boy Alley, Crow Cross and Turnmill Street – known for centuries as a place where robbery victims could be tipped into the open sewer of the River Fleet (search the area around the river's outlet, even today, and you may find fragments of human bones).

Even worse than the many whorehouses or the secret passage-riddled Rising Sun pub was the Red Lion Inn in West Street, a known highwayman's haunt and cheap lodging house. A contemporary illustration shows it straddling the stinking Fleet, its crumbling walls adorned with a sign offering "Good lodging for travellers". Who were likely to wake up, if they did wake up, robbed and naked, in the river below. Some didn't make it that far. When the inn was demolished in the 1840s, the secret spaces beneath it were reportedly scattered with human remains.

Scratching the surface

All of this is only part of London's metropolitan mirror, the hidden honeycomb of the second city. There are many other known niches nestling below: a tiny room beneath The Monument that enabled its hollow shaft to be used as a huge telescope. The Kingsway Tram Subway, site of Holborn and Strand underground tram stations, which at its Southampton Row entrance is the only place in London you can still see tram tracks in the road. Ice cream pioneer Carlos Gati's 1860s King's Cross ice wells, which could store 750 tons of imported Norwegian ice. The Camden Catacombs, a complex of stables, canal basin, cellars and horse-pulled railway below Camden Market. The Temple of Mithras, only discovered in 1954, a relic of the religion that dotted the Roman Empire with underground places of worship whose floorplan would be mimicked by the Christian churches that replaced them.

And more. Icehouses. Kilns. Wells. Cesspits. Dungeons, debtors' prison cells and village lockups. Priests' holes. Lost tombs below churches that were sealed because of the risk from the diseased bodies they contained. Plague pits whose memory is still so potent that building work pauses when they are uncovered.

In many places in London our street level is nine foot above its Roman-era equivalent. That's three yards of buried roads, villas and temples between us and then. Plus, the bearpits, houses, fortifications, churches and inns that replaced them. And that's before you think about what's underneath that Roman strata from which just those nine feet and two millennia separate us: the cellars and hypocausts, prehistoric mines, grain stores, graves, hiding places and deneholes below even that level.

For most people these places are of no interest, or too claustrophobic, or best forgotten. For others they are time capsules, a secret panel into the past. Through a trapdoor, below a flaking concrete seal or manhole cover the time machine is waiting. Find a way in and it is as if there really is a magic door at the back of the wardrobe.

Labyrinth legends
Alongside the recorded sites are the truly secret places known only to countless men in pubs. The world below stimulates a capacity in the human psyche for imagination, mythmaking

and paranoia. Ask around and you will hear stories of impossible bunker complexes. Of a secret Victoria Line station below Buckingham Palace. Another underneath the Houses of Parliament. How just outside the gents' toilet at the ICA is a ventilation grille for the secret state fortress whose door is next to the Duke of York Steps (Subterranea Britannica, whose members have done more than anyone to publicise and preserve what lies beneath, has shown it to be an entry to the ICA boiler house). A half-remembered ARP first aid post transmutes into a secret hospital awaiting the victims of the Third World War. A three-man Royal Observer Corps post turns into a vast refuge for fleeing civil servants. A decrepit public shelter in Epsom is "revealed" to be a secret refuge for the royals. A wartime arms factory becomes the place where the RAF hides crashed flying saucers, or the location of the legendary "strategic reserve" of steam locomotives squirreled away for post-holocaust use.

Thankfully, what is really beneath us is as fascinating as anything that Chinese whispers or urban paranoia can misremember or invent. It's true that there are probably no vast invasion defences below London whose existence has not yet been rumoured or revealed, no forgotten 1940s hospitals with their mattresses still rolled, awaiting patients who died peacefully in other beds in other decades. No one has recently discovered an air raid shelter that was sealed intact with everything in it: rows of gas masks and tin helmets hanging next to Bakelite telephones that will never ring to announce the All Clear above, while against the postered walls cobwebbed tea urns lean, waiting to serve the occupants of the bunks still clustering in the corridors into which no glimmer of light has penetrated for fifty years.

But we're looking.

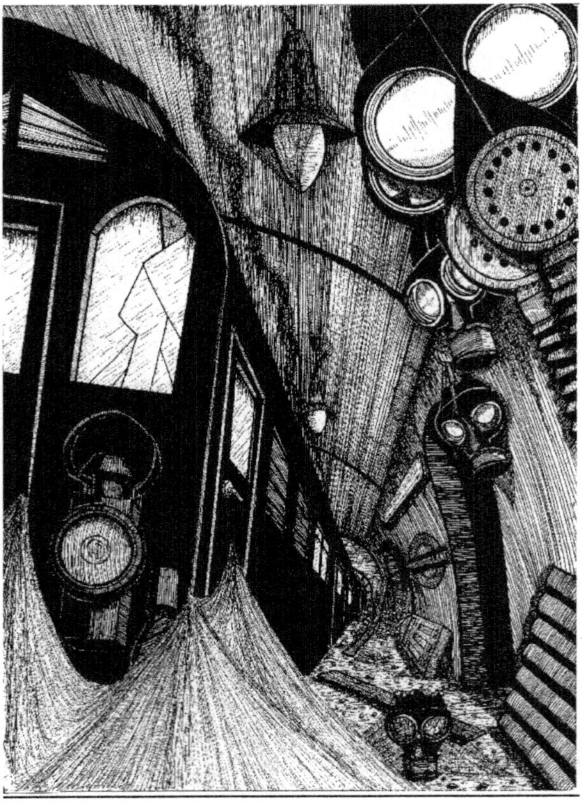

Further Reading

The Spanish Civil War and the International Brigades

Alexander, B, *British Volunteers for Liberty: Spain 1938-1939*, London, Lawrence & Wishart, 1982. Memoirs of ex-Commander of the British Battalion.

Atholl, Duchess of, *Searchlight on Spain*, London, Penguin, 1938.

Beevor, A, *The Battle for Spain*, London, Weidenfeld & Nicolson, 2006.

Borkenau, F, *The Spanish Cockpit*, London, Faber & Faber, 1937. Eyewitness account by Republican sympathiser who did not flinch from recording the endless murders as well as incidences of militia cowardice.

Brooks, S, *Armoured Warfare*, London, Imperial War Museum, 1980.

Bradley, K and Chappell, M, *International Brigades in Spain 1938-39*, London, Osprey, 1994.

Brone, V, *The International Brigades*, London, Heinemann, 1965.

Buckley, H, *The Life and Death of the Spanish Republic*, London, Hamish Hamilton, 1940, reprinted 2013 by IB Taurus. A long, heartfelt cry of pain at the injustices wrought on the people of Spain, and then on the cruel farce of British and French "non-intervention". Written by a conservative, Catholic, *Daily Telegraph* correspondent, whose humanity shines through his masterly reporting.

Cook, J, *Apprentices of Freedom*, London, Quartet, 1979. Reclaims the history of the British International Brigaders as mainly from the shipyards, mines and hunger marches, rather than the privileged Oxbridge young. Highly recommended.

Copeman, F, *Reason in Revolt*, London, Blandford Press, 1948. A bully, but also an eyewitness.

Elstob, P, *The Armed Rehearsal*, London, Martin Secker & Warburg, 1964. Great, lightly fictionalised account by ex-volunteer Republican fighter pilot.

Fraser, R, *Blood of Spain*, London, Allen Lane, 1979. The people of Spain are given a voice in their own history.

Gurney, J, *Crusade in Spain*, London, Faber and Faber, 1974. Astute, pithy, sometimes witty, occasionally angry mix of disillusion and betrayed idealism by Chelsea sculptor turned International Brigader. A key book.

Langdon-Davies, J, *Behind the Spanish Barricades*, Martin Secker and Warburg, Ltd, 1936, reprinted 2007 by Reportage Press.

Lee, L, *As I Walked Out One Midsummer Morning*, London, Andre Deutsch, 1969. A thing of beauty. Brilliant, impressionistic evocation of Spain just before the war. Lee's (much) later book on the conflict, *A Moment of War*, cannot be treated as a truly accurate account.

Mitchell, D, *The Spanish Civil War*, London, Granada Publishing, 1982. Visual, accessible history written to accompany a Granada TV series made just as it became possible for participants to begin to talk about the war after four decades of silence.

Monks, J, *With the Reds in Andalusia*, London, John Cornford Poetry Group, 1985. Inspiring ground level account by Irish International Brigader. (Also includes the information that British cinema stalwart James Robertson Justice – crusty old Sir Lancelot Spratt in the "Doctor" films – had been an International Brigade captain.)

Orwell, G, *Homage to Catalonia*, London, Martin Secker & Warburg, 1938. Essential.

Preston, P, *The Spanish Civil War*, London, Harper Perennial, 2006. Typically fair-minded and accomplished analysis from this expert historian.

Ryan, F (ed), *The Book of the XV Brigade*, Madrid, Commissariat of War XV Brigade, 1938.

Sansom, CJ, *Winter in Madrid*, London, Macmillan, 2006. If looking for a very, very brief history of the war then the Historical Notes at the end of this WWII-set novel are probably the best four-page summary of the conflict and its immediate aftermath available.

Thomas, H, *The Spanish Civil War*, London, Eyre & Spottiswoode, 1961 (revised 1977). The definitive history.

Tremlett, G, *The International Brigades*, London, Bloomsbury Publishing, 2020. Recommended.

Wyden, P, *The Passionate War* (New York, Simon & Schuster, 1983). Highly readable history of the International Brigades, despite devoting rather too much space to swaggering war tourist Ernest Hemingway. Also available in Spanish as *La Guerra Apasionada*, Barcelona, Ediciones Martínez Roca, 1997.

Zaloga, SJ, *Spanish Civil War Tanks: The Proving Ground for Blitzkrieg*, Oxford, Osprey Publishing, 2010.

Underground London

Connor, JE, *London's Disused Underground Stations*, Colchester, Connor & Butler, 1979.

Drummond, T, *The Second City*, London Unlimited, December 1989. Since this magazine article was first published Mail Rail has been first mothballed then opened to the public (along with some of the ghost stations and deep level shelters), and Wood Lane redeveloped

Emmerson, A and Beard, T, *London's Secret Tubes*, Harrow, Capital Transport, 2004. Definitive research into the capital's state/military subterranea.

Lawrence, D, *Underground Architecture*, Harrow, Capital Transport, 1994. The London Underground's glory years as a world centre of design excellence.

Subterranea Britannica, *www.subbrit.org.uk*. If you have a longing, an almost physical need, to explore beneath the earth which no one else seems to understand, then this is where to go.

Trench, R and Hillman, E, *London Under London*, London, John Murray, 1984. *The* book on the subject. Unmissable.

Wolmar, C, *The Subterranean Railway*, London, Atlantic Books, 2004. As good on the social effects of the coming of the underground railway as you'd expect from this expert journalist.

Jacob's Island

Dickens, C, *Oliver Twist*, London, Richard Bentley, 1838.

Doré, G and Jerrold, B, *London: A Pilgrimage*, London, Grant & Co, 1872. Doré's illustrations of the London Docks, the East End and, in particular, the underclass of what was then the world's greatest city can still shock and astonish.

Maps: The development and degradation over the centuries of the area known but never named on them as Jacob's Island is charted in many old maps of London. Follow it in them by looking for the tell-tale Neckinger estuary at St Saviour's Dock, east of and opposite the Tower of London.

Mayhew, H, *A Visit to the Cholera District of Bermondsey*, London, *The Morning Chronicle*, September 24, 1849. Journalism at its best.

Mayhew, H, *London Labour and the London Poor,* London, Griffin, Bohn and Company, 1851.

Printed in Dunstable, United Kingdom